I0710553

Jason's Princess

A KING BROTHERS STORY

TROUBLE IN TIMBISHA TOWNSHIP
BOOK ONE

ELISE MANION

Copyright © 2014, 2016, 2018, 2024 by Elise Manion

All rights reserved.
No part of this publication may be reproduced, distributed, or transmitted in any form or by any means, including photocopying, recording, or other electronic or mechanical methods, without the prior written permission of the publisher, except as permitted by U.S. copyright law. For permission requests, contact author at www.elisemanion.com
No Generative AI Training Use.
For avoidance of doubt, Author reserves all rights, and there are no rights to reproduce and/or otherwise use the Work in any manner for purposes of training artificial intelligence technologies to generate text, including without limitation, technologies that are capable of generating works in the same style or genre as the Work, unless the Author's specific and express permission to do so is given in writing. Nor does anyone have the right to sublicense others to reproduce and/or otherwise use the Work in any manner for purposes of training artificial intelligence technologies to generate text without Author's specific and express permission.
The story, all names, characters, and incidents portrayed in this production are fictitious. No identification with actual persons (living or deceased), places, buildings, and products is intended or should be inferred.
Book Cover by Teri Green
Fourth Edition 2024
Paperback ISBN: 979-8-9882110-2-0

To my mom, who loves me unconditionally; to Nineveh, my best musical friend and resource to all things Assyrian; to Christie, my ZenFriend cousin and encourager of all things positive; and to Paula, my best high school friend, who no matter how much time goes by we can just pick up where we left off. Most importantly, to my husband, Tom. Without him, I wouldn't know the meaning of romance. I love you, baby.

Contents

Jason's Princess

It Began With A Fight

"Oh my god, this place is packed," Julie said as she and her best friend, Lauren, burst through the doors of Fun Park. "D'you think the whole school's celebrating tonight?"

"Most likely. Can't believe we beat the state champions by one point. All my nails are bitten off!" Lauren studied the fingertips of her free hand while slurping a milkshake with the other.

Julie scanned the combination mini-golf, bowling alley, go-carts and arcade. She recognized faces from Timbisha Township High School in every nook and cranny which was easy to do in the small Nevada town of the same name.

She glanced at Lauren. "What time do you have to be home?"

Lauren circled Julie looking around while doing so, then shrugged. "Whenever you do. Ten?"

"Eleven because of the game. Dad's picking us up from here."

Julie loved being in high school. If she kept her grades up her parents promised a little more freedom. Her father had even accepted her new friend. A *male* friend. As long as their friendship remained strictly platonic, and she socialized in a group, her father allowed it. Her knew friend also happened to be the youngest son of Mr. King, an old buddy of her father.

The King family owned a construction company and was well-respected in their community. Even though Josh came from money, he never acted like a snob. He'd befriended her on the first day in homeroom. Now she, Lauren, and Josh, stuck together like glue.

Josh's goof-off personality made him adorable. He always did something random and unexpected to make them laugh.

His two older brothers also attended TTHS. Julie hadn't met them yet but she'd heard the rumors. Together, the King brothers had quite the reputation—they loved to fight, and lived by a macho male code—*cross us and we'll beat your ass.*

Jason, the middle brother and a junior, had the worst reputation. According to the rumors told by other girls at school, Jason was the toughest fighter on campus, and went through girls like toilet paper. Julie rolled her eyes at the scandalous stories she'd read on social media.

The oldest brother, Jarod, was a senior. He'd started the "don't screw with us" rule before his brothers had even gotten to high school.

"Check them out," Lauren said, pointing to a group of girls twerking on a couple of tabletops. Julie recognized them from the opposing team's cheer squad.

Lauren shook her head in disgust before polishing off her milkshake with loud, gurgling suction from the bottom of the Styrofoam cup.

"They're HOT!" Josh, who'd snuck up on them, said as he waggled his eyebrows before doing a lot of hip swiveling back and forth.

"You're such a slut, Josh. Only you would think that's attractive," Julie giggled.

"Yeah, Josh. Let's see if you can out-dance those little girls playing dress-up," said a deep voice from behind Julie. A couple of guffaws issued as Josh almost knocked her and Lauren over to reach the voice behind them.

"Screw you, Jason! At least I like them my own age."

Julie turned in time to find Josh in a headlock with a big guy she'd never seen before. He had thick, brown, wavy hair with sun streaks indicating he spent a lot of time outside. A few inches taller than Josh and quite a bit wider, Jason had well-defined shoulders and arms. He wore loose jeans, a tight black t-shirt, and black boots. His bicep bulged as it wrapped around Josh's neck like an anaconda, and sported a clear plastic bandage with a brand-new black tattoo underneath. It reminded Julie of ancient Greece and wasn't the only image marring his skin.

Before she yelled for help, the beast proceeded to noogie Josh's head and spoke to him as if he were a puppy. "Who's a good little brother? Who is? You, Joshie, you're a good lil' brother. That's who!"

Josh half-laughed, half-screamed. "Let me go, you bastard! I'm telling Dad you beat me up in public!"

Another boy who now stood with Jason laughed out loud. "Come on, Josh. You know Dad would tell ya to get outta Jason's reach faster." This boy looked exactly like Josh only much older. They chuckled as Jason set Josh free.

Her heartbeat sped up at the confrontation and slowed when it ended. Although Julie's little brother liked to spaz out on her from time to time, rough-house games weren't something they engaged in at home. She stepped out of their way and crammed her mouth full of sticky candy, hoping the sweet treat would cover her nervousness.

Lauren gaped at the older boys then elbowed Josh, whispering, "Well?" She looked at his brothers, then back again. "Introduce us," she hissed.

Instead of cooperating with her best friend, Josh pulled Julie in front of Lauren. He laughed out loud at Lauren's expression before he introduced Julie to his brothers.

"Julie, these are my big brothers, Jason and Jarod."

Julie's eyes widened. Big didn't cover it. Josh appeared older than his age but these guys looked like full-grown men. In the half-second Julie contemplated this, Josh stuck his thumb over his shoulder. "The pain in the ass over here is our friend, Lauren."

Lauren promptly punched him in the shoulder.

Julie lifted a hand in response to Jarod's wave, trying not to laugh and spray the giant mess in her mouth all over their shirts. Not wanting to choke, she took her time chewing but the more she chewed the bigger the gelatinous wad grew. Then her glance clashed with Jason's. He had the most beautiful green eyes she'd ever seen and they bored into her like a diamond drill making her heart speed up again. As she struggled with the candy, Jason lifted his eyebrows, mocking her. She still couldn't speak.

"Nice meeting you, Jujyfruit," Jason said indicating the yellow box in her hand before he sauntered off, turning his attention to some other boys entering the arcade.

Julie looked at her feet, embarrassed, but finally able to swallow the candy.

"That guy is ridiculously good looking!" Lauren said, bouncing on her feet.

"He thinks we're children, Lauren."

"Maybe, but he waved! I can't believe how much he looks like Josh, though. Maybe our dorky friend is worth keeping around after all." She began to giggle at her own joke.

"What are you talking about? Josh's eyes are blue. Jason's are an amazing green, and he doesn't look exactly like Josh."

"Jason? No, no. I'm talking about Jarod!" She squealed when she said his name.

Julie stared at where the guys stood grouped together. Their pack had grown in size. Jason glared at her again.

He probably thinks I'm the lamest baby ever.

Playing it cool, she looked around as if searching for someone else but her eyes kept landing on Jason. She tried hard not to be angry with herself about the humiliating situation, when another boy shoved Jason in the shoulder and headed her direction.

She searched to see where he might be going. Nobody stood behind her. He smiled as he reached her.

"Hey, I'm Billy." He stuck his hand out.

She blinked and put her hand in his. "I'm Julie."

"You're a freshman, right?" He kept looking at Jason with a weird half-smile on his face.

"Yeah." Not wanting to be further embarrassed she put up her guard.

"Well, my friend over there has a few girlfriends already. I wouldn't count on anything serious happening with him if I were you."

"I'm not counting on him at all!"

"No? The way you're staring, I thought you might be interested in him. My apologies, but you seem like a nice girl. I wanted to warn you about him. He's not a very good guy when it comes to the ladies. You know, he likes 'em older, and to be with more than one at a time. That sort of thing."

Ew. Why is he telling me this stuff?

"Aren't you his friend?" Julie's stare collided with Jason's again. His green eyes shimmered, his eyebrows scrunched into an angry V.

"Yeah, I am. That's why I know so much about him." He did the half-smile-half-smirk thing he'd been doing since he walked up to her, then glanced back at Jason and shrugged his shoulders. Billy turned back to her and asked, "Wanna see a movie with me some time?"

Julie jerked her attention from Jason's heavy stare to Billy's bright expression and made comparisons; not quite as big as Jason; icy, light blue eyes instead of green; and platinum blond hair. Billy dressed in new jeans, tennis shoes, and a leather jacket. He reminded her of a modern-day Prince Charming, and he patiently waited for her answer.

"Sh... sure. I'd like that. I need to talk to my parents first."

"Great! What's your num—" He trailed off suddenly as shouts filled the space. Some kids from the losing team crowded into the arcade. They pushed smaller kids off the machines and trash-talked anyone from Timbisha High.

"Excuse me," Billy said as he hurried over to the King brothers, who'd already made a beeline for the action.

Julie and Lauren watched in horror as the confrontation unfolded.

When Jason and his brothers had the creeps' attention, their ringleader stepped up toe to toe with Jason, who towered over the punk. Jason spoke softly, Jarod and Josh backing up their brother.

Creepy Kid didn't like what he said and swung a fist at Jason's face. Quicker than Julie's eyes could follow, Jason was on the kid, punching so fast she couldn't count the strikes. Josh and Jarod busied themselves keeping the other boys back until they too were engulfed in the fight. Billy, on the other hand, kept the girls and younger kids out of the way while yelling encouragements to Jason.

When all was said and done, everyone involved in the fight had been thrown out by security. As they escorted Jason to the front doors, he looked Julie's way before being tossed outside.

CHAPTER 1

Stalked By A Toad

Julie Armstrong lived her life for the only family she had left: her seventeen-year-old brother, Charlie. At twenty-five, she had hopes and dreams of starting a family with Prince Charming, but Happily-Ever-After had been put on hold. As Charlie's sole caregiver, she played many roles—parent, counselor, teacher, protector, chef, cheerleader, and taxi driver—while running a small business to keep a roof over their heads and food on the table. She simply didn't have time to look for a good man, if one existed, which she sincerely doubted. The last good man she had known was her father. Unfortunately for both her and Charlie, their parents were dead.

So when the chance to go camping arrived the weekend before Charlie's senior year started, Julie couldn't help suspect she was being stalked by a toad. Oh, he was a nice-looking toad, physically fit with a well-defined body, bright green eyes which could see into her soul, brown hair kissed by the sun, and a killer smile. But the tattoos gave away his bad-boy nature, and he liked to boss people around; sometimes resorting to physical force if necessary.

Jason King was no Prince Charming.

"Is that the Kings' boat I hear?" Charlie asked as he came out of his tent, hair every which way and his voice rough from sleep. The ski boat had woken him up, just like it had Julie. He squinted into the morning sun and scratched his belly as he walked over to the ice chest to grab an orange juice. "I bet that's Jason behind the boat. He sure can wreck a wake!" He flopped himself onto a beach chair to watch the skier swish back and forth across the water.

"I'm getting breakfast started. Lauren should be up soon. Do you want pancakes or eggs and bacon?" Julie got out the pans, hoping he would choose the latter. For some reason, bacon always tasted better when she camped. It reminded her of lake trips as a little girl, but it made her miss her parents even more than she already did. Funny how the smell of bacon could be bittersweet.

"Mmm, a bacon and egg scramble sounds great. Do you want me to help? I can mix the eggs for you." Before she could reply, he began rummaging through the ice chest again. With an *ah ha* expression on his face, he tossed her the package of bacon. She opened it up and put a few slices into the hot skillet resting on one burner of the small, two-burner camp stove, while Charlie whisked the eggs in a paper bowl. She could make it all in one pan since the old-fashioned coffee pot happily perked away on the second burner. As soon as the meat was cooked thoroughly, Charlie dumped the eggs into the pan.

An appetizing aroma of coffee mixed with bacon filled the air. Two seconds later, Lauren hurried out of her tent and down to the bathrooms. The campground was outfitted with plumbing, so they had flush toilets and showers. Lauren wouldn't be wasting time on a shower, though—not when a cool swim in the crystal-clear mountain lake was a few feet away.

When Julie's best friend in the world returned, they all sat down in front of the fire to eat. Soon, the Kings' boat pulled Jason to shore. Josh manned the wheel and Jarod sat in the back with the bright red "skier-down" flag handy in case Jason bit it.

As the boat slowed to do a drive-by along the tree-lined shore, Jason let go of the rope and smoothly coasted onto the beach on one ski. It was then Julie realized their camp was right next to the Kings'.

Yep, he's definitely stalking me.

"You guys up for some skiing?" Jason asked by way of saying good morning.

Honestly, the guy was so arrogant Julie almost couldn't stand it. She'd seen him every single day since King Construction had gotten the new shopping center deal. She had parked her food truck, Cafe Armstrong, near the site the day they'd broken ground, knowing it would be a steady source of income for the next eighteen months or so. Jason had come to her order window the first day and every day thereafter. If he wasn't so easy on the eyes she would've refused him service, but he had been polite, so she'd tolerated his efforts to get on her good side. Unfortunately for Jason, she held grudges and couldn't let go of the past.

Charlie tossed his paper plate and napkin into the fire and stood up. "I'm in, Jason," he said as he ran over to the tattooed god.

Jason smiled and clapped him on the back, then looked at Julie and Lauren. "We've got plenty of room for you two. Josh has a new wakeboard he wants to try out, if you're interested. Water's like glass right now."

"Jason King, didn't your mother teach you and your bullying brothers any manners? Out at the butt crack of dawn waking up the whole damn lake with that behemoth boat of yours. Jeez," Lauren complained.

"Go put your suit on, sleepyhead. The lake will do your disposition some good," he said, laughing at Lauren.

He gave Julie his killer smile. "Hop to it, Jujyfruit. We're wastin' daylight." He'd already turned to help Charlie with the vest when Julie rolled her eyes.

"He's called you that ever since we were kids. You have to admit it's kinda cute," Lauren said as she skipped over to the tent to change.

"Give it a rest, would you? I'm not getting involved with him."

"I wasn't aware he's asked you to 'get involved' with him." Lauren tsked at Julie. "I've never really understood why you don't like him. He's never been mean to you, he's always a perfect gentleman. Deep down you know Jason is a great guy. Look how he treats Charlie! A lot of women think he's a saint. And... he's first in line to take over King Construction, since Jarod got into law enforcement. You should at least attempt to be polite to the man."

"Fine, I'll be polite. For Charlie's sake," Julie emphasized. "But as far as what the other women in town think, they know Jason doesn't date. If we lived in merry ol' England in the 1800s, he would be described as a 'confirmed bachelor.' That's no Prince Charming in my book, Lauren." Julie walked into her tent to change her clothes and her mood. She didn't want to think about whether or not Jason was Prince Charming. She didn't want to think about him at all. Her life was her life, and she wouldn't cry about it. Charlie came first and that was how it was going to be until he went to college, God willing.

———

JASON COULDN'T KEEP THE SATISFIED SMILE OFF HIS face as he helped Julie into the boat. A little surprised she'd accepted the invitation, he knew she capitulated because Charlie would be trying the wakeboard. Jason wasn't insulted by it. The deep love she felt for her brother was one of the many things Jason loved about her.

Something clicked inside him the first time he'd laid eyes on Julie Armstrong, and it had stuck with him all these years, calling to him like a siren. Unfortunately, the feeling was not mutual. He could live with that and, in fact, he did live with it every day. Not wanting to ruin the morning with his wimpy, melancholy feelings, he shook off those thoughts and concentrated on this rare time of recreation with her.

As Josh slowly motored his way to deeper water, Julie and Lauren settled themselves in the open bow. Jarod went over some wakeboard tips with Charlie while Jason prepped the rope. The big MasterCraft ski boat had a padded stern for easy access into the water. Charlie sat at the ready, hanging on to Jarod's every word, excitement etched on his teenaged face.

"Once you're in the water, Jason will throw the line to you. The wakeboard is different from the ski, as your body is pulled to the side and not the front. You'll naturally want to turn your feet forward, but try to remember to keep them parallel to your shoulders. Got it?"

Jason listened to his protégé answer in the affirmative with a shit-eating grin spreading from one dimple to the other. The kid was eager and headstrong, something Jason understood which made him worry Charlie had something in mind he wasn't admitting to anyone else.

"Please be careful, Charlie." Julie had slipped into the back of the boat to settle on the seat with the red flag.

Jason immediately felt her nearness. He closed his eyes a moment before bringing his focus back to Charlie.

Damn, she's distracting.

"He'll be fine, Julie," Jason said before turning to Charlie with a look which brooked no argument. "Won't you?"

Charlie grinned and nodded his head. Jason raised his eyebrow. Yeah, the little shit was up to something, which made Jason grin too. He loved the kid almost as much as he loved Julie.

When the boat stopped, Charlie jumped in, flicked his wet hair out of his face, and signaled to Jason for the rope.

After catching it, he yelled, "Hit it!"

Josh throttled down, and Charlie popped out of the water like a cork.

Jason's face split into a wide smile but he wasn't surprised. The boy had always been athletic.

When Julie and Charlie had lost their parents, Jason's family had been shocked and worried Charlie would be orphaned. Julie surprised them all, though. At twenty, she stepped up and made the best home she could for the kid. However, Charlie needed a strong male influence around. Billy, Julie's boyfriend at the time, had not been a suitable role model for Charlie. So Jason took on the responsibility. He'd made sure to volunteer his time to any sports teams Charlie wanted to play for and had taken him out in the boat for ski lessons. He wasn't too worried about Charlie getting hurt because he knew the boy's capability.

He glanced at Julie and wondered how Charlie would've

turned out if Billy were still around. Jason could never stand the weasel, nor Julie's attraction to the creep. He didn't regret threatening bodily harm to Billy and getting the guy out of their lives, even though it had cost him Julie's affections. Jason made sure to be available for her, whether Julie wanted him to or not.

A shout from Julie had the hair on the back of his neck standing up.

Charlie had been hurt.

Everyone went into action at once. Julie kept her red caution flag high in the air, alerting other watercraft that a man was down in the water. Her eyes never left her brother. Lauren stood and helped Josh guide the boat at the wheel, while Jarod got an extra flotation device ready.

Jason jumped in the water for Charlie, who floated lifelessly.

Jason's heart leapt in his throat as he cradled Charlie's head, keeping his face out of the water. Charlie was breathing, but he had a gash on his forehead that bled profusely. Jarod leaned down to grab Charlie by the shoulders of his vest while Jason gained leverage on the bottom rung of the small ladder attached to the stern, pushing Charlie out of the water from the bottom.

"Oh my God, Charlie!" Julie cried and tried to wipe the blood from his face.

Charlie groaned, and Jason let out a relieved breath. He removed the board from his feet and examined him for more injuries.

"Hey, buddy. Open your eyes." Jason gently tapped his cheek. Charlie groaned again and tried to squint.

"How'd it look?" he asked hoarsely.

Puzzled, Jason asked, "How'd what look?"

"The three-sixty. I know I messed up the landing, but did I complete the rotation?"

Julie sat back on her heels in a huff while the men began to chuckle.

"You rocked the rotation but the landing took our breath away," Jarod deadpanned.

As Charlie attempted to move, Jarod said, "No, don't sit up yet. Let's slow this bleeding down first. Then we'll get the smelling salts for your sister. She looks a little green."

"Not funny, Jarod! I think I've aged ten years," Julie said.

"I'm fine, Sis. It's just a scratch."

"I don't know, Charlie. That wound looks a little deep to me. What do you think, Jarod?" Jason asked his older brother.

"He needs a stitch or two to close it up. Unfortunately, the first aid kit is back at camp. I've got some butterfly strips to hold him together until we can get him to the doc."

Even though Julie's hands shook, Jason was proud of her as she let the men take charge of the situation, sitting quietly with Charlie. Jason was afraid she would try to argue or blame him for the injury, but she stayed with her brother, making him as comfortable as possible while Josh slowly moved the boat back to camp.

Once on shore, everyone moved in different directions. Jarod retrieved his bag and the butterfly strips; Jason and Josh helped Charlie sit still for Jarod's ministrations, while Julie and Lauren grabbed dry clothes for Charlie's ride to the emergency room.

Jason had just gotten Charlie in his truck when Julie returned with her brother's clothes. "What are you doing?" she asked.

Here it comes, Jason thought. "Please get in the truck and I'll drive you to the ER."

"Jason, you don't need to go with us. I've got this," she argued.

"I won't ask again, Jujyfruit. Keep him comfortable if you must, but you're too shaken to drive anywhere." She was on an adrenaline rush and shouldn't be driving. He wouldn't let her risk them both after the scare Charlie had given everyone.

"If you hadn't followed me out here this weekend, he wouldn't have been behind your boat getting his head bashed in!"

Charlie put his hands to his ears and glared at his sister. "It's not Jason's fault, Julie. And stop yelling. My head is killing me."

That shut her up. Jason gave her a pointed look and was relieved when she got in the truck. As they drove off, Jason realized it was his fault. He had taken his eyes off Charlie for one second, distracted by Julie's presence. He had seen the look of determination on Charlie's face as he'd jumped in the water, and Jason had suspected the kid would try something crazy. So much for staying focused this weekend and having a good time. At least he would get to spend some more time with her on the way to the ER.

Shit. I really have it bad.

CHAPTER 2

Cafe Armstrong

On Monday morning, Julie parked Cafe Armstrong in its normal spot across the street from the construction site. Crews were already working. As she began prepping the small kitchen for the breakfast crowd, she wondered what she would say to Jason when he showed up. The camping trip had ended early, and the road trip back to camp had been a quiet one after they'd left the ER. She moved on autopilot now, thinking of him while making his regular order of breakfast sandwich on wheat toast, smoked gouda, fried egg with the yokes broken, and three crispy strips of bacon.

"How'd Charlie do this morning?" Jason asked, startling Julie from her thoughts. She turned to see his bright green eyes, which always reminded her of emeralds, staring at her from the window.

"It was a rough start, but he made it out the door on time. Wild horses couldn't keep that kid from school," she said with pride, passing her green-eyed stalker his sandwich through the window. An electric shock ran up her arm when Jason's fingertips touched the back of her hand. He grinned that wicked smile of his before taking a huge bite. She rolled her eyes before handing over his coffee. Always the first to arrive in the morning, they were still alone. It had become a ritual of sorts and was disturbingly comforting. She turned back to the small galley to continue her morning prep. She didn't *want* to like Jason, especially not after what he'd done to Billy.

"Why do you do that?" he asked.

Startled, she answered his question with one of her own. "Do what?"

Softly, he said, "Pretend I'm not here."

Always autocratic and confident, Jason King had never spoken to her this way.

Turning to face him head on, she found uncertainty in his beautiful green eyes. She'd seen the same look only once years ago when he'd been ushered out of Fun Park by security the first night they'd met.

Her heartbeat sped up but she schooled her features. "I can never pretend you're not here, Jason," she said sincerely. "Now, I need to get ready for the morning rush. Do you need something else?" She figured the uncomfortable tension would disappear if she stuck to being all business. Instead, she saw disappointment in his face before he masked it with a smile.

"No. You go ahead and finish prepping. I'll see you at lunch." He tossed his paper cup and napkin in the waste can she put out for her customers. He slipped his sunglasses into place before he walked back across the street to his trailer. His stride—which always held a bit of swagger—was now slower than normal. Seeing him like this cracked the hard shell of animosity she had toward him. However, it wasn't a big enough breach for her to do anything about it.

She shrugged and went back to her work but once she was

back in the flow, her mind wondered once again to the green-eyed devil.

With purpose Jason made himself an unwanted yet, permanent, fixture in her life when her parents had died. Of course, he'd always been present when she and Lauren visited Josh when they were in high school, but she'd ignored Jason whenever he'd been around. As soon as she'd been given full guardianship of her brother, however, she couldn't ignore him anymore.

At first, it was odd how he'd managed to be a coach in whatever sport her brother had shown an interest. Though Charlie had always been close with Josh, he downright idolized Jason. Julie allowed her brother to spend more time with all of the Kings because Charlie needed—no, craved—a male role model. Deep down, she knew he was safe with them, even if he returned home with more bruises and scratches than when he'd left. They were kind to Charlie, accommodating, and they treated him like a little brother.

When he returned home from visiting them, he was always more polite and respectful. Charlie thought Jason walked on water, but Charlie didn't understand; Jason had conspired against her at the worst possible time in her life.

She would be happily married to Billy right now if Jason hadn't interfered.

Not coming to any conclusions about Jason's behavior, she focused on the morning rush, which turned out to be crazy. Around ten o'clock she got a break and began prepping for the lunch service. She usually alternated her menus; every other day, breakfast would be hot and lunch would be cold, and vice versa on the opposite days. That way she only ran her grill once a day, which saved her on overhead fuel costs. The men appreciated the variety and were always complimentary. Sure, a couple of dorks flirted a little too much, but they were pleasant enough, and it was all good natured.

Besides, the more she smiled, the more tips she received.

The first group arrived around eleven-thirty. She had her salads, chips, and cold sandwiches ready to go.

"Three chili burgers, sweetness," said a huge beast of a man. She didn't recognize these men, and they obviously weren't familiar with her routine. She wondered which crew they were assigned to, as they weren't dressed for hard work. In fact, now that she took notice, these men were clean and tidy in casual jeans and t-shirts and they each wore light jackets, which were too hot for this time of year.

Maybe they work closer to town and are looking for different fare?

Smiling apologetically, she explained, "Sorry. Only cold sandwiches and salads today. The menu is on the white board to your left."

"Come on, honey. Just turn your little ass around and fire up the grill. We're hungry for something hot and meaty." He leered up at her, and his friends chuckled in a way that had the hair on her neck prickling in warning.

"I... I'm sorry. I don't have burgers today, or chili but I've got some fully loaded subs ready to go." Her polite smile slipped away as the men drew closer to the window.

"Oh, I bet you do, sweetheart. How 'bout I come inside and dive into that hot sub of yours, huh?" His cold eyes and empty smile drove a chill down her spine.

She looked out at the open area and saw no one else but these men. She always parked across from the construction site out of the way of the crews trying to do work, but it left her fairly isolated. Sage brush and small trees surrounded her parking spot, but she was in full view of the road and the construction office parking lot. At the moment, however, she was totally alone with these men who were becoming aggressive.

Don't panic, Julie. Someone will come soon.

The big man moved toward the side door of the truck and actually jiggled the latch. His friends laughed, egging him on while caging her in at the order window. There were two ways into her truck, the driver door and the rear.

He was accessing the easiest way inside—the driver side. Try as she might, her panic took over.

"You guys are going to have to leave if you don't want to order any food. The next group will be here soon," she said, but her voice trembled with fear.

I hope they get here soon.

"They'll have to wait to have my sloppy seconds," he said as he put his shoulder to the door. A surprised scream left her. The men alternated laughing and leering as one of them hung onto the window ledge to stare inside. Her mind went blank with shock, and her body didn't react. The lock on the door was insubstantial and wouldn't hold him off for long. The only objects she could use as weapons were her chef's knives. She grabbed the biggest one she owned and held on tightly.

Suddenly, shouts and what sounded like air being forcefully expelled from large torsos echoed around off the pavement.

"BACK TO WORK!"

"We don't work for you, King!"

"Then leave." Jason had shown up with Josh and five other men. Other vehicles surrounded Cafe Armstrong. Most of the men had stripped down to t-shirts and tanks in the hot sun. Jason's tight white t-shirt showed off his well-defined chest and six-pack abs. The ink on his arms became brighter against the white t-shirt, and some peeked out of his neckline. His jeans were worn and lovingly hugged him in all the right places. Julie's mouth went dry, but she assured herself it was from the fear and adrenaline running through her body and not the sight of Jason in all his masculine glory defending her.

Josh and the other men backed up Jason, who squared off with the large creep who'd tried to break down the door. She didn't know if these horrible men carried weapons. Fear trickled down her spine. She didn't want anyone getting hurt over her, especially not Josh. Somehow, she knew Jason would be fine as he settled his eyes on the ringleader. His body changed, as if wound tight on a spring, into full fight mode. Josh let go of his brother and moved out of his way.

"I said, get the hell off my site."

"Your site is across the street, King. We have every right to be here. Besides, I'm hungry, and this bitch hasn't served me what I came for. I'm not leaving until she does. I'll even let you watch if you're into that sort of thing."

Jason put his fist into the asshole's teeth. It happened so fast Julie wasn't sure what she'd seen.

All hell broke loose.

Josh and the rest of Jason's men squared off with the others. They created a circle around Jason and the hulk, all eyes on the fight between the two big men. For a moment she worried a knife would get pulled from their jackets but the fight didn't last long.

Man, she hadn't seen Jason fight since high school. He was unbeatable back then, and was downright lethal now. He'd gotten even faster with his fists. He hit the man twice more before the creep's knees gave out.

"Apologize to the lady. NOW."

The man whimpered and made a vague gesture toward

Julie. She saw Jason signal for Josh to let the other men go so they could collect their bloodied baggage and leave.

As they took him away, Jason called, "I don't want to see any of you near my site again. If I do, you'll get more of the same, along with a night in jail. Got it?"

"Are you okay?" Josh asked from the order window, out of breath. Julie's heart raced and her hands trembled. Not wanting Josh to see her shaking, she put down the knife.

"Yeah, fine. I'm...." She didn't complete the sentence. She was still in shock over what she'd just seen. Never before had any of her customers treated her this way. It had been a direct attack on her, and she didn't know why.

"Unlock the door and let me in, Julie, okay?" Josh had always looked out for her when they had been in school; they had always been friends. So she nodded but couldn't move, still trying to figure out the situation.

"Julie?"

"Yeah, sure." She didn't want anyone in her small galley at the moment, so she made the effort to step outside. As soon as her feet hit the ground, strong arms pulled her into a gentle embrace. She closed her eyes briefly, relishing the contact. No one had held her like this in years. When she finally opened her eyes, it was to see Josh a few feet away, concern etched on his whiskered face, his blue eyes intense. She tried to pull away from the man holding her so gently, but his strong arms tightened slightly, holding her in place, his large hand cupping the back of her head to encourage her to lean back against his chest, which smelled like heaven.

"Easy now, Jujyfruit. I've got you." It was Jason.

She stiffened, too stunned to move while fighting the tears in her eyes.

I will not cry in front of Jason!

But God, he felt good.

Seconds ticked by before she relaxed. Unable to help herself, she leaned into him and wrapped her arms around his big body. She didn't want him holding her, but she also didn't want to let go.

The adrenaline dump had her squeezing her eyes shut as tears slipped down her face without permission.

Calmly, over her head, Jason said, "Dennis, make sure those assholes leave the area."

"Yessir," Dennis said, and he was off.

Jason began to loosen his hold. She gripped him more tightly for one more second before letting go. She was a grown woman, for crying out loud and would not be weak. But he only turned her around so he could walk her to his trailer. Relieved, and a little ashamed, she clung to his side.

Stupid female hormones, she thought before she came up with a good excuse to let go of him.

"I need to finish the lunch crowd," she said when she tried again to pull away.

"Josh can handle it, and then he'll lock up your rig until you're ready to move it this evening," he commanded as they walked across the street to his office.

He's so damn bossy! But... she didn't let go the whole way there.

* * *

JASON HAD JUST GOT HER SEATED ON THE SMALL SOFA in his trailer office when his phone rang. The caller ID read "Sheriff Jarod King."

"Josh called. Do I need to send a car out?"

"No, the scumbags are off the site now. Dennis has a full

description of their vehicle and plates. I'd like to know who they are so we can figure out why they went after Julie." He wouldn't allow anyone to see how angry he was at the moment, though his heart still pounded from the incident. All he wanted to do was continue to punch that bastard in the face. Unfortunately, he knew how much his fighting bothered Julie. It would take a minute but he'd eventually get it together.

At the sound of her name, she looked up at him. He could see in her luminous brown eyes the shock was wearing off, thank God.

"I have some free time in about an hour. I'll drive out to the site, and your man can give me the details." Jarod hung up before Jason could reply.

He walked over to the office refrigerator to offer her something to drink. Anything to keep busy so he could calm down.

"Have you ever seen those men before?" she asked.

"No."

"Then how did they know your name?"

"I have no idea." He huffed out a disgusted sigh. He didn't want to talk about them because it only made him madder. So he focused on her care. "Can I get you anything? Are you cold? Hungry?"

"No, thank you. I need to check in with Charlie, though. I want to make sure his head is okay." She dug into her pocket to retrieve her cell phone and began texting. Her hands shook badly, which only pissed him off more. He also knew she was deflecting his questions and maybe even trying to ignore his presence but if talking to Charlie helped her calm down, then so be it. Jarod would ask more questions when he got there.

Jason hadn't recognized those men, but he'd recognized their type.

Bullies like that were the lowest form of scum, and he'd

been fighting them since he was big enough to throw a punch. His father ingrained in all three King boys the importance of protecting family and those weaker than themselves. Julie may not be his family, but she had no one to protect her except for him... whether she acknowledged that fact or not.

He studied her as she continued to struggle with holding the phone and texting. She looked tired, her beautiful face pale, even though they had spent the weekend at the lake, and her clothes were definitely looser than normal. He wondered what was keeping her up at night and why she wasn't eating. His curiosity morphed his anger into concern.

Taking a deep breath, he went behind his desk to check on some plans and wait for Jarod to arrive.

EYES DOWNCAST, JULIE FOLLOWED JASON FROM underneath her lashes as he went back to the plans lying on his desk. She couldn't look him in the eye; their embrace had elicited feelings she hadn't experienced in a long time. *It must've been the fear,* she rationalized as the motivating factor behind her long embrace and not because he was strong and warm—or that she was incredibly lonely. Her fear had made her feel vulnerable, and that made her mad at herself and at Jason, which was completely unreasonable... and childlike! Ugh.

As she waited for Charlie to respond to her text, she studied Jason and remembered the first time they'd met. It had been the beginning of her first year of high school. A junior to her freshmen, he seemed so much older back then. His piercing green eyes had starred in her dreams for months. It had confused her that she would dream about Jason's eyes while being in love with Billy. As she'd gotten older, she blamed it on teenage hormones. Unfortunately, those eyes still stalked her in her dreams, but now she blamed it on the fact that if it weren't for Jason, Billy would still be with her today. She had to force herself to remember Jason wasn't always the good guy, but a bully instead.

The night they'd met had also been the first time she'd seen the brothers fight. She hadn't been used to physical violence, and the brutality had not only surprised, but frightened her. Billy had protected some girls from the melee while Jason, Josh, and Jarod threw punches with anyone willing to take them on. Like Jason had done today, the brothers put an end to a problem. If the jerks from this morning had all decided to fight, Josh would have been just as dangerous as Jason. The difference between the two brothers wasn't just in looks and physicality, but in temperament; Jason acted like a dictator, while Josh was more down to earth, sweet and personable. Josh didn't cater to Julie's introverted tendencies. He made her come out and play, and had gotten her over some pretty big insecurities. She was blessed to have such a wonderful friend as Josh.

Julie came back to the present when her phone chirped. Looking down, she read Charlie's text:

> LIL BRO: WHAT'S UP

> ME: HOWS YOUR HEAD?

> LIL BRO: HURTS BUT OK

> ME: DO YOU NEED ME TO COME GET YOU?

> LIL BRO: NO. GROUP HOMEWORK AFTER SCHOOL. SEE YOU AT DINNER?

> ME: YA. LOVE YA :)

> LIL BRO: BACK AT YA

"He all right?" Jason asked quietly, not looking up from the plans on his desk.

Sighing with relief, she replied, "Yes."

"Do you want me to drive you into town to pick him up?"

"No, that's okay. I'll meet up with him for dinner this evening. He says he's fine, so I'd rather not worry him with this stuff on his first day back." She stood to return her phone to her pocket when Josh walked in.

He pulled her to his side first thing and kissed her temple. "I moved the truck in front of the office and locked it up," he said as he handed her the keys. "How're you doing? Did they hurt you?" His deep-blue eyes filled with concern. She loved him like a big brother and appreciated his tenderness even though she was beginning to feel silly. A few insults and they treated her as if she were an actual rape victim.

"I'm fine, Josh, really," she shrugged. "Thank you for finishing for me. You didn't have to do that." Once Jarod showed up, she would file a complaint to record the incident in case the men decided to harass her again.

What's this about anyway?

"I don't think you should leave by yourself, Julie. I'll follow you home when I'm finished here," Jason said, effectively dismissing her.

Like he was the boss of her.

Like he hadn't just been hugging the life out of her and being so sweet.

She hated that, but at the same time, she appreciated it. Talk about confusing. Maybe this afternoon's incident affected her more than she thought. She sat back on the couch next to Josh. He flipped on Jason's small TV, which sat on top of a filing cabinet. No one said anything until the door flew open to reveal an angry Jarod looming in the doorway.

"Plates were stolen. There's no way to trace who they are unless someone can identify them." He locked eyes with Julie. "Did you know them?" Then, more sweetly, "Are you all right?"

Wishing people would quit asking her that, she snapped, "Yes, I'm fine. And yes, I want to file a complaint, and no I do not want to sit at the police station going through mugshots because I didn't recognize any of them." She rolled her eyes at all three brothers. They looked ready to jump up at any moment to fetch her something if she needed it.

Jarod shared a look with Jason, who merely shrugged and went back to his papers. Then he looked her in the eye, all business again, and said, "Fine. I'll take your statement, but when you're done, I'll escort you home. Once there, I will do a search of the house to make sure everything is secure." Julie noted he wasn't asking. He was in full-blown cop mode.

Fine. She didn't want to go home alone anyway. The cold feeling she'd gotten from the way those men looked at her still lingered. Having Jarod check for boogeymen before Charlie got home was perfectly fine with her. Bonus points to Jarod for effectively getting Jason out of her hair. She didn't want him stalking her home; she was positive he would've insisted on it if Jarod hadn't made the offer—command—whatever. Jason confused her enough as it was already.

When she'd filled out all the forms and given her written statement, she stood to head outside. Jarod gave the same forms to his brothers, who were diligently filling them out. Leaving the trailer, she found several men leaning on cars in the parking lot doing the same thing. Jarod had demanded statements from everyone. She shook her head. He was so thorough she worried he might be suffering from OCD.

Hopefully, someone will recognize those creeps so Jarod will have something more to go on other than the stolen plates, she thought. She hopped into Cafe Armstrong's driver seat, twisted the key in the ignition, and followed Jarod's escort to her house.

Once he had done his inspection and deemed everything "clear," she thanked him for his protection and shut the door. Charlie wasn't home yet, so she sat herself on her couch and cried. Never in her life had anything so horribly confrontational happened to her. The only thing worse than today was losing her parents. She'd cried privately then, too.

Those men and their behavior had frightened her more than she let on. Had they sought her out? Had she been targeted? If so, for what purpose? She wouldn't ask those questions out loud because she had no answers, and she needed to get her emotions in check before Charlie came home. She decided not to tell him anything about this afternoon. He didn't need the worry.

Right then, Charlie walked in the door. He looked tired but happy. His smile faded when he saw her face. "What?"

"Nothing." She discreetly wiped her eyes. "How was your day?" She walked into the small kitchen and began fixing BLTs. Charlie followed her in and proceeded to tell her all about his first day of school, stories of his friends' summer vacations, and complaints about the amount of homework he would be doing this year due to his honors classes. As they sat down to eat, the phone rang.

"Hello?" she answered. No one was on the other end, so she hung up. Two minutes later, it rang again and was greeted with silence once more. Staring at the phone, she quietly set it down on the counter, trying to ignore the lingering cold chill in her spine.

"Who was it?"

"Don't know. They didn't say; maybe a bad connection?"

She wasn't going to worry Charlie but the phone rang again. Charlie grabbed it this time.

Clearing his throat, he puffed out his chest and in a forced, deep voice, he growled, "WHAT?" After a moment, he said, "Oh, hey Jason, what's up?"

Julie soughed out the breath of air she'd been holding. It must've been Jason with spotty cell service. She shook her head. It figured the big bully would be fraying her nerves again. Right as she was about to take a bite Charlie stuck the phone in front of her face.

"He wants to talk to you." He shook it at her and resumed shoveling food into his mouth.

"Hello?"

"Sorry to bother you, but I wanted to check to see how you're doing."

She smiled, knowing he couldn't see it. "I'm fine, Jason. Please don't worry about me."

"Sorry, Jujyfruit. I can't help it," he said quietly. Clearing his throat, he asked, "Can you come down tomorrow an hour later than normal? Dad wants to have a meeting with the men on each crew before we begin work. I don't want you alone out there until the men arrive."

Touched by his concern, she agreed to come later. She wouldn't mind an extra hour of sleep after the day she'd had anyway.

Unfortunately, she had a troubled night's sleep plagued by memories of the past, and the ugly faces of men who acted more animal than human.

CHAPTER 3

Not Telling

Jason hung up the phone with relief, knowing she wouldn't be on site early tomorrow.

Thank God.

He didn't know who those men were but didn't want to take a chance on them coming back when he couldn't protect her. He wasn't going to give up looking for them, either. Neither would Jarod or his father. No one was going to hurt her or Charlie—not if he could help it. She'd been through too much.

When Jarod left to escort Julie home, Jason and Josh discussed the possibilities of who'd hired those men and why they'd target Julie. One name came to mind, but Jason didn't want to believe Billy was back. He'd heard through the grapevine that Billy'd gotten involved with some pretty shady characters after his quick exit from town five years ago. Jason knew how dirty Billy could play. If he wanted revenge, Billy would go after what meant the most to Jason.

Josh let out a frustrated breath. "Why don't you tell her how you feel?"

Jason sighed. "You know why; Billy did a number on her, and telling her the truth would only make her hate me more."

"I think after all this time, you should tell her you love her. She's stubborn and alone, Jason. Not unreasonable. I swear, the way she looks at you makes me wish I would've tried harder to win her heart."

Jason caught the smirk on his little brother's face and gave him a shove. "Stop pissing me off, Josh. It's not helping."

"Look, I've known her a long time. The only reason she was so attached to Billy was because she was shy. He paid attention to her, was her first boyfriend, and he could talk a drowning man into a glass of water. Julie isn't a teenager anymore who only thought she was in love. Give her a chance."

Jason shrugged it off. He wouldn't tell her anything right now. She was shaken, but things between them had been good lately. They had a working relationship, sort of, and he got to see her every day. Hopefully, those barriers she'd erected against him would come down, and they could move on to something more personal. Holding her today had been earth shattering. And when she'd clung to him... he'd been surprised, *and* pleased. God forgive him for enjoying it, which made him feel like a bastard taking advantage of her emotional state.

God, I want to hold her again.

Changing the subject, he asked his brother how work was coming along on the engineering end. They discussed the project at length before Josh left. Jason figured Josh would hit a bar before heading home, probably with the plan of finding a companion for the night. His baby brother was a player. Josh's open face and friendly smiles had always helped him score with the opposite sex. Jason was no slacker, either. He'd had his fair share of female companionship, but nothing like the youngest King.

Jason locked the office and headed to his house. He owned a small three-bedroom/two-bath cookie cutter purchased for investment purposes. It was located in a new subdivision where King Construction had done work about three years ago. He kept nothing of value in his house, only using it as a landing pad until the right time to flip it came along. He kept all of his valuables at his suite at the family home. James and Camille King lived in a gated mansion on fifty or so acres of land located on the outskirts of town. They owned another ten square miles of land adjacent to that. His parents had divided up the property and willed portions of it to their sons. Someday, if Jason had a family, he would build his home on his portion of land. Until then, he lived lean and only for his work.

And for Julie and Charlie.

He sighed as he opened the front door of his mostly empty house furnished with the bare essentials. He flipped on the small television resting on the kitchen counter and prepared a dinner of stir-fry chicken with vegetables. Fast, easy, and filling. He chased his dinner down with a cold beer.

After a quick, hot shower, he watched the local news before turning in for the night, disappointed the game wasn't being aired. Nothing exciting was happening except for a rash of home invasions on the other side of Timbisha Township. Jason frowned. Mostly lower-middle class, it seemed a strange area to target. Most burglars hit the upper-class end of town in search of a more lucrative haul.

It was also not too far away from Julie and Charlie's house.

He thought of calling Jarod about the break-ins, but it was late. Besides, Jarod wouldn't divulge anything from an ongoing investigation. Jason was about to get into bed when his phone rang. He picked up the receiver and answered, but no one was on the line. Two minutes later the same thing happened.

The hairs on his neck stood on end. Changing his mind about calling Jarod, he picked up the phone.

"What."

Jason smirked. His brother wasn't known for pleasantries.

"What yourself. What's the deal with the break-ins on Julie's side of town?"

There was silence on the other end before Jarod lowered his voice. "Not much to tell. Some jewelry and small items of value taken, all done when the residents were out of the house."

"How close to Julie is this happening?" Jason's neck hair still bristled.

"A couple blocks. Look, Jason. I know what you're thinking and, believe me, the same thought crossed my mind. I'm keeping a very close watch on these occurrences."

"I know, brother. Have you told Dad?"

"Now why would I do that?" Jarod got sarcastic when challenged. Jason only chuckled.

"So Dad could, of course, confer with his head of security and help the sheriff's department out as much as possible?" Jason said sarcastically back. He knew how much Jarod hated it when Dane, their father's right-hand man and personal bodyguard, interfered with his investigations. Dane was retired F.B.I. He could dig in places where Jarod didn't have access, and Jason wanted Jarod to have all the help he could get, whether the sheriff wanted it or not.

"Dad watches the news. I'm sure he's running his own investigation, and I am positive if he found out anything, he would tell me. Go to sleep, Jason. I know you have to be up early for a meeting with Dad tomorrow." And with that, Jarod hung up.

CHAPTER 4

First Kiss

The next morning, Julie covertly watched Jason eat his breakfast of a multigrain muffin and an apple. Today, she would serve cold breakfast and hot lunch.

He had dark circles under his eyes as if he hadn't slept.

Probably entertaining a pretty guest all night long.

She frowned at herself; that wasn't fair. Even though he'd been his normal, autocratic self yesterday, he had stuck his neck out to protect her from those awful men, and acted like he actually cared about her feelings.

Jason looked up, catching her studying him, and smiled. "Good morning, Beautiful. How are you this morning?"

Raising an eyebrow, she answered, "I'm fine." She wasn't going to admit she'd had nightmares, how every creak in the house had woken her up in between the bad dreams.

He took a bite of his muffin and leaned against the truck. After swallowing his bite, he looked up at her. "Where do you get your pastries? These muffins are delicious."

"I make them at home over the weekend."

"Really? God, they're heaven, Jujyfruit."

She froze at the sultry tone in his voice, the softly spoken compliment brought tingles to her skin.

She shook off the feeling, and whispered, "Thanks." She tried again by clearing her throat. "I'm glad you like it. I wasn't sure about offering a split menu but the guys seem to accept it."

Smiling around a bite of apple, his green eyes glowed with humor. "Most men appreciate a homemade meal, especially one prepared by a beautiful woman." Never taking his eyes off her, he took another bite of his apple... and that was the second time he'd called her beautiful.

"Uh..." Her thoughts scattered.

Is Jason flirting with me? No. Way.

In all the years she'd known him, he'd never expressed anything other than tolerance. The only exception was when he was with Charlie. He was amazing with her brother. She could admit that because without Jason and his family's influence, Charlie would have suffered greatly after their parents' deaths. Jason had come into his life when Charlie needed it most, giving him something else to focus on other than the overwhelming grief that had been drowning him. Jason gave him the counsel and courage to grow and deal with the loss of their parents where she could not.

She would always be indebted to Jason for that.

She muttered an embarrassed, "Oh," and continued with the breakfast prep. She had muffins and pound cake. She used a toaster every morning, not considering the appliance a form of cooking. She organized disposable bowls filled with homemade granola cereal. Depending on the weather, the guys could eat it hot or cold, and she offered a variety of seasonal fruits and berries.

She overheard Jason speaking to the first bunch of hungry

workers, surprised he was still out there. He merely glanced at her, smiled, and continued to hang out with the men as they ordered their breakfasts.

"Hey, Julie, why the frown?"

She looked down to see a familiar face at her window. She pasted on a bright smile. "Ya caught me thinking too hard, Dennis. What can I getcha this morning?"

And so the morning went, seemingly normal except for Jason, who stayed until most of the men finished their breakfasts and began heading back to their various jobs. When the rush finally slowed down, she asked the question that had been on her mind all morning.

"Why are you still here, Jason? Don't you have work to do?"

"Nothing that can't wait 'til you're done."

Frowning, she asked, "Seriously. What do you think you're doing? Babysitting? Jason, yesterday was a fluke." She gave him the same face she gave Charlie when she wanted him to do something and he argued about it—the face which brooked no arguments.

Too bad she wasted it on Jason. "Maybe, but I'm not taking any chances. This is my site, Julie. And you fall under the same safety regulations as everyone else around here."

"Technically, I am not on your site. I'm across the street, so I don't fall under your jurisdiction at all." She smiled sweetly at him, but soon the smile faded as those emerald gems in his handsome face darkened to a glare. By the stern, commanding look and the confident tone of his voice, he wasn't going to be persuaded to leave.

Fine. If he wanted to hang out by her truck all day, it was none of her concern. She had work to do anyway.

As she turned to clean up breakfast and begin lunch preparations, he said, "Open the door, please. I need to speak to you in private."

"I'm really busy, and there's really not enough room in here. Can it wait 'til after lunch?" She'd never liked other people in her galley, especially large, green-eyed, tattooed men.

A few moments of silence went by. She hoped he would go away.

No such luck.

"Let me in, Jujyfruit. This can't wait."

She scrunched up her brow in thought. The usually patronizing nickname he'd given her all those years ago sounded more like an endearment this time. She unlocked the door and stepped back out of the way, too puzzled by the change in his demeanor to be worried about the size of her kitchen.

Her small truck became even smaller when his big body entered, and he closed the door behind him. Her eyes widened at their proximity, and her breathing accelerated. Panicking, she backed herself against the counter... an inch.

It's just Jason, for crying out loud! She was being ridiculous.

His eyes touched her entire body and she shivered.

He straightened, took a big, healthy breath, and let it out though his nose. He had to calm himself, too, which only enflamed her confused emotions even more.

Finally, he growled out, "Stop looking at me like that, babe. I can only take so much before I lose control and kiss you."

Stunned, her disobedient eyes went back to his face. Holy cow, he was right! Her eyes had been ogling him without her permission. Not knowing what to do with her embarrassment, she got mad.

"What do you want, Jason? I have work to do."

He chuckled, and she thought she heard him mutter the

word "you," but then, clearly, he said, "I'll be here during every meal service until next week. I've also hired some additional security until I can convince you to move your truck closer to the office. I talked to Dad, and he wants you to move onto site property."

He'd talked to James? And James wanted her moved to the construction site, too? Jeez, if it was so dangerous, why didn't they ask her to leave altogether? She wanted to argue, but he was right, it wasn't safe right now.

She nodded, resigned to his demands. Besides, she didn't want to move her truck to another location. She would have to deal with permits in town, and the income wasn't as steady.

"What? No argument?"

"What's to debate? You've already hired someone, right?"

"Well... yeah." He soughed out a relieved breath and grinned. His awkward behavior confused her. Jason was always confident and in control, the consummate autocrat. She furrowed her brow as she realized he was acting almost human —still a bully, but at least one she could deal with.

"Yes. I did hire someone. Thank you for making this easier."

She began to argue that point, but before she could get out a word, he flat-out changed the subject.

"What's for lunch?" He gave her that wicked smile again weakening her knees.

God help me. Once again, her breathing accelerated and her brain fizzled into an incoherent mess. She glared at him when his expression turned into a chuckle.

Liking this new side of Jason, she let herself relax and began explaining the day's menu to him, but panicked when she realized the time. "Crap. I need to get the soup made."

"Where's your marker? I'll go change your whiteboard to the lunch specials. What are they today?"

She handed him the pen and told him what to write. Once he was outside she could breathe again. As she began her prep work, he confirmed the menu with her and then stepped back inside.

"Hand me a knife and I'll help you chop."

"Don't you have your own work to do?"

"Actually, after this morning's meeting, I'm free until this afternoon. Besides, I have my cell with me for emergencies." He aimed his heart-stopping smile at her again. She was going to need a cardiologist at this rate.

"Uh... there's really not much room in here," she said, a bit breathless, but she knew by his glare (again!) he wasn't going to leave. "Fine. You chop the onions." She tried hard not to brush against him, only to find it impossible in the minuscule space of Cafe Armstrong.

His expression showed elated confidence, and she swore he wanted to fist-pump the air, as if he'd won a big contest. He suddenly stopped the motion as she handed him a knife. And then a miracle happened; she felt her face crack and smiled back at him.

She couldn't help herself. He looked so carefree and open, reminding her of Josh. It was a completely reflexive action on her part. She could feel her heart warm a little and further crack the wall of ice walled up around it to keep out this particular toad... No, he wasn't acting like a toad. He was more like a friendly frog today.

Jason couldn't believe how one woman's smile could be so beautiful. If he hadn't loved her before, he was definitely falling hard now. He wished he'd done this sooner, but he'd been a coward.

Fear of rejection is a bitch.

For years, he'd loved Julie knowing she'd hated him in return. When the horrible realization hit that they would never share the same type of relationship his parents shared; a life-long partner to love forever, he'd settled for what little contact she'd allow by mentoring Charlie. Yeah, he'd done it for selfish reasons but the boy turned out to be a terrific kid. He wouldn't take any of his actions back.

By doing so, his relationship with Julie turned into a weird partnership of sorts—not unlike a divorced parent situation—which barely sustained his need to be in contact with her. He'd hoped she might come around in those early years after her parents' death but, if anything, she'd only tolerated him and had become more distant. Things were only changing now because she had decided to feed his crews.

Thank God.

This morning was different, though. She kept smiling and, better yet, he had caught her eyes wandering over his body as if he were naked. If the circumstances hadn't been dangerous, he would have kissed her like he had threatened to do, but he still didn't know the reason for the attack, and until he did, he would stick close and stay alert, whether she felt happy about it or not.

Peeling the skin off the onion, he made his first cut into the pungent bulb. His eyes immediately began to water. "How many of these things do you need?" he sniffled.

"Two. I'm only making one batch today. Why? Can't you handle the burn?" she giggled.

Holy shit, she's flirting! YES!

The need to punch the sky was strong, but he remained cool and impassive. He didn't want to spook her.

Keeping his face serious, he said, "I can handle the heat, Jujyfruit. Can you?"

Her expression turned comical. *This is going to be fun.*

Goal for the day: Persuade Julie to initiate another hug.

He smiled to himself. He loved a good challenge, and Julie presented a challenge from which he could not walk away.

Eyes big as saucers, she turned back to her task. She stunned him with an abrupt change of subject. "I'm thinking about getting a gun to stash in Cafe Armstrong."

He glanced at her serious expression. Was she asking his permission? Hell, not only did she have it, but he would take her down and help her pick one or two out. Looking around at the tiny space, he asked, "Handgun or shotgun?"

"I... uh... I'm not sure. Shotgun, maybe? Before I do anything, I need to try one out first. You know, to see if I can even shoot. What do you think?"

He melted at her vulnerability. She had given him a huge gift by asking his opinion on something so important—her personal safety—trusting him with something which was obviously scary to her. Gentleness and encouragement were key to her situation, not intimidation. His father had insisted on personal safety for his family. He remembered his mother's reaction to the idea had been fear and apprehension. Once she'd started shooting, though, there was no stopping her from going to the range.

"Honestly?"

"Yeah. Tell me you think it's a stupid idea." She turned back to her work, trying to shut him out again.

Uh oh... Tread carefully. She's already intimidated, and it's her idea.

He scrunched his brows in confusion, trying to figure out what he'd said or done to make her react in such a way. It bothered him she would think he would treat her badly.

He continued the conversation as if she hadn't turned her back on him. "Truthfully, I would feel better if you practiced and carried both."

She whipped her head around in shocked amazement. "Really?"

"Yup. You should definitely keep a shotgun in here," he motioned to the small galley and continued, "as a precaution. I have a license for concealed carry, and I keep a handgun on me at all times. Everyone should exercise their right to defend themselves, Jujyfruit." He shrugged at the admission. Might as well get it out in the open, especially if she was going to be hugging him.

Which will be soon, he promised himself.

"What do you mean you carry a gun at all times?" Those beautiful brown eyes began to rove all over his body again, but this time it was in curiosity, not lust.

"Just what I said." He lifted up his pant leg to show her the compact .45 on his ankle, above his short work boot. Her look was priceless.

"You fought those men yesterday with a loaded gun on your person? Are you out of your mind?" She chopped the celery with new vigor. She was too adorable for words. He wanted to cuddle her until she was out of this annoyed mood, but it was a serious subject, and he wanted her to know she had his support.

"Of course I'm not out of my mind. With the weapon concealed on my ankle, I wasn't worried about the goon disarming me. If you really want to know, I prefer using my fists to make my point, but make no mistake, Julie, better me with the weapon than the asshole who's trying to hurt me or the people I care about. Understand what I'm saying?" He wanted her to know she was one of those people. She also needed to know the difference between being cocky and being prepared. She was dealing with a lot, and it was far past time he mentored her as well as Charlie.

"I don't know what to say."

He made the decision for her. "Let's do this: If you're serious about a firearm for self-defense, I'd be more than happy to take you and Charlie to the range to fire some rounds. Between me and my brothers, we should have more than enough firearms for you to choose from and try out. What do you say?"

He held his breath while she contemplated his offer. When it was apparent she still hadn't decided, he turned back to his cutting board.

"Is Saturday too soon?"

Hell no. It's not soon enough!

"Saturday is perfect. I'll ask my brothers if they can make it. If not, I'll ask if we can borrow their weapons, so you'll have a variety to choose from."

"Thanks, Jason. I really appreciate it. Charlie will have a blast too."

"Yeah, I know. The last time I took him to the range, I practically had to drag him out at the end of the day." He chuckled at the memory. The kid had been eager but clumsy. After a stern lecture on gun safety, Charlie pulled it together like he always did and made some great shots. But then, Charlie was a great kid who could do anything he set his mind to.

"You already took him to the range? Why didn't he tell

me?" Her expression was adorably put out. He seriously wanted to kiss her.

Damn, it's getting harder to keep my hands to myself.

"He didn't? Ah, well, don't take it personal, Jujyfruit. He probably considered it 'guy stuff' and didn't want to bother you with it. He could use some more practice though and with you there with him, he might feel more comfortable talking to you about it. At least, that's how it is with my brothers. Dad insisted we all learn to shoot, including Mom. She's a pretty good shot too." Jason smiled, proud that his mom could handle herself if she needed to.

"Does your mom carry a gun?"

"Yup. Dad won't let her out of the house without a weapon on her person, in her purse, or in her car. It's a dangerous world out there, Julie. I think yesterday proved how dangerous it can be."

She asked him more about his parents carrying weapons, conversing comfortably while they prepped for lunch. They lost track of time, and before Jason knew it, some of his crew were showing up at the window.

"Hey, boss. I'll take the lunch special!" laughed Josh.

Jason rolled his eyes at his brother. "I'll give you the special all right," he muttered.

When Julie smiled at his baby brother, a twinge of jealousy pinged through his chest, like it always did when they were together. He hoped someday soon Julie would feel as comfortable around him as she was with Josh. He understood they were just good friends, that nothing romantic was between them and never would be, but some days it was hard to watch the easy rapport between them. Jason had made good strides with her today, so he would remain hopeful.

They bumped into each other more and more as the orders

began to fly. He stepped out of the truck to give her room to work and made his way over to Josh, who was slurping a bowl of soup.

"How is it?"

"Good. She's a great cook."

"I helped her make it today."

Josh spit his spoonful back into the bowl.

"No way! How'd you get her to let you help? She always kicks people out of her kitchen." He took another spoonful of soup. "She's never let me help her, Jason. I think that's a good sign."

Jason told Josh all about the morning and the plans he had made with Julie on Saturday.

Josh nodded and winked. "Do you want to fly solo on this? I know you want to try doing something with her without the rest of us."

Jason appreciated the offer. "If you don't mind? I know you guys are close. How do I explain why you're not going to be there?"

"Honestly, I have a date, so we aren't making up a story. If she asks me later, which she will, our stories will be the same." Josh threw his empty food containers in the trash and clapped him on the shoulder.

Jason breathed a sigh of relief when the crowds began to thin. He stepped back into the truck to help Julie clean up.

"Jason, please. You don't have to help. Once I'm done, I'm going to drive the truck home." She was shutting him out again, the easy camaraderie of the morning gone and replaced with the usual coolness she seemed to reserve only for him. He didn't want things to cool off, so he grabbed her arm, stopping what she was doing. She looked up at him wide-eyed, and before she could tell him to back off, he leaned down and kissed her quickly on her surprised lips. Her eyes grew impossibly large when he backed up a step in case she decided to smack him.

Instead, she whispered, "Why did you do that?" Her hand shook when she touched her fingertips to her mouth.

Tucking a loose strand of hair behind her ear, he told her, "Because I needed to. Don't bother asking for an apology because you won't get one. Someday, I hope you'll let me kiss you again." When she said nothing but silently stared daggers at him, he shrugged and decided he'd better let her know what was what for the rest of the day.

"If you're leaving right after you finish cleaning up, I'll help you, then follow you home. If you want to move the truck back to the office and do cleanup there, that's fine, too, but either way, I'll be following you home today. Understand?"

Praying she wouldn't go completely ballistic, he stared her down. It took her a while to respond by throwing a dishtowel in his face which eased his tension and made him laugh out loud.

"Fine. Start wiping, *boss*," she sneered, letting him know she didn't respect the title one bit. He chuckled and began wiping.

CHAPTER 5
Working For The Weekend

The rest of the week flew by in the same way; Julie drove her truck to the construction site, parking near his trailer, and Jason would be the first to show up for breakfast. He usually stayed with her until the lunch craziness ended. The quick kiss he'd given her on Tuesday wasn't repeated, to her confused relief and dismay. She believed his sudden interest in her had to do with keeping her safe, nothing more.

They were developing an odd friendship of sorts. Close proximity in Cafe Armstrong's kitchen meant they had to talk to each other, mostly about their situation, but other subjects were brought up, showing her a different side of him. Oh, Jason remained the bossy autocrat, but he had a very caring side as well.

He had good rapport with the majority of his crew. He was fair and genuinely cared for each worker, but he kept himself guarded with all of them except his brothers. With Josh and Jarod, the atmosphere was completely different—competitive and comical. They were his family, but they were also his best friends.

She remembered a time when Billy had been counted as one of Jason's friends. Billy told her he'd loved Jason, though she never understood why. As her relationship with Billy grew, his friendship with Jason become strained, then distant, until finally they'd become outright enemies.

She recalled a night out the week before her parents had died. Billy favored one of the taverns in town. They'd been enjoying a local band when Jason and his brothers had come in looking for them. She couldn't remember all of the details because she'd had a few too many, but a brawl had broken out which ended with Billy in the emergency room for a broken nose. He'd withdrawn from her emotionally afterward, breaking her heart.

Then Billy left town. She'd just received notice of her parents' deaths so she blamed Jason for Billy's departure. Before the fight in the tavern, Billy told her Jason had been harassing him behind her back, and because the Kings were affluent in not only Timbisha Township, but the whole county, Billy could never make any charges stick against Jason. Especially not with Jarod making his way up in the Timbisha County sheriff's department. She'd tried to contact Billy's parents to find out how he was doing but they wouldn't accept her calls. He'd completely vanished from her life.

Left alone with a twelve-year-old brother whose grief was almost beyond them both, and no prospect of work or means of support, she had to rely on her parents' life-insurance policy. Luckily it paid off the small house they currently lived in, but with barely enough money left over for her to invest in her food truck. She'd had to drop out of school to make ends meet, but somehow she'd managed.

Lauren had done all she could to help, but she'd been a struggling student herself, and Julie wouldn't hear Lauren's desperate plan of moving in with them to help her with Charlie. One of them dropping out of college had been enough.

Through Josh's relentless persistence to help her, she'd found support from his family. While she hadn't been thrilled with Jason's involvement, James and Camille King had been a godsend to her mental and spiritual health, offering her parental advice, and encouragement and guidance for Charlie. At one point, when Charlie's grief had turned to unexplainable rage, Josh and his brothers absconded with him in their camp trailer. Julie wanted to go with him, but Josh had begged her to trust him, claiming Charlie needed a little "man time." After the week-long trip, Charlie returned to her a different kid—respectful, and less angry about their parents' death.

Unfortunately, Charlie had also come back singing Jason's praises and idolized him to this day. Julie'd been afraid Charlie would end up being a bully, getting into fights with everyone, but it never happened.

Julie would forever be grateful to Josh for that weekend.

Now that she thought about it, she should be thanking Jason as well. As much as Charlie liked Josh, Jason was his true hero. Begrudgingly, she admitted to herself Billy had treated her brother with indifference. She frowned at the realization.

Her cell phone rang as she got ready to start Cafe Armstrong's engine. She twisted the ignition and made sure her bluetooth connected before answering.

"Hello?"

"T.G.I.F." said Lauren.

"Back at ya. I'm getting ready to pull out of Jason's parking lot," she answered, as she put the food truck in reverse.

"Jason's parking lot, huh? How is the tattooed god this fine evening?" Julie could hear the teasing lust dripping in her BFF's voice.

"Bossy as ever. He's followed me home every night this week. He won't take no for an answer. It's easier to let him follow me than to fight with him. Besides, with all the weird burglaries happening in my neighborhood, I'm actually grateful he checks out the house before he lets Charlie and me go inside."

"Me too, Julie. We have absolutely no leads. There've been a few Secret Witness reports coming in, but they've all been a dead end."

Julie appreciated her friend's insider information from the sheriff's department. "How's work been for you this week? Still having trouble with the Homecoming Queen?"

"Marguerite," Lauren said as if something bitter stuck in the back of her throat. "She is an absolute troll. I swear, Julie, I don't know what I'm going to do. She's horrible to work with, completely unreasonable, selfish, manipulative...."

Julie had heard this rant before and Lauren filled the time with this tirade all the way home. It made Julie thankful she didn't work in an office. Operating her food truck business was hard and sometimes scary work, but she loved being her own boss.

Deciding Lauren had lamented long enough, she endeavored to change the subject. "Did you see Jarod today?"

"Of course. The good sheriff bestows his presence on us lowly surfs frequently when unsolved crimes are afoot," Lauren quipped before going into a whole different rant about Jarod and his nonexistent personality. "If I ever see that ex of his, I'll probably punch her in the nose."

Jarod's ex-wife had done a real number on him, changing him from a happy King to a bitter woman-hater. Still, Lauren's response made Julie giggle before ending the call.

She was still giggling at her friend when Jason did his home inspection.

"All clear, Jujyfruit. Don't forget, tomorrow we hit the range. What time do you want me to pick you up?"

"Not too early. I have morning chores. Noon?" She crossed her fingers.

"Noon it is. We'll grab a quick bite first. How's that sound?" His eyes shimmered a brilliant green in the setting sunlight, and his hopeful expression touched her heart.

"Sounds good. 'Night, Jason." She had a hard time getting her feet to move to the front door.

What am I waiting for? Just go in, Julie.

He stared at her for a minute before he sighed and said, "Goodnight, Jujyfruit." And with that, he started his truck and drove down the road.

CHAPTER 6

Change Of Plans

On Saturdays Julie caught up on household chores, did the grocery shopping, and baked her pastries for the week. However, on this particular Saturday she was supposed to go shooting with Jason. She got up early to try and fit everything in before noon. As she set the pans out for breakfast, Charlie shuffled into the kitchen, hair in his usual Saturday-morning bedhead, scratching his belly and squinting at the morning sun.

"Mornin', Sis."

"Good morning to you too. Why are you up so early? I figured you'd sleep in after your first week of school." She smiled as she began mixing the pancake batter. The ugly gash on his head looked better even with the sickly bruising around it. The stitches were due to come out next week.

"Yeah, me too, but apparently my brain is already in school mode, thinking I'll be late for something if I don't get up." He sauntered over to the coffee pot to pour himself a mug. "Are you shopping today?"

"Before we go to the range, yeah. What do you need?"

Apparently, he needed a lot because he gave her almost a full list of school supplies, snack ideas for quick bites when he was busy, and a short list of clothes.

She frowned at herself; had she forgotten to take him school shopping this year? What kind of sister was she? Looking at the list in dismay, she realized she'd be hitting the superstore as well as her regular business supply places. She needed to move her butt.

After breakfast, she headed into town in her small SUV, chewing on a thumbnail. Even with the backseats down, she worried she might not fit everything she needed into her vehicle. That was when she realized she hadn't worried about much all week.

Because of Jason.

He'd been a real help to her, and not only with Cafe Armstrong. He distracted her from all the scary thoughts which usually ran through her head when she was alone—things like bills, home repairs, and everything to do with raising Charlie. She had to admit even though being in his company had jacked up her hormones, Jason seemed to keep her from the day-to-day worries that usually plagued her.

I should buy him a card or something.

Rolling up to an intersection, still thinking about Jason and her mentally stress-free week, she hummed along with "Secret Smile" playing on the radio. Needing some gum while waiting for the light to change, she dug inside her purse. Out of nowhere, her car lurched forward with a bang and she thumped her head on the steering wheel. Realizing she'd been rear-ended she looked around spotting a black pick-up. It had hit so hard that her little SUV rolled into the crosswalk.

Thank God the air bags didn't deploy.

Confused, she checked and the light was still red. As she began to see if anyone else was hurt, the truck backed up and rammed her again, pushing her farther into the intersection.

What the heck?

Her engine died, which had her turning the key in a panic to get out of the jerk's way when she saw him back up like he was going to strike her again. Several cars pulled over, their occupants holding their phones either on calls or filming.

She heard sirens.

The driver of the black pick-up truck squealed his tires and flew past her.

Jarod's cruiser pulled into the intersection as the perpetrator sped away down the street, before the sheriff could make chase. When Jarod realized it was her, his eyes widened, and he ran to her door. "You're bleeding, Julie. Can you move?"

Stunned at what happened, she nodded the affirmative and put a hand to her forehead. It came back bloody.

"Stay right there," he commanded and returned to his vehicle. She could hear him speaking to dispatch requesting an ambulance and giving a description of the "subject's vehicle." Soon, two of his deputies showed up to take statements from the witnesses gathered around.

She'd just lain her head back on the rest when gentle hands touched hers, removing them from her forehead. "Let me see," he said softly. "You'll need stitches, and you've got a nice little goose egg. Are you competing with Charlie for the biggest forehead?"

"Funny, Jarod. I wish you hadn't called an ambulance. I can't afford one right now. I'm still paying for Charlie's adventure at the ER." She sighed and closed her eyes. So much for a stress-free week.

"Can you tell me what happened?"

She relayed everything she could remember, which wasn't much. One moment at the red light, the next getting slammed into the intersection. She described the dark truck as best as she could from her rearview mirror vantage point. The driver had only been a silhouette in a dark vehicle wearing a hoodie and dark glasses, but that was it. She couldn't determine skin color, age, or anything else helpful.

Josh's truck arrived. He skidded to a stop right before an angry-looking Jason flew out the passenger door and ran to her side.

"What happened?" he demanded, as he opened her door and helped her out of her SUV.

Good grief, she couldn't remember a time when she'd had this much male attention. As she told them the story again, the paramedics made it to the scene.

"Please, I'm fine. I don't need an ambulance." She kept saying it over and over again, but Jason was having none of it and guided her toward the ambulance.

"You are not fine, Julie. You have a giant, bloody lump on your head. I don't want you doing anything until they look at you."

He was in autocrat mode. Perfect. Well, she was in I-just-got-in-an-accident-and-I'm-ticked-off mode. She pressed her heels into the pavement to stop the bully from dragging her closer to the paramedics.

"Jason, you are so not the boss of me!" she yelled but immediately squeezed her eyes shut and grabbed her head. That's when he picked her up and carried her the rest of the way to the ambulance. She kept her hands clamped to her head and her eyes closed but rested her head on his shoulder. She whimpered as he walked, each step jarring her. Man, her head really hurt.

He stayed with her as the med techs went through their protocol, asking her questions, shining an annoying light in her face to check her pupils and examining her wound.

Jason's proximity calmed her, and at one point she realized he held her hand, offering comfort. His concerned, emerald gaze never left her face. He was even bossy enough to ask the tech questions about her health. She wasn't sure she appreciated that much concern but didn't bother contradicting him.

She closed her eyes briefly to gather her wits. When she opened them again, Josh stood at the end of the gurney, patting her ankle with a frown on his face.

"I moved your car out of the intersection. Doesn't seem to be any damage other than cosmetic. But if you want, I'll take it over to the garage where they can give it a better inspection. I wiped the blood from your steering wheel."

"Thank you but no, I need my vehicle. If it's drivable, I have a bunch of stuff I need to do today…"

Jason gently squeezed her hand. "You aren't doing anything for a while, Jujyfruit. You need to go home and lie down. If your head gets worse, they want you to go to the ER, and they want someone with you for the next twenty-four hours to make sure you don't have a concussion."

"Oh, for crying out loud, it's a little bump. I don't have a concussion." She couldn't afford to waste time napping all day.

"I'm sorry, Ma'am, but you do need stitches. I'd listen to your friends and take it easy. You're not going to feel like doing much of anything after they sew you up," the EMS tech said.

"I've already called Charlie. He says he has a project due soon and had planned to work on it after we went to the range today. Since that's not happening, I'm coming over to make sure you rest in order for Charlie to concentrate on his homework."

She gaped at Jason. This had to be some sick joke. She began to look for hidden cameras.

Ignoring her, Josh said to Jason, "If you have her covered, I'll take her SUV over to Gil's to have it inspected. Here's her stuff." He plopped down a pile of personal items from her SUV—purse, sunglasses, and some gum.

Where did he find the gum?

She closed her eyes and shook her head. She must be losing it.

"Really, you guys, this is ridiculous, you don't need to babysit m—"

Jarod strode up in the middle of her refusal to accept help. "Julie, listen to me. Someone is targeting you. As sheriff, I'm deputizing my brothers to escort you wherever you need to go, to stay with you 24-7, until we can figure this thing out. No arguments, you hear me?"

"You can't deputize your brothers to watch over me. That's an abuse of power, Jarod." She rolled her eyes, then groaned. *Man, that hurt.*

Jason leaned in to her and put his hand on her shoulder. His touch—though gentle and tender—felt like a tingling lightning bolt down her arm. "Please let us keep you safe, Jujyfruit. You live alone with Charlie. What if someone is targeting you? What if Charlie gets hurt because we didn't take this seriously, because *you* didn't take this seriously? You don't want that, and neither do we. Let us help you." He'd moved around in front of her for his speech, and now he brushed her hair off her shoulder. As he did she felt the light caress of his fingertips on her neck, giving her goosebumps. She couldn't look away from the mesmerizing green eyes which seemed to see right through to her soul.

Voice barely a whisper, she agreed with him. "Yeah... Okay, you're right. Thank you, guys."

Not wanting to pay for an ambulance, she let him help her to Josh's truck, where Jason got in the driver's seat. She dreaded the long wait at the emergency room. Her head hurt and she had blood on her shirt. All she wanted to do was go home, take a shower, and put on some comfy jammies. Then, she wanted to flop on the couch with a soft blanket and a cup of tea.

"Are you in a lot of pain? I'm trying to hurry without getting you in another wreck." He grinned at her.

She smiled and again started to say her mantra when he interrupted her.

"Yeah, you're fine, I get it."

THE EMERGENCY ROOM EXPERIENCE WAS EXACTLY AS expected since she'd refused the ambulance ride—sit and wait like everyone else. Julie sighed out loud while people crowded into plastic chairs lined up around the waiting area while others spoke to hospital representatives who hid behind computer screens. When someone eventually called her name, Jason stayed with her the whole time, listening as she gave the administrator her information.

After a quick triage, the harried nurse quipped, "Yup, you're going to need some stitches," and walked away.

Julie puzzled over that when the administrator said, "Go ahead and take a seat in the waiting room and someone will call you back as soon as we have space available."

Why do they call this the "emergency" room again?

Forty-five minutes later, another someone called out, "Julie Armstrong?"

Jason helped her stand. A swirl of dizziness hit but he supported her as they followed the nurse through the "No Admittance" door. A large nurse's station took up the center of the room, and all around it were stall-like rooms with sliding doors. The nurse opened a slider opposite the nurse's station marked 14, and indicated with a wide sweep of her arm. "Please have a seat on the gurney."

The nurse directed her first question to Jason. "Did your wife lose consciousness at any time?"

Before he could answer, Julie snapped, "I'm not his wife. And no, I did not lose consciousness." The blush crept up her neck to her face, and she jutted out her chin in embarrassment. Jason smirked but wisely kept quiet. Her eyes collided with his, and he gave her a full-wattage grin. She shook her head at him, but on the inside she was unsettled and confused. For a brief second she'd wondered what it would be like to be his.

Oh god, I must have a concussion.

The nurse smiled at Jason, openly flirting while she took Julie's vitals, asking her more questions about the accident and the pain in her head. Julie narrowed her eyes at the tart who purposefully bumped into Jason every chance she got. As Julie tracked the nurse's movements, she noted all Jason did was move away from her, never taking his brilliant green eyes off Julie.

For once, his gaze didn't disturb her.

She smiled when Naughty Nurse got frustrated and stopped flirting at about the same time an almost-doctor came in to sew up her forehead.

By the time they discharged her, Julie was cranky and hungry, which Jason said was a good thing.

"Do you want me to hit a drive-through?"

"No. Just take me home." Headaches and hunger usually put her in a bad mood. Add a hit-n-run, a goose egg with stitches and a flirty nurse to it and you got a seriously grouchy Julie.

She didn't say much on the ride home and she hoped he would drop her off, but she couldn't catch a break. He cut the engine and got to her side before she could get out of the truck by herself. He put his arm around her waist and held her hand as he steered her to the front door.

It burst open to her gaping brother.

"What happened?"

"Your sister was jealous of your head wound, so she got one of her own," Jason deadpanned.

She rolled her eyes, which still hurt like hell. *Dang it!*

"I got rear ended and bumped my head on the steering wheel, but I'm fine," she said quickly as she took in Charlie's concerned gaze.

Jason steered her to the couch when they got inside and began issuing directives.

"Charlie, why don't you fetch your sister her pillow and maybe a light blanket? Then go see what's easy to fix for lunch because she's hungry. Once I've got her settled, I'll come help you. Julie, put your feet up here and lean back... that's it," he said, taking total control of the situation, which both irritated and relieved her.

She wasn't in the mood to be bossed around, but on the other hand, she felt like crap. It was sort of nice being taken care of—not that he was taking care of her, but still. Not having the energy to overthink the issue, she let him do his bossy thing.

Within ten minutes, she had a paper plate in front of her

with a turkey sandwich and a small bag of chips, an iced tea, and two tall, handsome, very concerned men staring at her.

She stared back at them. They didn't move. "Aren't you two going to eat with me?"

That was all the prompting they needed, she guessed, because the words barely left her mouth as Charlie turned toward the kitchen to make himself a sandwich, and Jason asked him to make two for him. Then he sat beside her and grabbed the remote.

Taking the first delicious bite of her sandwich, she discreetly stole glances at Jason's profile. Damn, he was a handsome man. Too bad he could be such a bossy britches.

He clicked the remote until he came to a men's channel which aired a lot of fights. Sure enough, he stumbled onto a mixed martial-arts marathon. Or maybe he'd known it was on already? *Probably,* she thought as she continued to eat her mouthwatering sandwich. The naughty nurse who'd flirted with Jason had warned her she might have an upset stomach. She was glad the tart had been wrong.

Josh walked through the front door as they settled in for the next round of fights.

"Can't you at least knock on her door?" This from a disgruntled Jason.

She giggled.

"Yes, but why would I when I normally walk right in?" He laughed as he socked Charlie in the shoulder. Charlie laughed at him, too, while they did some complicated high-five maneuver. Their antics always amused her.

"Well? Don't leave me in suspense. What's the verdict on my SUV? Is it in my driveway or holed up at the garage?" Julie prayed it was in her driveway.

"It's in your driveway."

Yay!

"Damage is strictly cosmetic. Gil thoroughly inspected it himself. He said whenever you want to have the damage fixed, let him know; he'll charge you the 'friend' discount. After I told him what happened, he was amazed you hadn't lost any taillights. Just crunched the hatch on the back, and the spare tire will need to be replaced, but no serious damage." Shaking his head, Josh said, "It's lucky there was no cross traffic in the intersection, or you would've been seriously hurt." Concern etched into his handsome face.

Julie wondered about it herself. She'd had some time to think about the "accident," and the more she pondered, the more she worried. The driver had purposely tried to push her into the intersection. She'd hit her head on the steering wheel on the first impact because she'd been distracted searching for her gum. Then, the jerk had tried to shove her into cross traffic. When he couldn't move her anymore—because her foot was on her brake—he'd backed up as if to ram her again. Thankfully, Jarod showed up when he did.

She explained all of it to the men. They stared at her in thought for a while before Jason made a call.

"Jarod, it's me. Julie just described the accident in more detail. I think you need to hear it in her own words. Yeah, okay. See you soon."

When he hung up she noticed he'd jostled himself closer to her, and now he blatantly put his arm around her. The pain meds must've kicked in because she liked it. He was warm and smelled so good. She closed her eyes and leaned into him.

He won't notice me smelling him, will he?

"The doctor doesn't want you to sleep for a while, in case of a concussion." His eyes had darkened into green flames.

Okay, she'd stay awake if he'd let her keep looking at his pretty eyes.

"I'm feeling a lot more relaxed than before but not sleepy. I promise to stay awake. When is Jarod coming over? Maybe I should write down what happened while it's still fresh in my mind?"

"That's a good idea, Sis. Let me get you some paper and a pencil, or do you want to tell it again while I type it out?" Charlie jumped up to retrieve the supplies, eager to help out any way he could.

"Paper and pen is fine, Charlie. It will keep me awake." She wasn't sure if that was true, and she dreaded having to leave the comfort of Jason's arms, but writing it down would give her something proactive to do. Maybe it would help her remember more details.

Halfway into her report, Lauren breezed through the door.

Jeez, it's like I'm living in Grand Central Station.

"I'm here," she rushed in. "What happened, are you all right? Oh my God, Julie! You have the same forehead as your brother!" The witch cackled.

Why am I best friends with her again?

While Julie wrote, she listened to Josh filling Lauren in on the accident. Jason would pipe in here and there while keeping his arm around Julie, ready to help her if she needed it.

Someone knocked on the door as she put her pencil down. Lauren hopped up to answer it. Her friend's demeanor subtly changed from matter-of-fact to sultry when Jarod walked through the door.

Good Lord, not this again.

"Hey," Lauren husked.

Jarod glanced at her with a puzzled frown and motioned toward Julie.

"Oh, of course, of course. Please come in." When she ushered the hunky law man into the living room, Julie noted the excited gleam in her BFF's eyes and the sashay of her curvy hips. She started to roll her eyes at Lauren, but the stab of pain in her skull stopped the action mid-roll. Lauren grinned like a vixen.

CHAPTER 7

Lauren's Got A Crush

Jason handed the report to his brother. Julie began to look a little ragged. He frowned and got her situated comfortably again, then casually slipped his arm back around her shoulders.

Where it belongs, he thought.

"What'd you find out?" Jason asked, all business again. He ignored Jarod's raised eyebrow at the familiar way he snuggled up to Julie.

"Not a damn thing. Witnesses at the scene said the truck looked to be in a hurry. Didn't like how Julie took her time. Plates were stolen, of course. There's a definite pattern, but I have zero leads, Jason. You know how I hate that shit. Pardon my language, ladies."

Jason could relate to the disgust in his brother's voice. It was so damn frustrating not knowing why someone was trying to hurt her.

While everyone sat in contemplation, Julie's body relaxed against him. Her head fell against his shoulder, and her breathing deepened. He grimaced to himself. With a concussion, it wasn't good for her to sleep too long, but he hated to wake her up. He sighed, wishing he could just sit here alone with her to think about everything. He looked around the living room and studied all the people who cared about her.

Charlie had moved his project from his bedroom to the dining room table, which was situated in their small "great room." They lived in a small, older home where the living room, dining room, and kitchen were connected at the front of the house, divided only where carpet met linoleum.

Jason took note of all the personal touches Julie had installed to make the small space seem homey and comfortable: an electric fireplace which also doubled as a television stand, furniture purchased from a discount store with fluffy, soft cushions to encourage a person to relax and take a nap, like Julie did now. The walls were painted in warm, earthy hues. A narrow bookshelf held her paperbacks, some DVDs, and knick-knacks, along with pictures of Charlie at all stages of child-hood, as well as some of her, and their parents. A plant stand stood in the corner with a pretty pot on top.

Lauren, always busy, fixed something to eat for his brothers and Charlie. Jason wasn't sure, but Lauren seemed to be giving Jarod a little more attention than normal.

Huh. I'll have to talk to Josh about that and get his thoughts.

Josh was much closer to the girls than he and Jarod. Jason hoped the situation would change with Julie soon.

God, how I crave to be closer to her.

As he returned his focus to the fights he'd been watching, his mind wandered to the past. Billy kept popping into his head. He hadn't seen that clown since Billy left Timbisha, and he hoped to never set eyes on him again. But a prickly feeling crawled over Jason. Weird shit used to happen all the time back when Billy was still around.

He remembered seeing the delight on Billy's face whenever he'd pull a stupid prank on some poor, unsuspecting kid. He could be quite elaborate in his schemes, too, even when he was in his early teens. A natural-born liar and charmer. As far as Jason knew, no one had figured out how, or who, ruined the high school's plumbing. However, Jason was convinced Billy had coordinated the stunt.

By that time, Jason had realized Billy wasn't cut from the same cloth as he and his brothers. Billy possessed no honor and had only hung around Jason for a better social standing at school, and in Timbisha Township.

When Billy made his move on Julie before Jason got the chance, Jason had been done with the asshole. He'd only stuck around to make sure Julie didn't get hurt. As time wore on, Jason realized she'd developed a hatred toward him. He thanked Billy for that.

"Why don't you wake her a little bit before you let her get some more rest. Isn't that concussion protocol?" Josh had snuck up on him, releasing him from his disturbing flashback.

" Yeah. Good idea." He carefully disengaged himself from her soft, warm body while Josh helped rearrange the pillows on the couch so she could lie down more comfortably.

"Wake up, Jujyfruit," he whispered while gently rubbing her shoulder. Her eyebrows scrunched up in the adorable way they did when she didn't understand something, like why Jason was lying her down on her living room couch, he thought with a smile.

"What are you doing here?" she asked sleepily.

"We're all here, Julie. You were in an accident this morning, remember?" Josh said with concern.

"Oh. Right." She lay there for a second before she started sitting up. Jason pushed her shoulders back down.

"Everything is fine, babe. Lie back down. Lauren's here, too, and Charlie is doing his homework. You need to let the meds do what they're supposed to do."

Her fuzzy brown eyes tried to focus on him for a second before she relaxed back into the pillow. "'Kay," was all she got out before her eyelids slid closed again. He pushed her soft, brown hair from her forehead, exposing the bandage covering her wound. He waited for her breathing to even out before he stood and followed Josh to the kitchen.

Lauren handed him a beer.

"Thanks," he said as she refilled Jarod's glass of iced tea. "So what's up with you, Lauren?"

"I'm worried about Julie. She's been through so much. I don't understand who would want to hurt her, but when I find them, I'm kicking their ass." She closed the refrigerator door harder than necessary.

"Get in line," said Charlie.

Jason smiled at the kid, proud he understood the importance of protecting his sister. Charlie had been only twelve when they'd been orphaned. He'd resented his big sister taking care of him, not understanding she was the much better choice than foster care. The state would've taken him away if Julie hadn't stepped up, and God only knows what would have happened to him then.

Josh had witnessed the violent fight which led to Charlie spending the week with them, logging some man time. Jason had given Charlie a serious come-to-Jesus talk after Josh ratted him out. Big for his age, Charlie had towered over Julie by a head at the tender age of twelve. According to Josh, Charlie shoved Julie in a rage and would've hurt her if Josh hadn't tackled him.

The week-long stay with the Kings had been rough on the

kid, but by the time he was allowed to come home, he'd under-stood the importance of respecting his sister and himself; Jason continued to make sure of it.

Lauren slammed down her coffee mug. "Seriously, guys. What's going on? First the harassment at the construction site, and now a hit-and-run? It's no accident, and now I'm convinced those awful men from Jason's site were after her specifically." She looked at Jarod, who just shook his head.

Jason was about to ask a question when the landline phone rang.

"Hello?" Charlie answered. "Hello?" He sighed and hung up. The hair on Jason's neck stood on end when Charlie said, "No one there again."

"What do you mean by 'again,' Charlie?" Jarod asked.

"We've been getting hang-ups for the past few days. There's usually a pause before either I hang up or a quiet click. Not like it's a wrong number where someone hangs up fast, and not like a robocall termination. Someone's definitely on the other end. It's really starting to piss me off 'cause I know it's freaking out my sister."

"How often are you getting them?" Josh asked.

"Um...," he thought for a moment, "since Jason followed her home Monday night."

Jason ran his hands through his hair. Same day of the attack. Someone knew how to find her.

Son of a bitch.

"I've been getting hang-ups since then as well. They were bad enough the other night that I had to turn off my phone," he admitted.

Jarod stood up and started pacing the small kitchen. When he bumped into Lauren for the third time—who smiled sweetly at him—he moved into the living room. "Have you received any suspicious calls on your cell phones?" Jarod directed his questions to both him and Charlie.

Both shook their heads no.

"I don't know about Julie, though. I don't think so. Definitely none on my cell," Charlie said. "I've been star-sixty-nining to see if I can get a caller I.D., since we don't have that feature on our plan. But it comes up 'caller blocked' or 'unknown.' A business wouldn't block their call, right? They'd want you to know their business name."

"Not usually, but it can say 'blocked.' Mostly, it's either 'unlisted' or something close to that," Josh answered as he put a reassuring hand on Charlie's shoulder.

The more they talked, the more the hair on the back of Jason's neck prickled. Billy's face kept creeping into his mind. Quietly, he asked, "Has anyone seen Billy around lately?"

Silence.

"Why would you bring up that name, little brother?" Jarod's eyes became shards of ice as he looked at Jason.

"Because it feels like I've seen this kind of crap before." After a moment of silence, he shrugged. "Hell, Jarod. You know as well as I do we haven't been plagued with this kind of stupid shit since the bastard left town. This all feels familiar."

After a moment of contemplation, Jarod said, "I need to get back to the station. I'm going to run a few names through the system and see what comes up. You let me know if anything else happens." He started walking toward the door, Lauren hot on his heels, when he turned back to Jason. "Don't leave her alone."

Charlie began to argue when Jarod said, "No, Charlie. I want both my brothers either here or close by. If you and Julie split up, then I want a brother with each of you. If Jason is right, and it's Billy we're dealing with, I'm not taking any chances with either of you. Got it?"

"Yeah, I got it, Jarod." Charlie didn't look too happy about it, but he didn't argue any further.

Jason would have to fill Charlie in on how spooky Billy could be. He doubted the kid had been privy to all of Billy's antics. Hell, Julie hadn't guessed what Billy had been up to half the time. That's what made him such a threat. He'd been way too charming and could easily convince people to do things for him.

And he had been even more persuasive when he'd been in a romantic relationship. Hell, Jason had witnessed Billy cheating on Julie so many times, but she'd refused to believe it. The more Jason and his brothers tried to convince her Billy was no good, the more she dug her feet in to defend the prick. Even Josh couldn't bring her around to the truth; she accused him of having a bias against Billy because he was Jason's brother.

He followed Jarod and Lauren. *For heaven's sake, what is her deal?* "What do you want me to do?"

"Stay here today. If you can finagle an overnight invitation, then take it. I'd feel better if either you or Josh could be with them 24/7. I'll run the names of the creeps Billy used to hang with through our database, like I said, and let you know if anything turns up. I'll also speak with the local police departments in nearby towns. Find out if anything odd's going on in their jurisdictions."

"You mean like the break-ins?" Jason asked.

"Yeah, exactly like that. Shit, Jason. I didn't put that together. I must be off my game."

"What do you need me to do, Jarod?" Lauren asked.

"Stay close, be her friend, and keep me informed of any and all odd reports that come through the station. We all know how stubborn Julie can be. But even worse, we all know what Billy is capable of if, in fact, it is Billy we're dealing with." Tipping his hat in goodbye, he stepped off the porch and headed to his cruiser.

"My God, that man is hot when he's in charge." She winked at Jason and stepped back into the house.

Jason chuckled and followed her inside.

I guess Josh won't have to fill me in after all.

Lauren had it bad for Jarod. He wished her luck.

CHAPTER 8

Optimistic

After gently waking Julie for the second time to make sure she was responsive, Jason relayed Jarod's instructions to Josh.

"Tell you what," Josh said. "You need to stay the night, not me. Julie needs to learn to trust you, and you need to be more honest with her about your feelings, right?"

"Yeah...," Jason said, entirely too suspicious of Josh's motives.

"And I need to meet up with Amanda Baxter tonight." Josh smiled.

There it is.

Jason chuckled, shaking his head. "Fine, but you need to do me a favor first."

"Shoot."

"Stay here as long as you can while I run an errand or two."

"You got it, big Bro." Josh clapped him on the shoulder and went to help Charlie finish his homework.

Jason called a cab and headed to his house. He needed his truck and personal things for an overnight stay. It pissed him off he was nervous about it. He definitely wasn't looking forward to the inevitable fight with Julie when he told her his plans. Sure, Jarod wanted him to "finagle an invitation," but geez, easier said than done. It would never happen.

So, he'd do what he was good at; inform her he was staying. Period.

After collecting what he needed for the weekend—*Am I being optimistic or what?* he thought to himself—he checked his messages. He had two hang-ups with "unknown" in the caller I.D. Not wanting to miss the chance to catch the prank caller, he forwarded his landline number to his cell to see how many calls he got over weekend. Then he made sure everything was locked up tight.

When he stepped through Julie's front door with his bag, the phone in her house rang. Lauren picked it up and waited a beat, grimaced, and hung up. She looked at him but didn't speak. Another hang-up.

"Where's Charlie?"

"Shower. Josh left to get ready for his date with that Baxter troll." Lauren rolled her eyes.

Laughing, Jason stowed his duffel in the spare bedroom. He'd prefer to sleep in the same room with Julie, but regretfully that would never fly. So he sucked it up and lowered the futon. It had a crap mattress which his back would not appreciate. He rummaged through her linen closet for some sheets and blankets to make up the bed. When he finished, he put his toiletries in the hall bathroom next to Charlie's, who was now out of the shower.

Jason ignored the pleasant feeling coming over him at seeing his stuff in her house.

Shaking off his odd mood, he sauntered back to the main

living area. Lauren was fixing dinner; the smell made his stomach rumble.

Charlie sat kicked back in the recliner watching the fights.

Julie was still curled up on the couch. He sat in the open spot on the end by her feet. He casually placed his hands around them and gave her lower legs a little rub. He'd woken her when he'd left, but she still needed to be roused a few more times in the next couple of hours. He figured she'd probably be cranky for sleeping so long.

She didn't disappoint him.

"You're tickling me. Stop it," she groused.

He chuckled but didn't release her.

She blinked her eyes open.

"How're you feeling?" he smiled.

"Like I got hit from behind and smashed my face into the steering wheel. How're you feeling?" she grumbled.

Jason and Charlie laughed out loud at her crabbiness.

"Oh, good, you're awake." Lauren floated into the living room and sat in the hard-backed rocker. It was an old-fashioned, feminine contraption that Jason refused to sit in... ever.

Julie removed her feet from his hands and sat up, blinking her eyes and looking around, a bit disoriented. He tried to steady her, but she deflected his helpful hands with a good swipe of her own.

"What time is it?"

"Five-thirty. Are you hungry?" Lauren asked with motherly concern.

Julie shook her head in the negative before grabbing it in both hands. "No, thank you." She pressed the heels of her hands to her eyes. "I have so much to get done before Monday—"

Jason lost it.

"For crying out loud, woman, give yourself a break! You were in a wreck today, and your head has a goose egg the size of a mountain. Forget about Monday because...You. Are. Not. Going. To. My. Site. It's too damn dangerous right now."

"What do you mean, I can't go to the site on Monday? Jason, you said your dad wants me there. That's my livelihood. I can't miss work. I have bills to pay."

"You can't pay bills if you're in the hospital or dead, Jujyfruit."

"Yeah? And what about Charlie? I need groceries for the week or he won't have any lunches. And I can't buy groceries if I don't have any money. And I won't have any money if I CAN'T GO TO WORK!" Yelling must have hurt because she grabbed her head and squeezed her eyes shut.

Feeling like a bastard, he scooted closer to her and put his arm around her shoulders, bringing her head down to his. "Hush now, Jujyfruit. We'll figure this out."

Even if it meant he had to lock her up in her room.

***

MAN, MY HEAD HURTS.

She rested her forehead against Jason's warm, hard chest and breathed in his magical scent. It soothed her and helped her think more rationally.

What was she going to do if he didn't let her park her truck on the construction grounds? She'd have to park it somewhere else; the site for the new shopping center was the perfect location. It provided steady income, and King Construction employed lots of people from her community. There weren't many other projects going on in town with as many workers needing to be fed every day.

She could move her truck to the town square area, but the county demanded permits for those locations, which cost money she didn't have. With Jason booting her off his site, she would have to deal with the local bureaucracy and spend some of her savings to get set up. She didn't even want to think about the time wasted in finding a new reliable location.

Good grief, he was going to bankrupt her.

"I'm thinking of applying for a job at the diner bussing tables," Charlie announced.

She looked over at her brother with wide eyes. "You're what? No, Charlie, you need to focus on school. We've talked about this."

"I know, but I hate that you work yourself to the bone for us, Sis. You shouldn't have to do all of it. I'm perfectly capable of putting in a couple of hours a week clearing tables and washing dishes at Molly's. It would give me spending money, and you wouldn't have to give me an allowance." He'd put the foot of the recliner down, and now leaned his elbows on his knees, looking her square in the eye.

"I probably won't get the job. Even though helping you in the truck and in the kitchen has given me some idea of how a real restaurant works, maybe it won't be enough experience."

"To bus tables? You don't need any experience to do that, Charlie." Lauren shook her head. "Is the 'help wanted' sign still up?"

"Yeah. At least, it was yesterday."

"Maybe you should go in and talk—"

"No, he shouldn't!" Julie panicked as tears pricked her eyes. "He needs to concentrate on his schoolwork! When he has free time, I want him to have fun with his friends. He doesn't need a job right now. He'll have plenty of time to work when he's a grown man." She wanted his last year of high school to be the best and full of memories, like hers had been. She didn't want him to have to enter the cold, hard world before he was ready. She knew how that world worked, and she didn't want him exposed to it yet.

"Let's drop this subject for now," Jason said gently. "We can talk about it after you eat something."

"I have to use the bathroom." She needed an escape before the first tear fell.

She stood, pushing Jason's ever-helpful hands away, and stormed off to the small bathroom in the hallway. She opened the door and found more shaving equipment than Charlie owned.

What the hell?

After taking care of some rather urgent business, she washed up and headed back out to face the troops. Charlie was putting napkins and silverware on the table. Lauren set a bowl of salad in the middle, while Jason followed with some French bread. She glanced in the kitchen and saw the telltale signs of spaghetti noodles and meat sauce in two separate pots on the stove. Lauren had stacked dinner plates next to them buffet style. The scent of garlic and oregano filled the house.

Her stomach rumbled so loudly it rattled her teeth.

Chuckling, Charlie offered, "You can go first, Sis."

Fine with her. She picked up a plate and loaded it up. Lauren made *the best* spaghetti. It was also the only thing Julie's BFF knew how to make, so the recipe had obviously been perfected. Taking a seat at the table, she added salad and a slice of soft, buttered French bread to her plate. Jason placed a large glass of iced tea in front of her with a lemon wedge on the glass.

Jason was being nice.

Julie realized his behavior today, although aggravating at times, had been for her benefit. He had sacrificed his entire

Saturday to take care of her, and she'd done nothing but snap at him... or sleep on him.

Well, heck, she thought. She should probably apologize or at least thank him for helping her out today. And she would do that, right after she crammed more spaghetti in her face.

Gosh, I'm really hungry.

Charlie sat in his normal spot across from her, Jason to her left and Lauren to her right. Her table only had four chairs. It was bar height, so when Charlie had more friends over, they stood around it pub-style. She'd found it at a secondhand store and she loved it. Jason, however, was so big that when he put his feet on the footrest under his chair, his knee bumped hers. She thought of moving over but realized the action would be insulting. Jason didn't seem bothered by it, so why make a big deal?

Looking at Charlie across from her, she noticed how handsome her brother was becoming, even with stitches in his forehead and an unshaven face.

Frowning, those whiskers reminded her of something...

"What's with the extra shaving kit if you're not going to shave, Charlie?" she teased.

Looking truly puzzled, he squished his eyebrows together as he chewed the obscene amount of food in his mouth. When he finally swallowed, he asked, "What are you talking about?"

"She's talking about my toiletries on your bathroom counter." Jason looked at her when he spoke.

"*Your* toiletries? Why are your things in my brother's bathroom?" Her voice rose an octave and she started to panic again, damn it. Why would he bring his personal stuff here?

"Because I'm staying the night. Josh had plans or it would be him. Jarod wants us with you, and that's exactly what we're going to do." He shoved another forkful of spaghetti in his mouth as if this were no big deal—as if he spent the night at her house all the time.

"No way, Jason. You are not spending the night here."

"Yes, I am." He put his fork down and turned to face her. She could see Lauren in her periphery, grinning like the Cheshire cat. She would find no help from her so-called BFF.

"Someone's trying to hurt you. We don't know how far this person will go. Until Jarod finds some more leads, my brothers and I are going to stick to you and Charlie like glue. There's nothing to discuss. Don't worry, I made up the futon in your spare room. You don't have to wait on me. I live alone, I can take care of myself. And believe me, Jujyfruit, even if you tried to force me to leave, you'd never get me out the door."

His green eyes burned like fire. He wasn't asking her if he could stay. He was telling her, and there was nothing she could do about it.

Before she could really rally herself for this debate, Lauren interrupted. "He's right, Julie. Having Jason here will make me feel better as well." She gently squeezed Julie's shoulder to soften her betrayal.

"Let him stay, Sis. We can have a game night or something while he's here. You can school him in Monopoly like you do everyone else." Charlie wiggled his eyebrows up and down, grinning ear to ear.

Shoulders slumped, she relented. "Fine. What's for dessert?"

They all laughed, and the atmosphere relaxed again.

Once dessert had been eaten and the dishes put away, Charlie got out the board game. Julie enjoyed the interaction with Jason. Usually when she kicked butt during a Monopoly game, a lot of pouting and name calling ensued. Jason seemed to take it all in stride. He even laughed out loud a few times.

The phone rang twice while they played, with no one on the other end. Julie also noticed Jason checking his cell phone but never having a conversation with anyone.

Maybe he was receiving those alerts from his current girl-friend. She wasn't going to ask, and he wasn't sharing with the rest of the class.

Lauren stayed until almost midnight. She hugged everyone goodbye and threatened to kill Julie if she didn't get some rest.

Julie walked her friend to the door. "Thank you for staying today, making dinner, and keeping us company. I really appreciate it."

"You know I love you, Julie. Of course I was going to stay today. I'm coming over tomorrow, too, so by Monday, you'll be sick of my face." She hugged Julie goodbye and walked to her car.

Julie watched her pull out of the driveway before she locked the front door and flopped back onto the couch.

Jason still occupied the spot he'd claimed the whole day—the end where she usually put her feet. He looked tired but comfortable, like a man looked at the end of a hard day before going to bed. His head rested on the back of the couch, and his stockinged feet were crossed at the ankles on her coffee table. The remote was in his hand, and he had managed to put the fights back on the TV. His t-shirt was untucked, and he leaned on one of her throw pillows at his side. The tattoos on his arm shown colorful and ornate.

He was simply beautiful.

She swallowed a lump in her throat.

Jason looked as if he belonged there, like he was the missing piece of her home she'd been searching for since her parents were taken from her—like something she'd never find. Even stranger, she'd never pictured Billy filling that void.

Her eyes began to water, and she forced the tears to dry up before he noticed. She didn't like being so emotional in front of people and attributed her lack of control to her forehead bump.

Stupid steering wheel.

Jason turned to her at that moment. His eyes a brilliant green under heavy lids. She suffered a brief spat of jealousy over his thick eyelashes. Letting go of the pillow, he reached over and laced his fingers through hers.

"Hey. You feeling all right? You need a pain pill?" He gently rubbed his thumb on the back of her hand; it was surprisingly comforting.

She thought about it and, yes, her headache was back in full force. She gave him a small smile. "I should probably take one. I slept so much today, I won't sleep tonight without it."

She was about to stand when he beat her to it.

"I got it," he said, and he was up and in the kitchen before she could object. In a flash, he was back with a bottle of water and a small white pill. She took her medicine like a good patient and handed the bottle back to him, but he shook his head.

"You need to drink it. I know it's late, but you didn't have enough water today."

He sat back down on the couch, a little closer this time, and took her hand again. She didn't know if it was the head injury, the medication, or just plain loneliness, but she couldn't bring herself to tell him to let go. Tonight she would pretend things were different between them. She would accept his comforting presence, and in the morning, when he left, she'd feel much better. She'd be able to run her errands and finish her preparations for the week ahead. She wasn't going to worry over where to park her food truck or how her monthly bills would be paid.

And she certainly wasn't going to worry about the four "wrong numbers" she'd received tonight.

No, she'd relax on her couch with a strong man until she couldn't stay awake any longer, and tomorrow things would be a whole lot clearer.

Slowly, her eyes sank closed as her head rested on Jason's strong shoulder once more.

CHAPTER 9

Errands

"**D**amn," Jason groaned as he rubbed at a sore spot on his lower back. Sleeping on the fold-out had been even worse than he imagined. His back would never be the same after tossing and turning on the lumpy padding the futon company called a "mattress."

Even worse, he'd received two more hang-up calls forwarded from his house. He'd unplugged Julie's landline after he carried her to bed, not wanting the phone to wake her or Charlie in the middle of the night.

After a quick shower—which did nothing for his sore muscles—he got the coffee going and started frying potatoes. She had plenty of eggs, and he found some bacon in the door. A skillet scramble sounded good for breakfast; easy to make and filling.

Afterward, he'd take her shopping.

He let his mind wander as he mixed the eggs. With any luck, the shopping wouldn't take too long, and they'd be able to hit the shooting range if she felt up to it. Guns were loud, after all, and she'd banged her head hard in the "accident." The reminder had him seeing red. He'd spent most of the night thinking about how to keep her safe until they could resolve this situation.

He'd also realized she was correct; he didn't have the right to keep her from her work. As much as he wanted to take care of her and make all her financial problems go away, he knew she'd never accept his help. If he kicked the stubborn woman off his site, he wouldn't be able to watch over her at a different location. Hell, she probably wouldn't tell him where she'd be parked, either!

The extra security due to show up on Monday had already been hired. In retrospect, having her on his site was the best way to keep her safe, especially with the truck parked next to his office trailer. She'd be easy to get to if she needed him, and he could even remount some of the security cameras to keep Cafe Armstrong in view, as well as the people coming and going on the site.

Why didn't I think of that before?

He gazed into his empty mug.

Coffee should be considered a superfood.

Charlie shuffled into the kitchen, scratching his belly, and he stopped short. In stunned disbelief, he said, "You're not my sister."

"No shit, kid. Are you hungry? Coffee's ready and the food's in the skillet."

Charlie stood staring at Jason for a minute before he moved to the cupboard. He grabbed a mug and poured some coffee. He took his time to doctor it with milk and sugar. He set down the spoon, nodded once as if satisfied with his concoction, blew on it and took a sip... all while casually eyeing Jason.

"So..."

Here it comes.

"...how was the futon?" Charlie smirked as he proceeded to fill his plate with the scramble.

Jason punched him in the shoulder, and they both started laughing. He grabbed his plate and sat down next to Charlie.

After an hour or so, Julie hadn't appeared, causing Jason to worry.

"Your sister should be up by now, right?"

"I'll check on her." Charlie padded barefoot down the hall into Julie's room. Jason heard their muffled voices before Charlie came back. "She's getting into the shower now. She doesn't need any help. She promised not to get her head wet in the spray."

"Did you remind her not to?"

"Yeah." He pointed to his forehead. "Mine don't come out 'til Thursday."

"How are you washing your scalp?"

"I duct taped a piece of plastic wrap over the wound. Then when I get out of the shower I use a washcloth where the duct tape was." Charlie made hand motions over his forehead to show where he meant.

Jason tried not to choke on his laughter. "Did you loan Julie any duct tape and plastic wrap?"

Charlie looked puzzled over his question but said, "No, 'cause if she got the duct tape in her hair, we'd probably have to cut it out. I couldn't stand doing that to her."

"Yeah, I'd probably be pretty pissed at you, too, if we had to cut off all of her beautiful hair. So what is she using to keep the water off her wound?"

"I guess she's using a shower cap."

Jason shook his head. Of course that's what she's using. He

got another cup of coffee; the caffeine had obviously worn off, and his brain was disengaging again.

As he put the carafe back on the burner, he heard Julie's door opening. She sashayed down the hall in her soft, blue bathrobe. Her hair was indeed dry, but she'd pulled it back into a ponytail.

"Morni—" She stopped dead at the sight of Jason in her kitchen. After a slight pause, she cleared her throat and said clearly, "Good morning, you two. Have you eaten, or are you waiting for me to make breakfast?"

Jason studied her for a minute. "No, we've already eaten. How about you, though? Can I fix you a plate?" He gestured toward the breakfast he still had warming on the stove. She followed his glance, and he swore he heard her stomach growl.

"Oh." She turned those pretty brown eyes on him in surprise. "You cooked?"

"Well, duh. I live alone, Jujyfruit. I cook all the time or else I'd starve."

She laughed at that and grabbed a plate. Surprised she didn't bother with coffee, which was always his first plan of action in the morning, he watched her load up on the meal. She pulled one of the tall chairs from the table. She was about to sit when she stopped midway and walked back over to the coffee pot. He grinned at her antics. When she filled her mug, he thought she would go back to her plate, but she grabbed a small bottle of pills and a glass of water.

"Are you in a lot of pain?" he frowned.

"No, actually, I'm not taking the pain killer. I think I can manage with some Tylenol today. I don't want to spend the day trying to stay awake. I have a lot of stuff I need to do." She stopped to take a deep breath. Then she calmly looked at him with round eyes and asked, "I don't want to be impaired if we decided to go to the range. If... If you still want to show me?" She looked unsure but hopeful.

He smiled and told her, "That's my plan, too. I thought I'd take you wherever you need to go this morning, and then we can hit the range for an hour or so, later this afternoon. I don't want you to overdo it. We'll see how you feel after the shopping."

She sat at her plate with a big smile on her face. "Thank you, Jason. That would be great. Charlie, do you want to go with us?"

"As much as I want to see you with a gun in your hand, I have to meet with my study group to finish our project." He shrugged his shoulders. "Marco's picking me up around noon. We thought we'd grab something to eat and then head over to Ryan's house to work on it."

"Sounds like a plan then." Jason walked back into the spare bedroom to retrieve his cell phone and made the call.

"Do you have any small-caliber firearms at your house?" Jason asked Josh as soon as his little brother picked up.

"Smallest I have is the .44 revolver. Why?"

"I'm taking Julie to the range this afternoon, and I didn't want to break her arm off. I'll call Mom and see if I can borrow her .380. What are your plans today?"

"I'm hooking up with a lucky lady sometime this afternoon. When do you need me to relieve you from your babysitting duty?" Josh chuckled and Jason didn't appreciate it.

"First off, I'm not babysitting, and second, Charlie is going to be with his friends starting at noon. He won't be alone, but Jarod wanted him watched. What do you think we should do?"

"Call Jarod. If he wants me to tail the kid while he's with his friends, I will, but I honestly think Charlie will be all right, as long as he's not alone."

Jason agreed because nothing, so far, had been directed at Charlie. All the incidents had been focused on Julie, except for the phone calls.

"I'll be staying here at night, so you don't have to worry about that part. I'll see you tomorrow at work. I need to talk to you about where I want her truck and what I want to do with the security cameras around the office trailer," Jason said before they said their goodbyes and disconnected the call.

When he returned to the living room, he found Julie sitting on the couch with Charlie, fully dressed with a look of expectation on her smiling face. She stood when she saw him and grabbed her purse. "Ready to go?"

"Uh... Yeah, sure." He patted the various pockets in his cargo pants and then grabbed his sunglasses off the coffee table. "After you."

When they reached his truck, she hopped into the passenger seat with a look of determination on her face and closed the door. Seeing she was a woman on a mission, he grinned before hurrying to the driver's seat. As he backed out of the driveway he asked, "Where to first?"

There were only two wholesale grocery outlets in the area; one in Timbisha proper and the other was the Costco located just over the county line.

Once there, he grabbed the industrial-sized carts and pushed while she filled them with everything she needed for the next week.

They talked amicably all morning. By one o'clock, he was getting hungry, and his truck was pretty full. She looked like she was running out of steam as well. He pulled into a drive-through and ordered for the both of them. She didn't complain that he had taken charge, for which he was thankful.

He handed her the drink cups and bags and headed for her house.

"How did you know what I wanted?" She looked at him out of the corner of her eye.

"I didn't. I ordered two of what I like. It's the main sandwich at that restaurant. Why? Do you want me to go back?"

She grinned and shook her head. "No, it's what I normally ask for too, so no worries. Thank you for driving me around today, Jason. And thank you for lunch. I really appreciate everything you're doing for me." She briefly put her hand on his thigh before returning it to the bags in her lap. He felt the touch all over. He cleared his throat as he shifted in his seat to get comfortable.

"You're most welcome. I'm glad I can help." He glanced at her before returning his gaze to the road. She was looking down with a small smile on her angelic face.

God, he loved her.

CHAPTER 10

Annie Oakley

Getting smashed in the head must burn a lot of calories, Julie thought as she shoved her burger and fries down her throat like she hadn't eaten in a week. She tried to wipe her mouth as daintily as possible after making such a pig out of herself.

How embarrassing.

"What's the matter, Jujyfruit? Think I haven't seen a hungry woman eat before?"

The big jerk laughed.

She narrowed her eyes at him as she put her wrappers in the garbage and began unloading the items needed to be refrigerated.

"Point me in the right direction to help you get ready for the week," he said seriously.

They were back at her house, having already brought the groceries inside from the truck before digging into their food. She really did appreciate what he was doing for her. She gave him direction on where to put things. She stored most of the items in the garage on either the storage shelves or in the spare refrigerator-freezer, which she'd bought secondhand.

She'd converted the small single-car garage into her Cafe Armstrong food pantry some years ago. Charlie helped her put up the shelving, and Josh had done the electrical work by installing outlets for the fridge. He'd even added extra storage space in the rafters with a pull-down ladder for convenience.

Josh'd enlisted his brother's help in the conversion. Jason had walled off the room with insulation in front of the garage door. They'd left the door on the outside, so from the street it looked like a normal garage. It was a good way to secure her inventory. They sealed and painted the original cement floor to keep bacteria from growing while also allowing easy cleanup should any spills occur.

"If you don't mind, I'd like to go to the range now," she said. They were done putting everything in its proper place, and she was becoming anxious about the guns. Not knowing anything about firearms, she found the whole subject intimidating and scary. She wanted to be able to protect herself in the future because those men had made her feel small and powerless, and she never wanted to feel like that again.

"Of course. I'm ready when you are, Jujyfruit," he answered, as he put his hand out for her.

With a smile, she took it and let him lead her to his truck.

On the way, he gave her pointers and talked about what she could expect. The closer they got, the more nervous she became. At this rate, she was going to embarrass herself by not being able to hold the gun steady.

Breathe. JUST BREATHE.

He pulled into a gravel lot and got out. After opening her door, he lifted a canvas bag out of the back and put the strap over his shoulder. Once again, he held out his hand for her. She didn't hesitate to take it, and he walked her to the front door.

"We'll check in first and get you some eye and ear protection. At this range, we can fire the guns I've brought with me," he said, patting the bag he carried. "Or, you can rent weapons to see which ones you're more comfortable firing. There's a selection on the wall behind the counter; you'll see when we're inside. Is there anything in particular you'd like to shoot?"

"I... I'm not sure, but I was thinking a small pistol and a shotgun. What do you think?"

She looked up at him and got lost in his eyes... again, and had to look away. He was too good looking for his own good. This new Jason, who treated her like a mature woman and not a child, was getting to her. No, it was more than that... Jason treated her like a friend.

"I think we should stick to the pistol for now and move to the shotgun later if you don't get too tired. Deal?"

She smiled. "Deal."

"Why don't you go ahead and get your I.D. ready while I fill out the proper forms?"

She nodded her head, reaching for her wallet while he held the door open for her.

The lobby was not what she expected. It reminded her of a jewelry store with glass cases and items along the back wall. However, instead of having sparkly gems on display, this place had sparkly guns on display both in the cases and from floor to ceiling being the counter.

Lots of them, in all sizes, shapes, and colors. Her eyes wandered in all directions at the variety.

A woman also worked behind the counter, along with two other employees. Instead of soft classical music being piped in from an expensive sound system, muffled *BOOM BOOM*

*BOOM*s issued from the indoor range. The percussions vibrated the floor and she could feel them in her chest as if she were at a rock festival.

Jason propped himself up at the counter and started filling out the forms, whatever they were for; she figured liability, maybe? She didn't know what to do with herself, so she stood close to him while he wrote and noted he knew all of her information my heart.

Not wanting to think about that too hard, she looked toward the big glass window, and the people in the indoor range. An equal amount of women as men fired their guns, and she even spotted a couple of kids who looked to be in their early to mid-teens practicing their marksmanship.

That made her feel a little less anxious. She was never comfortable being in places where men were the dominant presence. Not that she didn't like men; she just didn't like the feeling of being out of place.

"Do you have your I.D.?" Jason asked quietly.

She handed it to him. He stacked it on the forms he'd filled out for her and himself, grabbed it with one hand, and placed his other hand at the small of her back, steering her toward the register. She tried to stifle the shiver running up her back at his touch. It obviously didn't work because she felt his thumb caress a circle on her spine.

They went through the process of checking in at the counter. Jason explained how this would be Julie's first time shooting a gun, so the floozy flirting with Jason—*ahem*, Julie caught herself, *the nice lady at the counter*—chatted with her and put her at ease. She asked if Julie wanted to try out at any of the guns in the display case to rent. Confused by the shear amount to choose from, she declined.

After being instructed to put on their eye and ear protection, all three of them headed for the doors to the range. Once the range master gave the all clear the counter lady ushered them to their lane. Julie's heart rate sped up.

This is it.

Their "space" looked like a small stall which sat between dividing walls on each side of a "counter" separating them from the other shooters, who now studied their targets and reloaded their firearms.

Julie paid close attention as Jason flicked a switch on the left side of their stall and heard a motor running reminding her of a garage-door opener. When it stopped, she realized he'd reeled in the target hanger from down the range lane. She was mesmerized by the play of his muscles as he clipped a picture of a zombie to the chain before hitting the switch again. The zombie floated out to the middle of the range like a two dimensional ghost.

With his back to her, he held up a gun with lots of buttons on it. He took a cartridge-thingy out of the bin that had contained the gun and a box of bullets. He put a few bullets in the thingy and then slammed it into the base of the "handle" of the gun.

She jumped when he jerked the top of the gun back with force, then quickly let it go with a snap as it slid forward to its original position.

Her focus bounced between Jason's muscular body and what he did with the weapon. She tried to concentrate more on what he was doing rather than on the man himself.

Overhead, the range master declared the range "hot."

Startling her, Jason said, "Okay, Jujyfruit. Are you ready to shoot your first weapon?" The big grin on his face immediately put her at ease.

"Do your worst," she said, trying to play it cool and failing miserably.

"All right then." He positioned her in the center of the stall, her back to him, as she faced down range toward the zombie target. She noted the earphones she wore allowed her to hear his speech clearly, but when someone fired off a round, the sound was muffled.

"The gun in front of you is my .380 Smith and Wesson Bodyguard. Its small caliber is perfect for concealed carry. My mother carries the same weapon, so you should be able to handle it." He cleared his throat and took a breath. "Now, pick up the gun with your right hand. Make sure you keep your finger off the trigger and point the muzzle down range toward the zombie. That's it. Good. Now... I want you to bring your left hand up like this..."

From behind, he took her left hand in his and wrapped it around the gun, arranging her fingers and thumbs in a firm grip. Keeping his left hand on her left elbow, he reached around her with his right and began pointing to the top of the gun with his index finger.

With him touching her everywhere, it was hard to concentrate. She steadied herself with a deep breath and focused on the sound of his voice rather than the warmth emanating from his body.

It's just Jason, for crying out loud. I can do this.

"This notch right here is the rear sight. When you're aiming at the target, you want to line the gap with the white dot on the notch at the front of the muzzle, which is the front sight." He gripped both of her lower arms, just keeping his body from touching hers, his head to her right side as he gave steady, easy directions.

His voice held a calming tone but his proximity did funny

things to her. Jason's magical scent surrounded her and only intensified the warmth she felt from his body. All his nearness kept her from thinking too hard about pulling the trigger.

"I've already chambered the round for you. I want you to place your finger on the trigger, but don't pull it back yet... Good. Okay, now line the white dot up with the rear notch, and then put both of those things on the zombie's chest. Good. Do you have it lined up?"

"Uh-huh," she breathed.

"Perfect. Now, I want you to take a breath, exhale, and slowly squeeze the trigger, all while keeping your hands as relaxed as possible."

You've got to be kidding, Jason.

She shook the thought from her head, took another deep breath, and exhaled as she pulled the trigger.

The thing exploded in her hand, almost hitting her in the nose. Her hand throbbed and there was a burning sensation on her forehead.

Son of a bitch! That hurt.

She let out a squeal and tried the drop the gun on the counter, but Jason's strong hands held her steady.

Chuckling, he said, "Calm down, you're all right. Look. You even hit the target." He sounded like he was proud, but she was still too startled.

That was terrible, she thought. The gun seemed to have come apart in her hand, and she definitely wasn't pulling that trigger again.

She shook her head and tried to move away from him when he calmly removed the gun from her hands and placed it back on the counter. He took her by the shoulders and turned her to face him.

Sputtering, she grumbled, "Let me go... I need to leave."

He bent down to look her in the eyes, almost touching his forehead to hers.

"Julie, calm down a minute. You can't leave the range while it's hot; people are still firing. Look at me, damn it."

She stopped squirming and met his beautiful green eyes. "My hand hurts and my forehead hurts," she whined. Her eyes began to water and she fought viciously to keep from losing control.

He scrunched his face up in concern. "Did the casing hit your wound?" He lightly brushed his finger over her bandage.

"I don't know. What the hell, Jason? You gave me a broken gun!" The adrenaline rush left her body. All the anxiety of the day kicked in her fight-or-flight response, making her angry.

"I didn't give you a broken gun. It's a semi-automatic. That's how they work." He shook his head at her, and she felt a hot blush blooming on her cheeks. He put his hands back on her shoulders and said, "Guns are loud, Jujyfruit. There's gun powder in the bullet. When it's fired, there's a small explosion, for lack of a better explanation, that pushes the projectile through the muzzle of the gun and into the air toward your target. In an emergency situation, if you don't hear a loud bang, that's when you're in real trouble. Understand?"

She took a deep breath and nodded her head. She really didn't understand but she didn't want to disappoint him either. He gave her shoulders a small rub again, and then he turned and reeled in the target. A grin split his face.

What now?

"You hit the zombie in the chest. Is this where you were aiming?" He pointed to a burned hole in the paper. She looked at the picture. No, she'd been aiming a lot higher, but it looked to be in the middle of the body.

That had to be good, right?

"Not exactly, more like here." She pointed.

"Damn, Jujyfruit. For your first time, that's not too shabby. Let me load you up again, okay?" His expression held so much hope, and tugged at something in her heart. She wouldn't deny him his efforts to teach her to shoot. She gritted her teeth and put her fears aside before nodding her agreement.

Over the next thirty minutes, she fired that broken gun over and over, aiming at the zombie's chest. He had holes all over him, and Julie had hot brass casings in her bra. Her arms were tired and her hand killed her. Her head hurt so badly it had gone numb.

But Jason's excitement was incentive enough to stay a little longer. He'd shown her how to put the bullets in the cartridge thingy, which she now knew was a magazine, and how to shove it hard into the stalk and then chamber a round. He'd talked about something called "slide bite," so she had been careful where she placed her hands and thumbs while firing the weapon.

He hadn't fired a single round. He'd stayed with her, showing her how to calculate distance to the target and how to aim better. This was the first time she'd had this much one-on-one time with Jason, other than when he had helped her in her truck or protected her from imminent danger. He was a good teacher too. She especially liked how he didn't get upset or annoyed when she didn't understand something or when she didn't follow his directions exactly as he'd explained them. His patience with her made her feel more confident than she had in a long time.

She realized something in those moments while they checked out of the range...

She truly liked Jason King

CHAPTER 11

Prepping

Jason listened to the endearing way Julie talked about their range experience on the drive home. Animated, beautiful, and smart, her excitement made him fall in love with her all over again.

He thought he could spend every waking moment with this sweet woman and never tire of her. He'd been a victim of love-at-first-sight the instant Josh had introduced her to him, but this was the first time he'd had the chance to spend quality time with her. Billy had swept her up in the blink of an eye, and even though he couldn't stand the douchebag, he'd respected the fact she'd belonged to someone else. Jason didn't poach. Period.

Over time, he'd gotten the reputation as a ladies' man because he didn't date in the traditional sense. Why bother when the woman you loved was in a relationship with someone else? Dating was basically the means by which a man got to know a woman to see if she was the one with whom he would spend the rest of his life and have children. Since Julie, the only woman he wanted, was already taken he didn't see the point in dating. When he needed the comfort of a woman, he had no problem finding one. In the morning (if he stayed that long), it was always "Adios muchacha."

Sure, he had female friends, like Lauren, but he rarely spent much time conversing with women. Listening to Julie talk was a joy he'd missed out on—or maybe it was just Julie he'd missed. He didn't know but he wasn't willing to give it up again now that her barriers had come down.

"Next time we do this, can I try a revolver? They don't kick the casings out when you pull the trigger, right?"

"Next time? Does that mean you want to go on another date with me?" Her shocked expression made him grin. He may not have meant to say the d-word, but her reaction was completely worth it. "Don't worry, Jujyfruit. I won't hold you to it. And yes, you can try my revolver. It's bigger than the Bodyguard you practiced with, but I'd like to see how you handle a bigger caliber."

After a quiet moment, she said softly, "Jason, thank you for today, for not laughing at me. I appreciate you taking the time to show me this stuff."

He nodded while he drove, too moved to speak. Every time she began to soften toward him, his brain function slowed to a crawl. He was used to her animosity but delighted with this sweetness. She was like a timid rabbit that wanted to be loved and cared for.

Desperate not to scare her off, he changed the subject. "What are we preparing for breakfast and lunch tomorrow?"

Smiling, she said, "It's muffin and cookie baking day. I'll let you put the granola in the cups for single-serving cereal as well... if you want?"

Before he could accept her request, her smile morphed into a startled expression. She stared at something on the side of the road to his left. At first, he didn't recognize the man standing on the sidewalk. When it hit him, he almost drove off the road.

Billy.

Jason jerked his attention back to Julie. "Hey, are you all right?" Eyes as round as saucers and her complexion white as the walls in his empty house, she held one hand to her forehead and the other to her stomach.

Concerned, he began to pull over, but she stopped him.

"I'm fine. Can you take me home?" Jason thought she looked like she would break... or puke, he wasn't sure which, but he didn't want her to do either in his truck.

"That's where we're headed anyway, babe. I think I might need a drink."

She didn't respond. She seemed to be lost in her own thoughts.

Damn it, he wouldn't let that son of a bitch take her away from him again. She'd been opening up to him, and now that he'd spent time with her, he wasn't letting go. Oh no, he planned on getting as close as he possibly could.

Jason's cell rang as they walked through Julie's front door. He looked at the caller I.D. before answering.

"What's up, Josh?"

"Guess who's back in town."

"Billy. We saw him on the street. Where did you see him?"

Julie looked at him when he said Billy's name. He shook his head and motioned for her to continue into the house. He listened to Josh on the phone while following her into the kitchen.

"I got a call from Charlie. He's pretty upset. Wants to make sure Billy didn't go to his house. He doesn't want him there."

"Have you called Jarod? He'll want to reopen the investigation."

"Yeah, I think you're right. I need to call Dad too. What are your plans for tonight? Do you need me for anything?"

Jason pondered that for a second. "Nah, enjoy your evening. Julie enlisted me as a sous chef, and Charlie should be home any minute, so I've got this handled. I'll see you in the morning if I don't hear from you later tonight."

"You got it, Bro." Josh clicked off and Jason studied Julie as she made preparations to bake. His eyes widened at the mountain of supplies spread across her small kitchen.

Holy shit! How much are we making?

"Do you mind if I turn on the news?"

Julie shrugged her shoulders as if to say she didn't care.

Frowning, he grabbed the remote. He clicked on his favorite local channel and walked back into the kitchen. Julie had laid out an assembly line of items for him to put together; it was the hot cereal detail. She explained how she wanted it done and walked him through the first couple of bowls. She must have been satisfied with his work because she turned to her big KitchenAid and began making the batter for her muffins after the second bowl.

The news droned on as they worked together until an alert came on. They both stopped working to listen to the news segment:

"This just in; police believe several break-ins in the northwest area are related after a fifth home was reported to have been broken into. Police have no suspects at this time."

The hairs on the back of Jason's neck tingled. Billy's reemergence in town, the break-ins, and the two incidents with Julie were no coincidence.

Julie was back to being quiet and distant with him, which he didn't appreciate one damn bit. Determined to keep her in the here and now, he brought her attention back to him. "All done with the granola, babe. What's next?"

She jumped at his voice. "What? Oh... sorry." She glanced for a moment at the pyramid pile he'd built with the cups. He relaxed at her amused expression. "Now that's cute. However, I hate to be the bearer of bad news. They need to be loaded into the plastic tubs in the pantry marked 'cereal.'" Chuckling, she went back to work.

Relieved at her slight smile, he did as instructed. "Okay, Jujyfruit. Be right back."

He retrieved the bins from the pantry and set them on the floor by his pyramid pile, then loaded the cups into the bins. He made sure the lids were on tight before stacking them by the front door.

"Those need to go in my SUV." She didn't look up from spooning batter into the muffin cups.

"I'm driving you to work tomorrow, and I don't want these items in the back of the truck all night where they can be stolen or tampered with."

"You are not driving me to work tomorrow."

"Yes I am; no arguing. You heard what my brother the sheriff said about your safety. With Billy back in town, Julie, I'm... *we* aren't taking any chances." He continued moving the bins next to the door, not explaining his hunch to her about Billy and the break-ins.

"What do you mean, 'with Billy back in town'? What does Billy have to do with me not being safe?" Her face was so cute when she got angry or puzzled. Right now, she was both. Not wanting her to defend her ex—because honestly he might break something if she did—he quietly pointed out some facts.

"Well, I think it's odd that you were attacked twice in one

week, only to find out Billy is back. Billy left town under some ugly circumstances..."

"Circumstances you caused! Don't blame Billy for having to leave town, Jason. Don't you dare! I know what you did to him." She practically threw her muffin tin in the oven. Jason wondered whether the muffins would come out crooked or straight.

"What do you mean, what I did to him?" He was careful not to sound angry. He didn't want to go into any details with her because Billy's betrayals would hurt her more than anything, and she was very delicate right now. Everything he did, he did for Julie. And for Charlie. He didn't want them hurt any more than they already had been.

The front door slammed startling them both.

"That asshole is back in town!" Charlie yelled. He stormed through the living room, his arms loaded with bags, poster board, and what Jason thought might be clothesline, but he wasn't sure. Charlie dumped his stuff on the dining room table and faced them, hands on his hips and staring in disgust and what looked like a little bit of fear on his angry face.

"Watch your mouth in front of your sister," Jason warned quietly.

Charlie threw his hands in the air. "Sorry." He clearly wasn't. "But has he called you, Julie? Have you spoken to him? Because if you have, I don't want him here. Don't you dare invite that jerk over. Please?" he asked desperately as he stomped off to the bathroom.

Jason puzzled over Charlie's outburst before asking Julie what it was all about. She looked at him for a second and then began to mix a second batch of batter.

"Julie? Why does your little brother hate Billy so much?"

"I don't know," she said with a sigh. "I'm not sure if

Charlie ever liked Billy, but the last year we were together, Charlie wouldn't be in the same room with him. It bothered Billy, you know, hurt his feelings. I talked to Charlie about it, but he would never tell me the problem."

She shook her head in contemplation. "I figured he was being a typical twelve-year-old boy who didn't like his sister's boyfriend. In those days, Charlie wasn't very nice to me either. I think it was hormones or something. When Mom and Dad died, he was absolutely unbearable to be around."

She looked up at him then. "You remember? That's about the time Charlie knocked me down, and you guys took him away for a while. He came back a different boy, Jason. I figured the three of you had threatened to break his legs or something if he didn't straighten up, but I didn't care what you did, as long as I got my brother back."

Jason was lost when she looked into his eyes and said softly, "I never thanked you for that."

He put his hand to her cheek, about to tell her she didn't need to thank him when Charlie stomped back into the room.

"And he's still just as big of an asshole as he ever was, still hanging out with the same creeps, too."

"How do you know all of this? I thought you were working on a school project?" Jason asked.

"We were, but we decided to go to town for something to eat when we finished. And there they were, sitting in a booth at Molly's Diner, yucking it up and harassing the waitress. Whatever. I wish he'd stayed gone."

Charlie went to the fridge and grabbed the milk. He slammed it on the counter before turning to grab a glass out of the cupboard. Julie stopped him before he got there. She gently opened the cupboard and handed him a glass, all while giving him a warning glare, which kind of scared Jason.

"Tell me why you hate him so much," Jason said. He didn't like the underlying fear in Charlie's face. He understood the disgust but not the fear.

What had Billy done to this kid?

Charlie poured some milk in the glass before returning the carton to the refrigerator. He seemed to be sorting out his thoughts, deciding on something. He lifted the glass to his lips and took a swig before setting it back down. He put both hands on the counter as if to brace himself before he looked up at Jason.

"Because he's not a loyal man."

He looked Jason straight in the eye when he said this and then pointedly looked at his sister. Jason said nothing. He waited for Julie's reaction.

"What do you mean, Charlie?" Her brow crinkled up in that cute way, but her voice held a little bit of fear.

Sighing, he stood up straight and faced his sister. "I mean..." He took another breath before he closed his eyes. Jason was about to offer encouragement when Charlie spoke up.

Staring his sister in the eyes, Charlie said, "He was cheating on you, Sis. I caught him one night at the diner with another woman."

Jason held his breath.

Julie shook her head. "Billy had lots of friends in this town, Charlie. It doesn't mean he was cheating on me. I'm sure he was just friends with whoever you saw him with."

Rage marred the kid's face. Jason made his way closer to Julie in case Charlie lost his temper.

"Does it mean he was just friends if he had his tongue down the girl's throat? Does it mean he was just being friendly when he threatened to hurt Trevor if I told anyone? Does it mean he was being a nice, *friendly* guy if I told Marco about it and mysteriously Trevor died the next day? He was here, and when I found Trevor in his tank with his shell crushed, Billy winked at me, Julie. I never understood what you saw in that creep."

Charlie had worked himself up again. He breathed liked he'd run a marathon; his face was red and blotchy. It was only a matter of time before he punched something, and Jason would make sure it wasn't Julie. He cleared his throat to get Charlie's attention as he moved in front of the kid's sister.

"No, Jason, don't tell me to calm down," Charlie yelled. "I thought I'd never have to see him again, but now he's back. What's worse is people still love him. He has a way of conning everyone into thinking he's such a great guy when actually he's an incredible asshat!"

Charlie stomped down the hall again, this time slamming his bedroom door.

"Who's Trevor?" he asked.

"A turtle Josh gave him for his birthday one year. I thought the smelly thing had died on its own. Charlie never said anything about it." She turned back to her muffins.

Jason narrowed his eyes at her back. He wanted to shake her. Instead, he calmed himself by focusing on the cooking while planning on how to keep them both safe now that Billy was back in town.

CHAPTER 12

Someone Blinked

Julie woke with a screaming headache. Monday mornings had never been her favorite things, but with stitches and a goose egg, it was almost unbearable.

Days like this made her wish she worked a regular nine-to-five office job, like Lauren, so she could call in sick. She couldn't do that as a self-employed entrepreneur (she laughed at the title she gave herself), so she forced her tired and sore body out of her warm, comfy bed and shuffled her way to the bathroom.

Going mostly by feel, she plugged in her curling iron, turned on the radio, and started the water. After stripping out of her jammies, she reached for her toothbrush. She sleep-walked through the rest of her morning routine.

After dressing, she made her way down the hallway to the kitchen where she found Jason and Charlie scarfing down muffins at the counter. Nothing made her happier than seeing men eating food she'd made with her own hands. It gave her a purpose in life, satisfying some inner female instinct to nurture and care for someone. After her parents' deaths and Billy's abrupt departure, she'd spent her entire adult life caring for her brother and making ends meet, instead of looking for a husband to start a family. So she compensated by preparing simple, healthy meals for her customers and the people she cared about most.

"Coffee?" Jason handed her a steaming mug with cream and sugar. She looked in the mug and noted the color—a beautiful caramel. She sighed in delight on her first sip.

He'd made it perfectly.

"Mmm... Thank you, Jason." She smiled at him as she tilted her head to verify. "Or did Charlie make this one?"

She looked questioningly at her brother, who shook his head. She glanced back at Jason with an impish smile. His lips lifted up on one side, showing off a dimple in his tanned, handsome face. His thick hair was still damp from his morning shower.

"No, smart ass, Charlie didn't help me," he said quietly with the same comical gaze.

Not taking offense to his name calling, she said, "Well, thank you very much. It's just how I like it."

Keeping her eyes on his intense green ones, she put the mug to her lips and took another sip. Those gems stayed focused on the mug, following it to her mouth as she drank. She unconsciously licked a drop off of her lower lip.

His eyes darkened. He shifted his feet and looked up to her eyes.

Her breathing began to quicken, and her body felt things it hadn't felt in a long time, if ever.

"Somebody blink, 'cause I need to go to school," Charlie sighed as he rinsed his mug in the sink.

Julie jumped back from Jason, eyes wide.

He shook his head and moved toward the sink with his own mug.

Charlie grabbed his backpack, which was stuffed with all the project materials he'd put together the night before. "Science is first period, so I have to meet up with my group to put this thing together for the presentation."

Jason cleared his throat as he rinsed out his mug. He put it in the dishwasher and reached for Julie's.

"We're taking my truck this morning, Charlie. Go ahead and put your stuff in the back; it should be fine on the way to school."

"I'll follow you in Cafe Armstrong," Julie said.

"It's already been moved to the site. You're with me."

She watched in startled shock as he picked up a couple of her muffin bins and walked out the front door after Charlie.

She grabbed the other bins and followed him outside. "When?"

"I talked to Josh last night after Jarod called. The prank calls plaguing you match the pattern of the ones I'm getting. Jarod asked that you and Charlie not be alone on your way to and from school and work, so Jarod brought Josh over late last night and followed him to the site in your food truck."

He stopped, took the bins she held, and placed them with the others in the back of his truck. "He wants to play this safe. He's got a funny feeling about all of this, and I have to agree with him."

His eyes darted up to the wound on her forehead before he opened the passenger door for her.

When she got herself buckled in, Charlie spoke from the backseat. "Why would someone target the two of you? You never hang out together."

His question reflected the thoughts that were going through her head.

Why me and Jason?

It didn't make any sense. They had no connection with each other, besides Josh. As far as she knew, Josh had no enemies, except maybe a jilted lover or two. But she didn't believe any of those women would connect Julie to Jason. Besides, nothing had directly happened to Josh. No, none of this made any sense.

Jason started the engine and turned his head to back out of the driveway. He placed his right arm on the back of Julie's seat, the leather squeaking as he adjusted his big body. His voice close to her left ear, he said, "I don't know, Charlie, but Jarod's working on it. The calls came from disposable phones. They're impossible to trace. But Jarod's going to interview employees of the stores in the area that carry disposables and hopefully get a hit on the sales. Of course, if they were bought with cash, which is likely, there's no way to find out who bought them. He said he'd look at any video footage for patrons, see if anyone is recognizable. It's a long shot, but it's something at least."

Julie held no hope Jarod would solve the prank calls. If she had caller I.D. she could screen her calls and not answer numbers she didn't recognize. Maybe that would discourage the caller enough to stop. She added "calling the phone company" to her growing to-do list

JASON HEADED TO THE CONSTRUCTION SITE AFTER dropping Charlie off at school. Julie *seemed* in better spirits. The little spree of flirting over the cup of coffee this morning had been encouraging and his blood still sang through his body. If Charlie hadn't spoken up, he would've kissed her silly to prove how much he cared for her.

Shaking those fiery thoughts from his head, he pulled into the makeshift parking lot outside his office. Cafe Armstrong sat to the right, so he parked next to it.

Right away, he noticed the new security cameras hanging at odd angles, wires showing.

What the hell?

Giving nothing away, he watched Julie get out of his truck and open up Cafe Armstrong. She began her morning checks, starting the generator and getting things going. When she turned to retrieve the bins from the truck, he stopped her and handed her a couple, then grabbed the rest. Not wanting to alert her anything was out of the ordinary—and since she hadn't noticed the damage—he stepped inside the little galley behind her and began unloading her items. He heard the crunch of tires on gravel and he went to the cafe's window. He caught Josh's attention once he'd parked his pickup next to Jason's.

"Hey, Bro. Does she need any help?"

"Yeah. Can you stay with her a minute while I open the office?" He looked meaningfully at his little brother and then glanced at the cameras.

Josh followed his gaze. His eyes widened before he nodded. "No problem." He kept his voice as carefree as ever, but his expression spoke volumes.

Jason trusted Josh would keep Julie busy while he checked things out.

Giving his brother a brief nod, Jason jogged up the steps to his office. His neck hair prickled as he put the key in the lock and opened the door.

At first glance the small sitting area looked just as it always did, until he flicked the lights on and took in his workspace. All of his files had been turned out of the filing cabinet and strewn everywhere; his chair was in the corner on its side; drafts and blueprints were either crumpled or torn; his computer was demolished; and, most importantly, the security-camera monitor had been smashed. A cool breeze blew in through the broken window.

He pulled his cell phone out of his pocket.

As Jarod answered the phone, Jason heard someone behind him. Startled, he quickly turned to find Josh standing there with his mouth hanging open. Josh was the engineer for this project; seeing the plans everywhere seemed to make him sick.

Jason spoke into his phone, "Hold on a minute." Then to Josh he said, "Go back to the food truck, and don't leave Julie's side."

Josh looked up from the mess and nodded before walking back outside.

Once he was gone Jason gave his attention to the sheriff. "Sorry, Jarod. I've got a situation here. I'm gonna need a deputy to file a report on this mess."

"Anyone hurt?"

"No, not that I know of. My trailer's been ransacked, and the security monitors are destroyed."

"I'm on my way." He hung up on Jason before he could reply.

Jason called his dad next to tell him the situation. James had been kept up to speed on everything from the altercations with the strangers to Julie's car accident. If Jason knew his father, James would put his main guy on it to help in the investigation, digging where the law, and Jarod, couldn't.

"We'll catch this son of a bitch, son. You just keep that

sweet girl and her little brother safe. Dane seems to think he might have found the stripper. He's still doing some checking before he conducts an interview with her. If she's the same person who can identify Billy, then we'll pressure her to file a statement with the sheriff's office, so Jarod can reopen the hit and run case."

"Thanks, Dad. I'll keep you informed of what's going on here." He hung up and walked out the door.

His hungry workers had already lined up for breakfast. Josh was outside the food truck with a disgruntled look on his face. Julie must've kicked him out, which Jason found hilarious under the circumstances.

Josh handed him a cup of coffee. "Well? What'd Jarod say?"

"I asked for a deputy; he's coming himself." He rolled his eyes. He loved his big brother, but Jarod had responsibilities, and Jason didn't want to take him away from other cases. He could handle the situation here for now. He needed Jarod investigating instead of babysitting. "I called Dad too. He's got Dane on it and says they may have found the girl."

Josh's eyes widened. "You mean the stripper who was in Billy's car the night Julie's parents were run off the road? What was her name?"

"Candy or something."

"Where did Dane find her?"

Jason took a sip of coffee. Looking down at his cup, he said, "Dad said she's working a pole at Fantasy Five."

Disgusted, Josh shook his head. "Figures. Billy always had an eye for the trashy side of life. That place is a real dive." Josh threw his empty cup in the garbage. "Doesn't Jarod plan his weekend surveillance routes around that place? Lots of drug and other shady deals go on there. I know a squad car is called out there at least once a week."

Jason understood how his brother felt. Knowing the types of women Billy had cheated on Julie with made Jason's skin crawl and his blood boil. Prostitution was legal in most Nevada counties, and Timbisha was one of them. He hoped the bastard had used condoms, but the topic was too personal to ask Julie.

He squeezed his eyes shut and shook off his rage. "Dad's team is running a check on the stripper," he said. "We'll know more later today, I hope."

Jason caught Julie's eye to silently ask if he could come inside. The lines had died down, and he thought he'd help her prep for the next service before Jarod showed up. He didn't want to disturb the crime scene in the hope the sheriff's department would find something—hell, anything—to lead them to a suspect.

He stepped inside the tiny kitchen, relieved at Julie's welcome—her beautiful face a balm for his troubled heart.

Sweetly, she asked, "Everything okay? You and Josh looked like you were having a pretty intense conversation." She pulled out the onions, tomatoes, and lettuce from the small cooler. He grabbed a couple of tomatoes and started slicing.

He took a deep breath to force the anger from his voice, wanting to spare her from the violent emotions brewing inside him. "My office was ransacked last night. Some security equipment is destroyed. Until Jarod gets here with a team, I'm not allowed inside. Do you mind if I help you with breakfast?"

She stopped working as he spoke. "Of course it's all right." Pausing in thought, she then asked with concern, "What do you mean 'ransacked'? Is anything missing?"

He focused on the adorable, confused line between her eyebrows. He wanted to kiss it to distract himself from what was happening in his office. Instead, he answered, "Not sure.

All the site's blueprints are either torn or destroyed, but it's not really an issue. The company keeps duplicates." He moved on to the onions. "Jarod's on his way over to investigate the scene."

"Will you be halting construction on the shopping center? While they investigate, I mean?"

"No. Dad wouldn't stop work unless he was court ordered to do so or if injuries were involved." He shook his head at the horrible thought. If whoever's doing this is looking to shut down the company, Jason sincerely hoped they wouldn't go as far as to physically hurt people.

Except, Julie had been hurt in the hit and run.

Tearing himself away from the painful memory, he sliced the onions with more vigor before helping Julie assemble sandwiches.

Jarod showed up right before lunch. He brought in a few deputies to help catalogue the damage and run some prints. Not wanting to get in anyone's way, Jason stayed in the kitchen with Julie.

The more time he spent with her, the more he wanted to keep her. Trying to remain aloof was getting harder and harder. He wanted to make Julie see he wasn't the bad guy. He thought he was getting through to her. He wouldn't leave her side until she was safe, that was for damn sure.

Lunch came and went as usual except for the fact he did the serving and was not working out of his office. Frustrated Jarod hadn't communicated with him since his arrival, Jason finally left Julie to the cleanup and ventured into his own trailer. Police tape crisscrossed the doorway. He stepped into his office, ignoring it.

It's overkill anyway.

Jarod spoke with some sort of technician about evidence. Jason almost had hope they'd find clues on who did this.

"I want the results as soon as possible," Jarod said to the tech.

Jason approached them. "Find anything?"

"Nothing of significance. I think we might have a partial print, and we found some hairs in the file cabinet, but they could be yours. I put a rush on it. Pray the lab isn't backed up."

Jarod moved around Jason's office, checking this and that. "I spoke to Dad. He told me about Candy, or whatever she's going by these days. I'll check on her myself and see what we can come up with or if it matches up with what Dane can find. I don't usually like working with P.I.s, especially one who used to be a fed, but in this case, I'll make an exception."

Jason nodded his agreement. "Can I start cleaning this mess up, or does some fancy technical machine need to come in and collect data?"

Jarod laughed. "No, little brother, this isn't a sci-fi movie. Give me ten more minutes, and we'll be out of your hair."

Jason clapped his brother on the back before he headed back out to the food truck to check on Julie.

He'd just stepped into Cafe Armstrong when Jarod cursed loudly. He turned around to find Jarod running to his squad car.

"YOUR HOUSE IS ON FIRE!"

Julie screamed, "WHAT?" from behind him and started pushing him out of the way.

Jarod backed his cruiser out of its space and yelled out his window at them. "Jason's house is on fire! Fire department is on scene now!"

Stunned, Jason watched in disbelief as his brother-the-sheriff tore out of the parking lot faster than light.

Jason stood there with his brains scrambled and offline.

Julie knocked him on the shoulder. "Gimme your keys!"

She had her hands all over him in an attempt to find them. Kind of enjoying her touch, he let her search him while his mind tried to reboot to get his body moving again.

More quickly than he would have liked, she found his keys hanging on his belt loop. Then she yanked on his arm and shouted to his baby brother, who'd returned from the other side of the site.

"Josh! Jason's house is on fire! We're going!"

"What? Are you serious?" Josh got out of his truck and ran to them.

Jason still couldn't make his mouth move.

The bastards have resorted to arson.

Julie explained the situation to Josh, then both of them shoved Jason into the passenger seat of his own truck.

"Do you need me to drive, Julie? How's your head?"

"I'm fine, Josh. Follow me to his house." She jumped into his lifted pickup like a pro and started the engine. Unknowingly turning Jason on, she impressed him with how she'd taken over. His desire for her helped tamp down the ever-present rage which again boiled inside him. She backed up, put his big truck in drive, and flung gravel as she peeled out of the parking lot, Josh hot on her tail.

Arson. Someone's playing a very dangerous game.

She reached over and took his hand. "Talk to me, Jason. You're scaring me. You're not having some sort of breakdown, are you?" She alternated watching the road and looking at him as she sped down the two-lane highway.

"No, not a breakdown. I'm good. You're doing great, keep driving." No way would he admit that her take-charge attitude had sent blood to *all* his extremities. No sirree.

But then he saw the smoke and his blood turned to ice.

Shit.

Still a few blocks away, a couple of emergency vehicles passed them on the way to his house. After turning onto his street, Julie had to stop about four houses down from the scene. Authorities blocked the road and his neighbors, the ones who were home during the day, had gathered to watch the spectacle.

The three of them got out of their trucks, gaping at the sight. Julie reached for Jason's hand. He held tight. She was his anchor, even if she didn't know it. As long as she was with him, holding his hand and lending her support, he felt better.

He stood in a pissed-off daze, clinging to her like a lifeline as firefighters worked to save his house. When the roof caved in, Julie released his hand. He thought he'd die in that brief second until she wrapped her arms around his waist and hugged him tightly. Josh and the rest of his neighbors around him let out a sad moan.

"Oh, Jason," she began to cry.

He couldn't bear her tears. He wrapped his arms around her and kissed her head. "Don't you cry for me, Jujyfruit. There wasn't anything in there that can't be replaced. Hush now."

He kissed the top of her head again as she clung to him.

Josh patted his shoulder. "I've got plenty of room at the townhouse, brother."

"No, I won't impose, but thank you. I'm sure the insurance company will set me up with temporary digs."

Julie tried to pull away from him, but he wouldn't let her go. When she struggled softly, he looked down. Her big, brown eyes were luminous with unshed tears.

"You can stay with me as long as you need to. Besides, your things are already there." She looked down before she hugged him again. "I like you being in my home, Jason."

He went from wanting to punch something to feeling his heart beat out of his chest. Her sweet admission meant everything to him. God help him, he'd burn down his house ten times over if it meant Julie admitted she cared for him.

"I like being with you, too, Jujyfruit. I'll stay as long as you let me. Thank you, babe." He squeezed her against his side, loving how perfectly she fit against him.

He glanced at Josh, who wore a sad smile on his face. His brother understood. Josh was just as worried about the danger now that it had escalated to fire.

While the house burning down, along with most of his clothes, was a total pain in the ass, he hadn't been lying when he'd said it could all be replaced. This house had been minimally furnished with the bare necessities. He'd kept nothing of sentimental value inside. He'd purchased it as an investment and a place to crash at night when he worked in town. It wasn't home to him. So while most people would have been completely devastated, he was merely put out.

Julie eventually stopped crying, thank God. He would explain things better tonight when they were home. He had lots of calls to make. He had a fireproof safe to retrieve when the fire department gave him the all clear. Hopefully, it wouldn't take too long to deal with the insurance company.

He didn't let go of Julie, and she didn't let go of him until Jarod moved toward them from the other side of the makeshift barricade, his face grim.

"Arson. They used gasoline, lots and lots of gasoline. It's all preliminary, but the fire chief says it's pretty obvious. When were you here last?"

Jason thought a minute. He hadn't been in the house since he'd gathered up his things Saturday afternoon. He gave all the information to Jarod, who asked multiple questions about how the house had looked when he'd left, especially whether or not he'd remembered to lock his doors. Jason was positive he had done a full lockdown.

"Good," Jarod muttered as he wrote the information in a small notebook. Once he finished, he said, "One of your neighbors reported a black pickup parked in your driveway before noon today. The descriptions of the truck and the men who got out of it match those of the suspects who harassed Julie at the construction site."

Loud sobbing was his only warning before a woman threw her arms around him, forcing him to let go of Julie.

"Oh, Jason! Are you hurt?" He looked down into emerald eyes that matched his own and a face full of concern.

"I'm fine, Mom."

"Give him some room, Camille," Jason's dad said. "He said he's fine, but you're frightening Julie."

"Julie!" she yelled, throwing her arms around his girl and showering her with motherly concern as well.

Julie mumbled something into his mother's hair before Jason reached over and untangled her from his mother's grasp. Once he had her free, he put her right back at his side, *where she belongs*, he thought and held on tight.

Jarod bristled. "Dad. What are you doing here?"

"Are you kidding? Like you could keep us away; and don't take that tone with me either, Jarod. You may be wearing a uniform and badge, but you're still my first born, damn it. I want you to let Dane," he gestured to the older man next to him, "do what he does best. I think you need all the help you can get on this case. These 'accidents' are getting way too dangerous."

James King was not someone you argued with, especially at a time like this. Jason grabbed his mom's hand and pulled her close. Both his parents wore the same look—fear and concern for their children. Jason had seen that look many times growing up, and he loved them for it.

His mom interrupted his thoughts with an invitation. "I've planned an impromptu family dinner tonight, and I want you all to come." She reached for Julie's free hand with her own and said, "I want you and Charlie there as well, dear."

"Thank you, Camille. That's very sweet of you to think of us."

Jason held Julie a bit tighter, glad she hadn't tried to weasel out of dinner either. Damn, she's cooperative today.

Then his mother looked at him with authority. "I'm having your rooms freshened up for you, honey. So don't even think about staying at a hotel or with Josh." She smiled at him and touched his cheek.

Before he could say anything, Jarod interrupted, "Mom. No. I've asked Jason to keep watch over Julie and Charlie. He's already set up in her spare room." Jarod abruptly turned to their father's head of security. "Dane, please come with me," effectively ending the conversation.

Relieved he didn't have to explain further why he was sticking to Julie like glue, he gave his brother an appreciative nod. Jarod winked at him before leading his father's man away.

CHAPTER 13
Caravan

Julie watched Jason's house be reduced to a smelly pile of ash. Desperate to offer Jason comfort she held on to him, relishing the contact. She'd harbored such bad feelings towards him for so long but now she suspected things weren't as they'd appeared to be. Everything from the altercations, the hit and run, and now arson, all shed light on how misguided and stubborn she'd been.

Jason was never the bad guy.

No one deserved to have their house burned down. Someone out there believed she and Jason shared a dangerous link and they wanted to hurt them for it.

But why? And who?

Fire fighters finally extinguished the large blaze but the black sticks and foundation still smoldered, the acrid smoke biting her nose and mouth. Jason had lost everything and Julie couldn't fathom being so calm after such a personal loss. Other than his momentary loss of speech, he acted like it was just another day. His strength amazed her. She'd always thought of him as too controlling and pushy, and she may have been a bit afraid of him. But now she saw him in a whole new light. She'd misunderstood his authority, because without the ability to command, his life would be in total chaos.

Absolutely nothing remained of the burning house. She texted Charlie to let him know what was going on and to dress appropriately for dinner with the Kings'. Jason hadn't let go of her except when he'd hugged his mother. Julie squeezed his hand as he pulled her toward his truck. He'd already confiscated his keys from her, recovering his control once again.

Thank God.

"I'll meet you guys at Mom and Dad's," Josh said, heading toward his own truck.

Julie waved at him before crashing into Jason's back when he stopped short. He tugged her closer as his body tightened. A small, black convertible pulled in behind both their trucks. A blond man with light blue eyes stepped out of the car. Walking toward them wearing a familiar smirk, he raised a hand in greeting.

"What the hell are you doing here, Billy?" Josh's question was laced with menace. Both brothers positioned themselves in protective stances on either side of Julie, almost blocking her from Billy's view, but Jason switched from holding her hand to pulling her close.

"Nice to see you too, Josh." Eyes the color of ice chips shifted toward Julie, sending a chill straight into her soul. "And what about my girl? No tearful hello from the woman who said she'd love me forever?" He tsked at her as his smile morphed into something marring a once-handsome face; all teeth and dead eyes.

"Why are you here?" Jason asked. He sounded relaxed, but

because he was touching her, she felt the tension vibrating throughout his large, muscular frame.

"I've wanted to say hello since I got back to town, but haven't had the time. I've been busy. When I heard about the fire, I thought I'd come by to offer my condolences. Need any help?"

Julie thought he sounded sincere, but she didn't really know him anymore. She realized she probably never truly knew him.

"Thank you for your consideration, Billy. I've got this handled," Jason said as he wrapped his arm around her.

"Yes, I can see you that do, Jason." She heard the contempt in his voice. "I just wanted to come by and let you all know that I'm here... to stay this time."

Julie held her breath when Billy leaned in close to Jason's face and lowered his voice. "You'll be hearing from me again. Have yourselves a good evening." Then he slithered back over to his expensive convertible and drove away.

Julie shivered and Jason's arms tightened around her.

"Let's get Cafe Armstrong and bring it to my parents' house. It's gated and will be safer than at your house out in the open."

"Do you honestly think that's necessary? Won't your parents mind? It's kind of an eyesore."

"Never mind the eyesore, Julie," Josh said with cold steel in his voice as he followed them to the vehicles. He was one of her best friends, so she knew when not to question him.

"Billy's showing himself now," Jason said, "and he's not afraid, Jujyfruit. His comment about seeing us again—that was a threat, babe."

She wasn't stupid. The man who'd left in the sporty

convertible wasn't the boyfriend of her youth who'd broken her heart. He was a stranger.

Trusting Jason she acquiesced. "Oh, all right, but I don't want to impose on your parents." All of a sudden, she had an intense desire to please him. She was sick of fighting him anyway. It didn't feel right to fight with him after what he'd lost today.

Josh said, "Dad will insist after we tell him about Billy's visit. The fire has them both so freaked out that Mom mentioned some nonsense about all of us moving back in with them." He shook his head but glanced at Jason in the brotherly way Julie often witnessed between them, like sibling telepathy. She and Charlie shared a common bond, but because of the age difference and the fact she'd transitioned from sister to guardian, their relationship felt different.

"We'll talk more tonight at dinner," Jason said, giving Josh a glare.

"I'll follow you two back to the construction site to make sure nothing else happens. What about Charlie?" Josh asked.

"Maybe James and Camille can pick him up? Let me know and I'll text him the plan," Julie said.

JULIE HAD ALWAYS KEPT CLOSE TABS ON HER business vehicle, Cafe Armstrong, and leaving it on the Kings' gated property didn't sit right with her.

She'd followed Jason in her food truck while Josh had followed her. She giggled when Jarod flashed his lights behind Josh, making quite an entrance into the palatial estate—a large duel-wheeled pickup fit for a construction boss, a food truck, another man-sized pickup, and a sheriff's cruiser.

All we need is a clown car. They made a comical parade through town.

Camille and James came out the side door, Camille waving and James directing everyone where to park. He looked like a person working at an airport waving in large aircraft. All he needed were the cone-shaped flashlights. Following his direction, she parked on the far side of the house out of sight of the road.

James strolled over to Cafe Armstrong as she was getting ready to lock the doors. "I've always wanted to see the inside of one of these," he smiled at her. "Mind if I come in?"

"Not at all." She opened the door wider and squished back as far as she could to let the big man inside. "It's not much to look at, James. It's all pretty basic. Just a small kitchen on wheels."

"You're too modest, Julie. I've tasted your fare, and you are a very accomplished chef." He gave her a wink before turning around and stepping out of the vehicle so she could lock up.

"And you have a way with words, Mr. King, but thank you for the compliment." She took the elbow he offered her.

James King had the same air of authority as his sons, but he was a lot like Josh—or Josh was a lot like him. They both had an open, friendly way about them which made people feel comfortable. Even though she was surrounded by wealth, she didn't feel out of place. The Kings were regular people who happened to have a lot of money which, she knew from Josh, was hard earned.

Maybe that made a difference because Billy certainly had never made her feel comfortable when they'd been in his element. A trust fund baby, his family came from old money earned from the silver mines in the early 1900s. She remembered now how he'd found delight in her discomfort whenever they'd been around his family.

Funny how she'd forgotten about that. She shook herself from the memory to concentrate on the people around her—people she truly cared about and who cared for her in return.

CHAPTER 14

No Choice

Jason enjoyed seeing his father escort Julie from her truck to the house. It gave him a sense of peace and rightness knowing how much his family loved her and her brother. He wondered how the evening would go, though, when she discovered they were all staying here until this problem was resolved.

"When are we going to tell her?" Josh asked.

"I think we should leave it to Mom. She has a way with Julie neither of us has."

"True enough, but what about her house? Aren't we leaving it unprotected?" Josh asked, concern etched in his brow.

"Don't worry about her house," Jarod said as he sauntered up behind them. "I've got a cruiser going by every hour, and I've talked to the neighborhood watch director. If anything suspicious comes within fifty yards of her property, we'll know about it." Jarod patted Josh on the shoulder while making eye contact with Jason. Jason nodded back at his older brother.

"What are you three hunks up to?"

Jason felt feminine arms wrap around his waist. He looked down to see Lauren's smiling face shining brightly at his.

"Planning your demise," Josh answered her, laughing and slinging his arms around her shoulders in a brotherly hug. "What're you doing here?"

"Very funny." She pushed him back playfully. "Camille asked me to spend the night. Said she was having a dinner party and couldn't live without my winning personality or my social skills in delicate situations." She grinned her special I-got-a-plan grin while she locked her eyes onto the sheriff.

Jarod groaned and stalked off.

"I meant with Julie," she said with a wink. "It's going to take some convincing to get her to stay here overnight. But it looks like you guys have brought the two most important things here already: her brother and her food truck. She can't put up too much of a fight with those two concerns taken care of." As she glanced at Jarod's departing back, she giggled, "Oh, this is going to be a fun night."

Jason rolled his eyes. He almost felt sorry for Lauren if she thought she could break through Jarod's stone-cold heart. His older brother only tolerated women when he needed them. They had spent many nights discussing the reasons why neither of them were married—Jason because he was in love with someone who hated him and Jarod because he didn't trust women. His ex-wife had made sure of that.

It was really too bad Jarod was so stubborn. Lauren would be good for him, Jason thought to himself.

They all walked into his parents' massive home. Even though Jason technically moved out of his childhood home when he left for college, he still loved this house. His father bought the property right when King Construction began to turn a big profit. The landscaping around the mansion was kept lush and green, fed by underground wells and groundwater. Natural hot springs were common in the region, making the desert landscape deceptive. The outlying acreage to the west remained natural and untouched, and the area to the east held paddocks for the myriad animals his mother liked to keep. The house, barn, and outbuildings were surrounded by a security wall. It was safe enough on its own but James had state-of-the-art security, as well as Dane and his team of merry men. They would be safe here tonight.

They went in the side door on the east wing of the house into the mud room which, in actuality, was a massive utility space which held a washer and dryer, a large bathroom, utility closet for his dad's tools, vacuum, ironing board, and other odds and ends. Coat hooks lined one whole wall with cubbies underneath for shoes and work boots, and shelving to hold various items.

The doorway led them into the smaller family kitchen his mother used every day. It held stainless-steel appliances—a stove, cooktop, sink, dishwasher, and wine cooler near the small wet bar—and marble countertops atop knotty pine cabinetry. There was a "small" table of the same knotty pine material with captain's chairs at the two ends; along one long side were four chairs, and along the other was a bay window and a padded bench seat. Jason and his brothers had grown up at that table, in this kitchen. Their dad had built another commercial-grade kitchen in another part of the house, used only for large social events for the company or for charitable events for the community.

Their mother had changed the color scheme several times

over the years. Currently, it was a sunny cream color with earth tones, gingham curtains, and throw pillows on the window seat. They found Charlie digging through the fridge looking for an after-school snack, as was his habit.

"Charlie! What do you think you're doing?" Julie exclaimed, looking appalled.

Jason laughed. Charlie knew this house inside out, having spent a lot of time here over the years.

"What?" Charlie asked unconcerned. "I'm hungry. Camille doesn't mind." He grinned at Jason's mom, who wandered over to Charlie, gave him a maternal squeeze, and helped him pull some snacks out of the fridge.

Julie scowled.

"Oh, don't you worry about Charlie, dear," his mother said. "He knows his way around my kitchen. He's a growing boy and he needs to eat often." She punctuated her statement with a sharp nod of her chin.

"Let me help you, Camille."

"Oh, no you don't. You've been through enough today. You relax with Jason while Charlie and I cook."

He leaned into Julie's ear. "Relax, Jujyfruit. This is helping my mom regain her composure after this morning. Look at her face. See how worried she is? Let her do this, okay?"

He watched his beautiful woman take in his mother's features and knew Julie would let it go. When Lauren jumped in to help, Julie didn't say anything, even though his mother wasn't shooing Lauren from the kitchen.

As Camille directed her two helpers, the rest of them gathered at the table. Jason led Julie to the bench seat while Josh squeezed in on the other side so she couldn't escape. Of course, she had no clue she'd been captured, but as soon as she got wind this dinner party was going to be an overnighter, Jason had no doubt she'd try to bolt. No one in his family wanted that. With his house burned to the ground and Julie being the target of two attacks, they weren't taking any chances until they could figure out Billy's game and put a stop to it. Between Jarod's and Dane's investigating skills, hopefully they could nail the coward in order to move on with their lives.

"Thank you for letting me store Cafe Armstrong on your property. I know it doesn't go with the landscaping," Julie said to James, who sat across from them.

"Don't you worry about that, Julie. It's our pleasure. Dane and Jarod wouldn't have it any other way. The danger is very real and I want to make that very clear to you, if you don't already know it." Softening toward her, he admitted, "Your father and I were friends, so I know he'd come back down from heaven to give me a good pounding if I didn't look out for you and Charlie."

Jason had heard this many times before, but he'd never discussed it with Julie and didn't know if she was aware of how close their fathers had been.

"Dad said you two knew each other, but he didn't say how close you were."

"Well, there was a time when we were inseparable, but we went to different colleges. Afterward we grew apart because we ran in different circles, but I always considered him one of my dear friends. I would be remiss if I didn't look out for my friend's children after he passed away."

Julie leaned into Jason. He doubted she was conscious of it. Casually, he put his arm around the backrest of the bench they shared. He caught his dad's smile. Julie remained clueless.

She was so damn cute sometimes.

They continued to talk as Jason's thoughts rambled on. His house had just burned to the ground, yet sitting this close to Julie—the love of his life—filled him with such peace he'd never be able to describe it out loud. Until the words *through good times and bad* fluttered softly through his mind.

Holy cow, he needed to focus on the conversation! He'd had those fleeting thoughts in the past, but they were always vague and completely out of reach. Could he hope for something he believed to be so far away? Maybe. Their rapport was changing for the better. He could hope.

It was late in the afternoon, but no one had had a chance to eat lunch with all the drama of the day. Charlie brought over a huge platter of sandwiches and set it in the middle of the table. Lauren set a bowl of salad next to it, and Camille passed out paper plates, napkins, and silverware.

Julie made a move to scoot out to help, but Jason instinctively put his arm around her shoulders. When she looked at him in question, he merely smiled and shook his head. "Don't worry about it, Jujyfruit. They've already gotten everything." He looked into her eyes as he pulled her a little closer to him. "Besides, I need you to stay close to me," he said quietly so no one but Julie could hear.

He loved it when her eyes widened and her face flushed.

She whispered, "'Kay," then turned her head toward the rest of the room. When they came around, she pulled two plates over to them and filled his plate with sandwiches and salad before she made her own plate. She was a natural born nurturer, and it turned him on something fierce. She met his eyes, took a huge bite of salad and chewed. He laughed before attacking his sandwiches.

Conversation took a backseat to the late lunch. Everyone filled their plates and their stomachs. Charlie asked questions about the fire and Jason's ransacked office. Jarod and James caught him up on everything, not sparing any details. Information was power, and everyone agreed Charlie needed to be as much on his toes about the danger as everyone else.

Lauren hadn't been told about the office destruction, so Jason filled in the places where the others couldn't. Everyone agreed Billy's appearance at the fire had been his way of making a threat. Jarod had his people on it, but Jason didn't think the law could do much at this point until another crime was committed. So far it had all been property damage, except for the hit and run on Julie, which could be construed as a random act of road rage. Otherwise, no one had been seriously injured. They had no proof Billy was behind any of it, nothing legally connecting the dots to him. Unless Jarod could tie either the truck, the stolen plates, or the men to Billy, he would remain on the streets, free to run whatever game he pleased.

"I think he's going to push us until we lose our cool and do something stupid. Trap us in some legal battle. That's usually how he got away with his pranks as a teen," James said as he put his napkin on his plate. "He doesn't realize most of us remember how he operates. I'm counting on him being just as arrogant as ever, thinking of himself as untouchable."

"He is untouchable, Dad." Jarod said. He gave their father his cop face, but James only winked at his eldest.

"Don't you worry about that, sheriff. You keep doing what you're doing. As long as you and Dane stay in touch with each other, we'll get him," James said with confidence.

"Dad, you know I can't share ongoing police investigations." Jarod rolled his eyes.

"I don't expect you to leak potentially dangerous information to the Taliban, son. I do expect you to protect your loved ones." James raised his eyebrow with that statement.

Jarod began to argue, but their mother interrupted. "If you two are finished bossing each other around, I think we should talk about tonight."

Jason took a deep breath. She was gonna drop the bomb. *Shit, here we go.*

"What about tonight?" Charlie asked around a bite of apple pie. The kid's stomach was an endless abyss.

"Jason, I've made up your room. Dane sent some of his men to Julie's to pick up your things. They also took the liberty of packing bags for both Julie and Charlie."

Julie went rigid in his hold. "What do you mean?"

His mother put on her don't-you-argue-with-me face and looked Julie right in the eye. "I've prepared rooms for all of you. You will be staying here until this mess is cleared up."

"But..."

"Lauren has brought her overnight bag and will be staying as well. I won't have my son out there where it's dangerous, and it's obvious whoever is doing this is leading up to do more harm than he's already done."

"Camille, I can't stay here. I have a home, work, and Charlie has school," Julie argued.

She is so in for it, Jason thought.

"I know you have a home of your own, Julie. But I insist you stay here where you'll be safe. That is *my* priority. I won't have Jason or Charlie in harm's way. Would you?" She raised her eyebrows at Julie.

Jason wasn't sure if invoking his name would really matter to Julie, but using her brother against her was the killing blow.

"Of course I wouldn't want them in harm's way. But Jarod said he had police watching the house—"

"He does, and he will keep your house safe. But it is only a house, dear. You are the people I love, and you will be safer here. Now, no more discussion. Your things are here and your rooms are being set up as we speak. Think of it as a family reunion of sorts. What do you say?"

"I don't have a choice, do I?" Julie looked at Jason, but his father and Jarod answered for him in unison...

"No. You don't."

CHAPTER 15

Room Of Doom

Julie studied their faces while Jason waited for her to blow up. Surprising him, and everyone else in the room, she said, "All right. You know what's best, and I don't want anyone else hurt."

Jason leaned in and kissed her temple. "Thank you," he whispered, as he let out the breath he'd been holding.

"Good, it's all settled then." His mom replied. "It's going to be so nice to have some female companionship in this house for a change. Have you girls ever seen my craft room?"

With regret, he let go of Julie when his mother ushered the women out of the kitchen to the part of the house all of the men feared; the room of doom.

That's what he and his brothers called it. His mother kept all kinds of *things* in there which did not interest boys; she'd use lace and ribbon and all kinds of fluffy girl stuff to punish them when they'd gotten into mischief as kids. Thankfully, he hadn't seen the inside of it since he'd moved out, and he didn't plan on revisiting any time soon.

"You know, she had me expand it," his father said with absolutely no emotion at all.

Completely horrified, Josh said, "No." He shook his head. "She didn't make you do it personally, did she, Dad?" Josh had spent a lot of time in that room.

"No, I had some men come do it, but she did make me draw up the design plans to organize all the crap she's got in there. Then she enlisted me to help put all that shit away. Worst two weeks of my life, and you know how much I love your mother."

Jason shuddered at the thought.

"What's so awful about Camille's craft room?" Charlie asked.

The King men proceeded to regale him with tales of their youth, the trouble they'd gotten into—even James—and the punishments Camille had come up with. Charlie seemed to be equal parts impressed with their mischief and horrified by what they'd had to do as punishment.

"She made you help with the decorations for baby showers? That's cruel and unusual punishment, isn't it?"

Jason said, "That's nothing, Charlie. When I got my first tattoo, I was only fifteen. I'd convinced the tattoo artist I was eighteen—she was super hot and I wanted to impress her, and she fell for it. Anyway, when I got home past my curfew, Mom was still up pacing. First she saw the hickey on my neck. Then she spotted the bandage on my arm. Concerned I got hurt, she insisted on 'looking at it to make sure I didn't have an infection.' I knew I was screwed, so I showed it to her."

"Did she completely freak out?" Charlie asked, his eyes as big as saucers.

"No, not completely. At first, I thought I was safe because my tattoo wasn't offensive."

Charlie looked at his arm. "Which one is it?"

Jason pulled up his left t-shirt sleeve. Taking up most of his tricep was a large superimposed XP. To the left of the symbol was a smaller upside-down V, and on the right was an upside-down horseshoe.

"What does it mean?"

"It's Greek. The center symbol is called a Chi Rho; it's a symbol for 'Christ.' This one," Jason pointed to the upside-down V, "is for 'Alpha,' and the other symbol is for 'Omega.'"

Charlie looked awed. "'Christ, the beginning and the end.' So, you thought if you got Christian ink, Camille wouldn't flip out?" Charlie grabbed his stomach and laughed great big guffaws. The kid knew Jason's mother all too well.

"Yeah, I was an idiot. I still love this tattoo, even though she made me help her with the Anderson/Vickers wedding." Jason wasn't sure if Charlie was too young to know who that was, but by the look on the kid's face, he'd made his point.

"I didn't think Camille could be so mean," Charlie said, a little dumbfounded.

Jarod piped up then. "Oh, she's mean, all right. Not only did Jason get stuck putting together all the pink birdseed packets, we," he stopped to gesture at Josh, "had to help when she found out we knew he planned on getting the tattoo." His brother shook his head at the memory. "I think she must've been short on help, now that I look back. She panicked and employed her children in slave labor." All three of them looked at each other for a moment and then busted up laughing.

"What's up, kid?" Jason said when Charlie's face turned melancholy.

Charlie shook his head and stared at his half-eaten slice of apple pie.

Josh clapped Charlie on the back as he returned with a beer. "You sure you don't want to talk about it?"

Charlie put his fork down but remained silent. Jason understood he had been close with Josh long before the Armstrongs died, but it was odd for Charlie to be reluctant to speak in front of them. James, who sat next to Charlie, put a fatherly hand on his shoulder, like he did with Jason and his brothers when something was obviously wrong.

Charlie looked up at him and smiled a sad smile. "I just... I miss my parents. Things were different when they were alive. Being here reminds me of those times." He shrugged his shoulders.

Jason wanted to hug him but knew the action would embarrass everyone at the table.

His father came to the rescue. "You know, Charlie, you're welcome to come visit us any time you like. Camille and I think of you and Julie as our extended family, and I hope you feel the same way."

Charlie cleared his throat. "Yeah, I know, sir. Thank you." Then, to cover up his quavering voice, he took a drink of his soda.

Into the quiet, Jarod's cell rang. Relieved by the interruption, Jason stood to put the dishes in the sink. He overheard Jarod saying he'd be right there.

"I'm needed at the hospital," he announced as he exited the kitchen.

"What's happening?" Jason asked before his brother could leave the house.

Jarod stopped but didn't turn. Jason could see he was debating whether or not to answer. When he finally turned, he wore his cop face.

"A woman's been admitted to the hospital, possible assault

victim. She works at Fantasy Five." Giving Jason a pointed look, he turned and walked out the door.

At the same time, Dane came into the kitchen from the other end of the house and spoke softly into their father's ear.

"You better get going. Jarod's already left for the hospital," James said.

"Yes, sir," Dane answered. "I'll call when I know more," he said, following the same exit route as Jarod.

"What's going on?" Josh asked.

James looked at Charlie pointedly before Charlie said, "What? No way am I leaving." The kid shook his head at them, refusing to be left out of the conversation.

Resigned to speak in front of Charlie, James drew a breath, only to blow it out as the girls returned from the Room of Doom.

"I think we can do something with that extra material for Cafe Armstrong. What do you think, Julie?" Camille said as they entered the dining room.

"What's going on? Where's Jarod?" Lauren asked.

"As I was about to inform my sons, Dane has gone to the hospital to interview a patient, a young woman. Dane seems to think she may be a witness to a crime. We won't know anything more until later. Jarod caught the case right before Dane informed me of the situation. Jarod's on his way to the hospital to speak to the woman."

Jason watched his mother absorb what his father said. Julie, Charlie, and Lauren all wore blank expressions, clearly not understanding the problem.

"Does she have something to do with the people who are trying to hurt you and my sister?" Charlie asked Jason.

"Maybe. We don't know yet."

"What crime did she witness?" Julie asked the room.

Jason looked at his family. He wasn't sure if he should say anything until they had more information. His dad answered for him.

"We think she's a witness to a hit and run from a few years back."

That sentence could describe any number of scenarios. Jason studied Charlie first for a reaction. His eyebrows lowered in puzzlement but accepted the explanation at face value.

Julie, on the other hand, became quite still.

Jason stepped up to her and spoke softly to her. "We don't know anything for certain, Jujyfruit. It's only a possibility."

"But you must have a pretty good idea about it, right?" Her eyes filled with tears and her voice shook.

"We've got a good idea, yes." James admitted.

Good. Jason never wanted to keep things from her again.

JULIE COULD NOT BELIEVE THE SIZE OF CAMILLE'S craft room. It was triple the size of the living room, dining and kitchen space of her and Charlie's house. The woman had her own hobby store in one room of her home! Julie didn't have an artistic bone in her body, so she couldn't fathom what even half the items were used for.

Camille enjoyed being a hobby enthusiast, and made different things for people. She used the room for other handy things as well, like wrapping paper. She had a bank of rollers which held an assortment of colors and prints, from holiday-themed to life events, such as birthdays and showers. It was amazing. She had enough workspace to accommodate someone wrapping small or large gifts or to work on crafts. Cubbies and bins were everywhere and little drawers containing an assortment of beads, baubles, and doohickeys.

Lauren opened and closed every drawer, cabinet, and storage container. She oohed and ahhed at everything. She even spoke to Camille in some weird crafting language Julie didn't understand.

"This is the newest section James helped me add. It's for my sewing." Camille showed them her state-of-the-art sewing machine, which had more buttons than an airplane cockpit. There was another worktable with a wooden measuring stick screwed onto the top, like something found in a fabric store. The opposite wall held bolts of material in a variety of colors and fabrics.

Julie was speechless.

"How is it you've kept this room from me all these years, Camille?" Lauren seemed to be only half kidding. Julie had heard that tone of voice before when Lauren thought she'd been cheated out of something grand.

"Because Josh made me promise not to show you two my 'Room of Doom' for fear I'd lure you girls into helping me with my hobbies, which would force him to spend more time in here with us." Camille rolled her eyes.

"Spend more time? I didn't think Josh was all that handy with a glue gun. Mechanical pencils and draft boards, sure, but ribbon and beads?" Julie was confused by the whole thing.

Camille's grin grew downright diabolical. "I used to punish the boys by making them help me plan for events like birthdays and weddings. They hate this room," she said, bursting out laughing.

"Why is that so funny?" Lauren asked with a suspicious grin on her face.

"Because this room is my escape from all of the testosterone in this house." She sighed. "I needed a retreat and a hobby that didn't include fighting, dirt, cars, sports, or heavy machinery. If the boys got into mischief, they ended up helping me with my projects. It worked pretty well, too, because if they knew they'd end up elbow deep in flowers, pink ribbon, or bird seed, they tended to stay out of trouble a little more often."

"That's positively evil. I'm impressed, Camille." Lauren high-fived Jason's mom.

Julie laughed outright. She couldn't see any of those tattooed gods working with all this fluff. Julie listened as Camille told story after story about the boys growing up, what trouble they had gotten into, and the many projects she'd worked on over the years for their small community.

"You know, we should collaborate on some events, Julie. Your culinary skills are superb. I know some clients who would love your style of cooking for their parties. Have you ever thought of expanding your business into catering?"

"I... wow, Camille. You've eaten my food?" Julie couldn't think of a time when Camille had been out to any of the sites for breakfast or lunch.

"James brings something home for me every now and then. I also have three sons who rave about your cooking. Word gets around, dear. You have quite the reputation around here." Camille smiled at the double entendre.

Lauren giggled and poked Julie in the ribs. "She doesn't get out enough to have that kind of reputation, Camille." She winked at Julie, who shoved her shoulder.

"Thanks a lot, bestie," she glared at Lauren. Then to Camille she said, "I have thought about expanding, especially when things quiet down on the shopping mall. I love Cafe Armstrong and the ability to move it wherever there's hungry people to feed. The downside, though, is when business is slow.

I still have bills to pay and a growing brother to take care of. I just don't know how I'd make it work."

She shrugged her shoulders and continued. "I don't know what I would need or what it would take to cater; I guess I could cook out of my truck, but don't most hostesses want caterers who provide dishes and linens and such? I don't think I could afford to expand that much."

Julie scrunched up her face in thought. She had to admit the idea had merit but she wasn't experienced enough to know how to make it work on her budget.

However, Camille wore big grin and Lauren hopped up and down, quietly clapping in excitement while she contemplated the pros and cons of taking on a new business venture.

"Julie, my dear, if you're serious about expanding, I would love to work with you. I have connections in this town." She tilted her head at Julie. "Plus, have you taken a good look at this room? I have party supplies, place settings, and a huge kitchen."

"Your kitchen's nice, but it's not that big," she said.

"No, dear. The *other* kitchen. The one James built into the house to host huge parties. It's commercial grade. Trust me; combining your business with mine would be of little to no cost out of your pocket. All we need is time to cook and plan."

Then Camille focused on Lauren. "And you, my sassy friend, would be perfect for networking and event planning. Your organizational skills make you a natural talent for these things. Plus, according to Jarod, you're a whiz with a computer."

Julie jumped when Lauren squealed.

Then all three of them laughed again.

"I certainly want to talk more about this, Camille," Julie said.

"I don't need to talk about anything. I'd love to do something like this with both of you. I'm sick of working in that office. It's killing my soul," Lauren complained.

"You're too strong to let them bother you." Julie gave her friend a side hug.

"Oh, Julie, you have no idea what that place is like."

Camille raised an eyebrow. "Are you saying you don't like working for my son?"

Lauren flushed a little but admitted, "I love working with Jarod when he's in house. But he's often out on calls. There's a lot of people in the office who live for their work, not the other way around. It becomes a small realm of dictators and power grabbers who make going to work on Mondays a real drag. I wish I could venture out into something more fun. I've often thought of being an events coordinator. How did you know, Camille?"

"Seriously? I've known you girls since Josh brought you both here all those years ago as 'friends.'"

Julie smiled at her. *Yeah, those days had been fun.*

"Josh, of course, thought he was going to be the only brother to bring home two girlfriends at the same time, something his brothers egged him on about for weeks. I took one look at you two and knew you were good girls and didn't have those kinds of ideas in your pretty heads."

She put her arms around both of their shoulders. Julie wrapped her arm around Camille's waist. Camille said, "Lauren, with your bubbly personality and savvy smarts, you were born to work with the kind of people I have been forced to socialize with since James began his business. So, what do you say, girls?"

For the first time in a long time, Julie was hopeful about

her future. She looked at Lauren, who was already nodding her head up and down enthusiastically.

"I can't wait, Camille!"

Then all three of them squealed like a group of teeny boppers at a Justin Bieber concert.

After a quick tour of "The Big Kitchen," they made their way back to the men.

As soon as they walked into the dining room, Lauren asked, "Where's Jarod?"

That girl has it bad, Julie thought.

Shaking her head and still a little giddy about the prospect of working with Camille and Lauren, a chill ran down her spine at the stoic expression on Jason's face. She was starting to understand him more; that look did not bode well.

Oh man, what did we miss?

James explained about a woman in the hospital who'd witnessed a crime and how Jarod and Dane had left to interview her. The fact Dane was on the same case as Jarod rang all of her warning bells. This woman, whoever she was, had something to do with Billy. Charlie asked the question that was running through her head.

"Does she have something to do with the people who are trying to hurt you and my sister?" Charlie swallowed a few times.

Jason answered him vaguely, so Julie turned her attention to him.

"What crime did she witness?" As the words left her mouth, Jason made eye contact with the rest of his family. They knew something she didn't and she didn't like the feeling one bit and felt emotional walls rebuilding to guard her heart from betrayal.

James cleared his throat, drawing her attention away from

Jason's piercing green eyes. "We think she's a witness to a hit and run from a few years back."

All of the air left her lungs as the puzzle pieces clicked together. This woman, whoever she was, might have witnessed her parents' death?

And apparently, their car accident had something to do with Billy.

All eyes landed on her. She swallowed the lump choking her. "But you must have a pretty good idea about it, right?" She turned to Jason for verification while keeping her heartache in check. Her head throbbed and she swiped at her cheeks.

But again, James answered. "We've got a good idea, yes."

Julie waited a minute trying to compose herself. She cleared her throat to hide her sob. Jason stood and put his arms around her.

"You okay?" he whispered in her ear.

Not really, but she nodded anyway. He led her back to the table as Josh handed her a shot of something amber. She threw it back and felt it burn all the way down to her tummy. It helped melt the ice in her veins. Charlie had his face scrunched up as he put it all together.

"That son of a bitch killed my parents, didn't he?" Charlie stood so fast his chair toppled over backward. The ever-present rage living just under the surface had bubbled up and over-flowed. If he didn't get it under control, things would get ugly.

Josh stood in front of Charlie. Julie was thankful because she couldn't move. James had got to his feet to stand in front of Camille and Lauren.

"We don't know for sure what this woman knows, Charlie. But yes, we think he was involved in the hit and run, and she witnessed it," Josh said, careful not to get too close to her brother. Everyone knew better than to touch Charlie when he was angry. As the two of them stood toe to toe with each other, Julie didn't miss their similarity in height; Charlie was maybe an inch shy of Josh's six-foot-two-inch frame.

When did he get so tall?

"How long have you suspected? How long have you been keeping this from us?" Charlie gestured between himself and Julie by thrusting his arm in her direction. The motion caught Josh in the chest, who didn't react. It hadn't been deliberate but Charlie stared at Josh, chest heaving as his anger tried to take over.

Julie had never seen her brother challenge any of the Kings, especially not Josh. Sure, they'd rough-housed and she remembered him coming home years ago a little battered, but they'd explained their tussles had all been in fun, not in anger. She prayed Charlie would keep his head now and not let his emotions make him do something he couldn't take back.

James answered the question. "I've had suspicions since the day they died. I could never prove anything though. Dane's been investigating this case for five long years, Charlie. I want Billy behind bars as much as anybody. I want my friends to finally be at peace. I especially want my family, which I hope you will consider yourself a part of, to be safe. Do you understand what I'm saying, son?"

His calm and honest words were a balm for Julie's troubled heart, but Charlie's face crumpled, and he sat back down with his head in his hands.

Charlie took a soft intake of breath before his shoulders began to shake. Josh sat down next to him, rubbing his back. She was by his side in less than a second, Jason taking the seat across from Charlie. She knelt in front of her brother on the hard floor, her hand on his knee, rubbing sympathetically.

"They're going to arrest him, Charlie," she said softly. "You know that, right? Because I know it. Please don't cry; you're making me cry too, dang it."

She looked over at Jason, who stared at Charlie. She wished Jason would offer him some comfort. She hated seeing her brother like this. Josh continued to rub his back for which she was grateful. Camille and Lauren returned from the safety of the kitchen where James had stood over them waiting for Charlie to calm down.

He sniffled and Camille rushed over with a box of tissues. When he looked up, Charlie's face was ragged and wet but, thankfully, he'd stopped crying.

Jason asked in his calm, quiet way, "What did he do to you? I know there's more than just him cheating on your sister and smashing your turtle after you told your friend about it."

"Billy killed Trevor?" Josh's question was laced with so much menace that Julie stepped away from Charlie and sat across from him, next to Jason.

Charlie swallowed and told Josh the story. Josh shook his head in disbelief. "Why didn't you tell me what that bastard did? I gave you Trevor for your birthday."

"I know, but I was scared. After I buried Trevor in Mom's flower bed, I came back into the house to wash up. Billy was waiting for me in my room. I can't remember where Julie had gone, the store I think. Anyway, he sat on my bed flipping through my homework like he was grading my papers. He had a red marker and was putting marks all over my work. I asked him what he thought he was doing, and he said he was making sure I knew how to keep a secret."

"He was harassing you," Jason clarified.

Julie reached over to grab Charlie's hand. How could she not have known what her boyfriend had been doing to her little brother? She was an awful sister.

"Yeah, I guess you could say that. From the time Julie brought him home to meet Mom and Dad, he would do weird shit to me." He shook his head at the memories. "I'd finish my homework and put it in my backpack. When I got to school, it wouldn't be there. Things I used all the time went missing out of my room, and I'd find them in weird places—like one time I couldn't find my headphones for a week. I found them in the freezer. Or my controllers for my GameCube would end up in the bathroom cabinet under the sink. Just weird, stupid stuff. If he was around when I found them, he'd make an odd comment like 'should be more careful with your possessions, Chuckles.' I hated when he called me that. Jackass."

Julie took a deep breath as Charlie told them more of Billy's pranks, and it made her stomach roil. She thought she'd been in love with the jerk, and she hadn't believed her brother when he asked her to make Billy back off. She would never forgive herself.

Jason put his arms around her as she met Josh's eyes. He'd tried to tell her but she hadn't listened to her friend either.

She hadn't understood boys at all.

She'd been a gullible idiot blinded by a lousy crush she'd confused with love.

"Go on, Charlie. What else did he do?" James stood behind her brother now, a fatherly hand on his shoulder, offering encouragement. She was so grateful to this wonderful family.

Charlie swallowed and tried to speak again. His voice wavered a bit and was a little too quiet.

"Two days before Mom and Dad were killed, I was out with Marco and the guys. We weren't where we were supposed to be. Marco's older brother had a car, and he'd driven us out the county road to Fantasy Five. We were being stupid. We wanted to see what the girls looked like; maybe try to sneak in.

I know it was a dumb thing to do," he said quickly, glancing around at all the adults.

Julie only smiled at him and waved her hand for him to continue.

"When we got there, the place was packed, and Marco's brother had trouble finding a place to park. He finally found a spot at the back of the building. We thought we could sneak in that way, you know, through the staff entrance. Maybe even catch a peek at some of the girls arriving for work. So Marco's brother thought up a plan for him and his buddies to go through the front, and then they'd come to the back and open the door for me and Marco. While we waited, Marco had to take a leak, so he wandered into the trees to piss. I stayed out by the car, watching the back door to make sure we didn't miss his brother."

Charlie put his head in his hands again and rubbed his face hard, like he wanted to scrub whatever he was trying to tell them out of his head. He looked back up at Julie. "I saw Billy hurt someone," he whispered.

CHAPTER 16

Coming Clean

Every muscle in Jason's body tensed. Billy was a sick bastard. Having Charlie confirm it for him turned his stomach.

Julie put on a brave front for her brother, but she was losing the battle. Tears gently fell down her beautiful face. Jason held her hand hoping he could lend his strength through touch.

His mom and Lauren took a seat at the table to hear Charlie's story.

Josh pounded the table, startling the women.

Jason glared at him.

His dad pulled up a chair on the other side of Charlie. He hadn't released the fatherly hold he had on the kid's shoulder. "Go on, son. Who did Billy hurt?"

"A woman—I think she was a dancer. She had on a lot of make-up, or at least a lot was smeared all over her face. She wore a tiny costume, but it was torn at the neckline. She kept pushing her clothes back into place and crying when she ran inside the back door. She had come from around the other side of the building. I could hear laughing. Marco was still in the trees, and I leaned on the trunk of his brother's car in full view under a light in the parking lot. There were three of them. Of course, Billy laughed the loudest. I didn't recognize the other creeps. When Billy saw me, he stopped laughing and stared in that weird way he always did by tilting his head, as if he was thinking of something interesting. He spoke to his friends, who went back to the bar and then he made his way to me."

Charlie kept his cool. Jason knew telling this story, a horrible story the kid had suppressed for so long, had to be killing him. If he could take away the pain, he would in a heartbeat, but Charlie was as brave as they came.

Jason hoped Charlie realized he was safe now, surrounded by his family.

James kept his hand on Charlie's shoulder and encouraged him to continue.

"First, he wanted to know what I thought I was doing in a shit hole like Fantasy Five. When I told him, he laughed, and asked if I was looking for some..." He stopped and looked at all the women.

Jason was proud of him for that, because Billy was a crude son of a bitch.

Charlie shook his head and edited what he was about to say. "He asked me if I wanted to hook up with the woman I'd seen running into the bar. He said she had been a fighter but a 'prime piece.' He made some other disgusting comments about her before he laughed again. Then, he got right in my face and screamed that I better get my ass back in the car and leave. He said he'd kill my family if I said anything about what I saw."

A tear rolled down Charlie's cheek. "Two days later, Mom and Dad were dead," he said brokenly. "But I swear I didn't tell a soul!" he pleaded. "The bastard killed them anyway!" He openly sobbed now as he pushed back from the table to walk down the hall.

Jason let go of Julie when she got up to follow her brother. His mother and Lauren tried to follow as well, but James stopped them. "No, Camille, let them grieve. Julie needs this moment alone with her brother."

"You're not the boss of me, James. I'm going to my friend," Lauren said as she turned to leave, except she ran into Jarod on his way into the room.

"No, he's not your boss but I am, and you need to stay here, Lauren." Jarod spoke softly. For once, Lauren didn't argue. Jarod rubbed both of her shoulders and looked her in the eye. "Just give them a minute, Sassy, then you can go to them. I'd like you to stay with us while I tell everyone what I found out at the hospital."

Lauren straightened and said, "Of course I will, but don't you want to wait for Julie and Charlie? They should hear what's going on, right?"

"We're right here," Julie said from the hallway.

Jason got up and went to both of them, hugging Charlie first, then slipped his arm around Julie so he could kiss her forehead. His mother grabbed Charlie's arm in a motherly embrace and led him back into the room. Charlie accepted her comfort and made a heroic effort to keep his anger in check.

"Eh hum," Jarod waited for quiet. "The woman's name is Christina Mason—goes by Candy. She's in ICU. Her doctor says she has extensive injuries to her face, arms, and lower abdomen, and some internal bruising as well. They did a rape kit on her. We're still waiting for the results."

"Is it standard procedure for you to be personally called to the hospital for this type of thing?" his mother asked.

Jarod sighed. "Yes. Fortunately, this type of thing doesn't happen very often around here, or I'd go crazy."

"Is she awake? Were you able to question her?" his dad asked.

"No. I waited for her to come around, but they're keeping her sedated. She's in rough shape, Dad. I left a couple of deputies at the hospital in case someone comes for her again."

Jason's stomach rumbled, startling Julie. "Are you hungry?" she asked as she sniffled and giggled at the same time.

"I guess I am," he chuckled.

His mom sprang into action. "Well, that's good because the chili's ready. I think we need some sustenance. It's been quite an emotional day for all of us." She gave Charlie a squeeze as she went to get the food. Lauren excused herself from Jarod's side to help.

Jason knew Julie wanted to help, but he didn't want to let her go, as usual. She smiled at him when he held on tight. "I need to feel useful," she whispered in his ear.

He let her go and whispered, "Hurry back."

Her gentle kiss on the cheek nearly had him shouting for joy. She was everything to him now, and he'd prove it to her. When this was all over, she wasn't going to get rid of him.

Dinner was unusually quiet while everyone contemplated the events of the day. Jason couldn't believe how much had happened. He'd woken up hopeful only to find his office trashed and his house burned down, and then he'd heard Charlie's heartbreaking story. Plus, the mysterious Candy ending up in ICU after Billy's unexpected reappearance.

Jason couldn't keep his mind on any one thing at a time.

After dinner, his mom moved everyone into the family room. A baseball game played on the TV with the volume low. A crackling fire burned in the stone fireplace offering life to the solemn room. Josh had brought down the Risk board game and was currently engaged in an epic battle with Charlie, Jarod, and Lauren. Dad gave pointers to Charlie every once in a while to keep the kid's mind off the terrible memories of the past. Julie glued herself to Jason's side on the couch.

"Any word from Dane, Dad?" Jason asked.

"Not yet, but that man likes to take his time. He'll want to stay at the hospital and wait for Ms. Mason to wake up."

"How will he get in to see her?" Julie asked.

"He has his ways, Julie. I think that's why Jarod doesn't like to work with him. He isn't limited to the letter of the law like my eldest so sometimes he comes by important information in ways that are not admissible in court."

"Then how is that helpful?" asked Lauren with an amused smile.

"Because whatever information he obtains, we can use it to our advantage by having the law investigate and find the proof."

"What he's saying is Dane likes to make more work for me," Jarod said, not looking up from the game.

Jason chuckled. "You're a lazy bastard, you know that, Jarod?"

Jarod gave him a one-fingered salute before moving a game piece.

Julie laughed and then yawned.

"Sleepy?" Jason asked her.

"Yes. I didn't think I'd be able to relax with everything going on today, but I'm beat." She rubbed her injured forehead with her hand.

"I can show you to your room," he said as he helped her up. Camille saw they were leaving the room and followed them upstairs.

"Here, Julie. Let me show you your room," she said, which irritated the hell out of Jason.

"Mom, I can show her."

"I know, dear, but I want to show her where all the linens and things are," she explained with a conspiratorial smile. "I took the liberty to put your clothes away for you, Julie." Apparently his mother wanted to play chaperone this evening.

He'd have to do something to ward her off.

It turned out his mom was working in his favor, though. She put Julie in the spare room across from his suite.

Thank God!

Camille winked at him when she left them alone in Julie's room, which was a simple guest room with its own private bath. There were four of those in this wing of the house. His suite was basically a one-bedroom apartment minus a kitchen. There were three rooms like his in the house; the other two belonged to his brothers.

"Holy cow, this house is ginormous." Julie walked up and down the hall and then returned to her room. It had a large queen-sized bed, a desk, a dresser, a nightstand, and a matching armoire, plus a full entertainment center. Compared to Julie's, the bathroom was luxurious. "This room is half the size of my house. I've been here more than a dozen times and never knew the estate was this big. How is that possible?"

"Because my mom didn't allow any girls in this wing when we were growing up." Chuckling, he grabbed her around the waist. "Do you want to see my room?" He waggled his eyebrows up and down.

He felt her giggle go straight to his chest when she said, "I'd love to."

He opened the door to find it exactly as he'd left it the last time he stayed here. He followed Julie's expression as she took it all in, waiting for her to spot the pictures he'd kept of her throughout the years. They lived on his nightstand, as well as some on a dresser and in the sitting area.

Seeing them now through her eyes, it kind of made him look like a stalker.

Damn.

"What are you doing with those?"

"Josh let me have them," he said quickly.

She crinkled her sweet forehead. "Why would you want them? Some of these are really old, Jason. I don't understand."

Shit. Time to come clean.

He sucked in a lungful of air and led her to the small sofa. He urged her to sit next to him and looked her in the eyes. "Do you remember the first time we met?"

Her eyes grew round. "Yes. You all got in a huge fight before security kicked you out of Fun Park."

"That's right. What else do you remember about that night?" He waited patiently while her face went blank. He knew this expression; she used it when she didn't want him to know what she was feeling.

"I met Billy too. What does that night have to do with you having all these pictures of me, Jason?"

He studied her, contemplating his next move. Today had been filled with one overwhelming revelation after another. He wasn't sure how she'd react to yet another bombshell. He didn't want to wreck the peace between them, but he knew if he didn't tell her how he felt it would all end badly anyway.

Screw it.

"That was the night I fell in love with you, Jujyfruit." He watched her carefully, preparing for the volcanic eruption which was sure to blow up in his face. But she gave great blank face when she needed to.

He waited, bracing himself for impact.

And waited...

"WHAT?!" she yelled as she hit him in the chest with a tiny, elegant fist.

Before he could grab her hand, she jumped up and made her way to the door. He shot from the sofa and spun her back around. He had to duck as the momentum brought her tiny fist around to hit him in the face. He grabbed both of her arms behind her back.

"Settle down, will ya?"

"That was the *meanest* thing you have ever said to me, Jason King! Why? Tonight of all nights? Did you think I'd laugh? Do I look amused right now?"

She gasped for air like she'd just run a marathon and her big brown eyes filled and overflowed with tears, spilling down her flushed cheeks.

Damn it! He hadn't expected anger.

He pulled her closer but she fought him. As he held her he whispered in her ear,. "I'm not lying, Julie. Calm down and let me explain."

He began to rock her as she struggled and cried into his chest. Finally, she relaxed and her arms went around him and knotted in his t-shirt.

He shuffled them back to the couch and sat down with her in his lap. She began to struggle again.

"Stop it, Jujyfruit. I need to get this out in the open once and for all. Have you ever known me to lie?" He had her there because he never lied.

She stopped and shook her head.

"Say it," he commanded.

"No," she whispered.

"No what?"

"You've never lied to me," she whispered.

He sighed. "Right. I've never lied to you, and I never will." He squeezed her hand and readied himself for what he was about to—finally—admit.

"The night we met, Billy and I made a bet. I mostly agreed to it because he'd been a giant pain in the ass, pestering me all damn day about the double date I'd had with some girls who weren't in high school. When I say 'double date,' I mean I had been with two women at once."

Her horrified expression made him talk faster.

"Both were consenting adults, so don't give me that look. Back then, girls—hell, women!—came easy for me, and I took advantage. At sixteen-going-on-seventeen, I was big for my age and full of raging hormones. If I wasn't fighting then I was..." Chagrined, he paused before admitting, "...looking to hook up."

She looked completely disgusted. He guessed she really didn't know much about males. He had to finish his story as quickly as possible before she bolted.

"I'm not sure I want to hear any more of this, Jason." She began to squirm off his lap. He let her move as far as the cushion next to him, but he didn't let go of her hand.

"Anyway, there'd been all kinds of girls at the football game paying attention to me and Jarod. Billy got a couple of numbers but, I don't know, I guess the girls didn't think he measured up, and he took exception to it. He was always jealous. Coming from a rich family, he thought he was entitled to respect, or at least the kind of respect an immature bully like Billy thought he deserved. If my brothers and I got attention he thought belonged to him, then he'd create situations guaranteed to put him in the spotlight."

"He used to do that to me, too, Jason. He didn't want

anyone talking to me without his approval. I thought he was protecting me, that he cared. I was wrong."

Jason's heart broke a little at what the little asshole had done to her psychologically. Needing to finish this tale before his anger ramped up again he continued...

"When we got to Fun Park, I saw you before I saw Josh. I knew he'd met you and Lauren at school because the two of you were all my little brother talked about. He had some stupid idea he was going to have two girlfriends at the same time like I did."

"Camille said something about this to Lauren and me while touring her craft room. I still can't believe Josh thought that about us." She giggled at this.

Relieved she'd found some humor, he said, "Of course he did. Anyway, I was curious about his new 'friends,' so I tried to see the two 'hot chicks' he kept talking about at the game, but I never ran into you guys. I knew he'd hit Fun Park afterward, so I talked Jarod into going with me. I didn't have to do much convincing because he was as curious about the two of you as I was. Unfortunately, Billy wanted to meet you, too. He was actually pissed he might have to compete with 'another Jason,' as he put it."

She rolled her eyes. "Jason, you do have a reputation as the ladies' man. Your crew talks about your exploits every day while I'm serving them lunch. You don't *date* women, but you're never without companionship. Am I right?"

No way was he going to admit *that*—his loveless relations with women—and let her distract him from his purpose. He grabbed her cheeks with his hands and kissed her long and deep. When he came up for air, he looked her in the eyes and pleaded, "Just listen to the story, sweetheart. No more interruptions, okay?"

She merely nodded, looking a little dazed.

Good.

"As I said before, yours was the first face I saw when I stepped through the door. You were smiling your beautiful smile and laughing at Josh. By the time I got close enough, you had turned your back to me, so you hadn't seen me yet. Since I was always messing with Josh, I thought it would be funny to steal you away from him. I decided to tease him, but it made you mad, right?"

She nodded. "I didn't know you, and you were so much bigger than us. I didn't like the way Josh hollered for help until I realized he was laughing and that you were his brother."

"When you didn't speak to me after he introduced us, I figured I'd blown it, so I got a little pissed. Girls *always* spoke to me, Julie. They went out of their way to speak to me. When your eyes met mine, my heart beat so hard, I thought it was going to break a rib or two. You were the prettiest thing I had ever seen. You didn't giggle or act like I was a prize to be won. You looked at me as if I were scum and it only made me more curious about you. So I decided to play it cool."

"I assumed you thought I was a baby," she said quietly. Then she surprised him with, "I dreamed about your eyes for a solid three months after that night, even though I was dating Billy by then."

"Really? Because I haven't stopped dreaming about you."

CHAPTER 17

Honor-Bound

Jason dreams about me?

She remembered how she couldn't get him out of her head. Billy had been very straightforward with her, showing an interest like no other boy had done before. In her young mind, she thought it meant something, but she didn't understand boys at all. As hard as she'd tried, though, she hadn't been able to stop thinking about Jason King.

"Tell me about the bet," she reminded him.

He inhaled, expanding his impressive chest. "Billy's shrewd. Unfortunately, I tipped my hand when I walked away from you, making you a perfect prize for his game. His goal was to steal any girl who I found interesting, and you'd definitely captured my attention. When you began to talk to him, I wanted to punch anything that moved. When the kids from the other school started picking a fight in the arcade, I was honor bound to put a stop to it. And because I was so mad at Billy for stealing your attention, it was a great release of frustration. I got carried away."

"What do you mean, 'honor bound' to fight?"

"Not to fight, exactly." He readjusted his position on the couch, turning to face her. "Jujyfruit, you've met my dad. What do you think he taught us? To stand up for those who can't stand up for themselves. We learned early if he ever found out we were picking on the weak, or bullying them, he would whip our asses. And he made damned sure if we allowed others to be picked on, we would get a beat down. Period. He taught us real men didn't prove themselves by starting fights but by stopping assholes who liked to hurt those smaller and weaker in order to gain power, money, or popularity. He taught us to fight for people who can't fight for themselves. Jarod, Josh, and I take this philosophy very seriously. Unfortunately, Billy's one of the biggest power-hungry cowards around. I'm sorry I didn't protect you from him."

She considered everything Jason said. In truth, Billy had acted funny all along, but she'd been too young and so in love with the idea of an older boy paying attention to her that she would've done anything Billy asked of her. She'd been impressed with his wealth, even though his family never treated her kindly, more like some social climber. In their eyes, she hadn't quite come up to scratch. They'd thought her beneath their son and that it was only a matter of time before he dumped her for a woman acceptable to their class.

In comparison, the Kings always made her feel welcome. She and Lauren had made fast friends with Camille and laughed their heads off at Josh and Jarod. Sometimes even at Jason, but he was usually too serious to goof around with; now she understood he hadn't disliked her, as she'd once believed. His disgruntlement had been born out of an unrequited love she'd known nothing about.

"Did you hate me? When I was here with Josh, I mean."

"No, but it was hard. I was in college by the time you guys

were juniors. You were still dating Billy while he dated anything that moved on the college campus. That's when I started hating him and started worrying about you."

"You worried about me?" Her heart thumped a mile a minute.

She watched his Adam's Apple bob once, twice... and then his green eyes focused intently on her face. "I witnessed the kind of girls he was with when he wasn't with you. I didn't know how... safe he was being with you, if you know what I mean."

She blushed from head to toe. God, had they practiced safe sex back then? Billy had insisted she take the pill because he'd hated condoms. He'd been her first and only lover, so she'd thought that's how all men felt about sex. She never had a clue he'd been cheating. She cringed remembering the embarrassing conversation with her mother and the appointment with the doctor.

She answered quietly, "I was on the pill, so no. Not very safe at all."

"That's what I thought." He shook his head in disgust. "I knew how he was. I should've known he would be that way with you. Whenever he wanted to brag about the two of you together, I would shut him down. I couldn't bear hearing it."

"What do you mean?" she screeched.

Billy discussed our sex life with Jason? Oh my God.

She wanted to crawl into a hole and never come out.

Jason pierced her with those deep-green eyes which seemed to know her private thoughts. "You know what I mean. Billy's not honorable in any sense of the word, Julie. He talked about all the women he slept with to whoever would listen, including you."

Mortified, she realized something very important—she was

probably the stupidest woman on the face of the planet and a horrible judge of character.

I'm such an idiot.

Finding it difficult to meet the eyes she loved so much, she asked, "Why did you want my picture if you knew how stupid I was?"

"Because I've always loved you. And you're not stupid, Jujyfruit, just stubborn. Once I confided in my brothers about what Billy was doing to you, we all made a pact to look after you. It was easiest for Josh because he was already your friend and still lived here. The bonus was he could keep an eye on Charlie as well, which meant Billy got caught doing a lot of shit. My friendship with him was over and he knew it. He still had his family's money to fall back on, but people in this town figured out he was a bad seed. Billy went a little crazy when he didn't receive the respect he thought he deserved."

"But I treated you horribly after my parents died and when Billy left me. I blamed you for his leaving."

"Yeah." He scratched his head. "Why did you blame me, anyway?"

"He always had fresh cuts on his face and neck. He said things had gotten bad between the two of you, that you were harassing him but he didn't know why. He said you bullied him. I believed him because I had seen you fight before. He said you were jealous of him. I didn't understand."

Oh boy, how she had not understood. Jason's eyes held no blame, no judgment, which helped relieve a bit of her shame at being such a gullible fool. She'd spent the better part of her young adult life pining for a man who'd been responsible for harassing her baby brother, and possibly killing her parents, all while being disgusted with the one man who claimed to truly love her.

Just shoot me now.

"You were under the influence of his charm. A lot of people fell for it. Hell, even I did for a time. But once he reveals himself, there's no mistaking the weasel that he is." Jason ran a hand through her hair, her scalp tingling at his touch. Her favorite emeralds turned dark as she gazed at his handsome face.

"You have no idea how frustrating it was for me." He tightened his hand on her scalp a moment before he gentled his touch again. It made her more aware of him. Made her blood sing. She didn't say anything, afraid he'd stop his confession.

"I thought if you found out about his cheating, it would kill you, and I didn't want you hurt. When your parents died and you stepped up to take care of your brother, I fell deeper in love with you because there's nothing more important than family. I admired you when Dad tried to help out financially and you wouldn't take it. I thought Mom was going to have a major conniption over that one, but Dad kept an eye on you to make sure you and Charlie were okay."

"Your dad knows my finances? What the hell, Jason?" How was she supposed to react to that? She'd worked very hard for what she had and was proud she'd made it work. Every sacrifice she'd made for Charlie was worth it as long as her brother would be able to attend a good college. She had a small nest egg and it would see them through. Now with the prospect of expanding her business with Camille and Lauren, she knew things could only get better.

"Dad was honor bound by the friendship he had with your father, Jujyfruit. They were closer than you think. Dad is listed in your parents' wills as a sort of silent godparent, for lack of a better term—at least that's what Dad said. Your parents had no way of knowing they'd die so young, leaving the two of you with the small insurance benefit you received. So Dad made sure everything went smoothly for you. Please don't be mad," he said quickly as she moved to stand.

"How did he make sure things 'went smoothly' for me?"

"When he learned you were interested in the restaurant business, he contacted the man who sold you Cafe Armstrong."

She narrowed her eyes. "And?" She could tell by the way he cringed there was more, and he didn't want to tell her.

"He...made sure you got a great deal. That's all." His smile was innocent and very un-Jason-like.

She sighed in frustration. "What am I supposed to do with all this information, Jason? What do you want from me? I don't know what to say to all this." She began to pace.

"You aren't supposed to do or say anything. I'm telling you all of this because our situation has changed, and you need to know everything. I'm tired of the secrets, and I can't stand to be without you anymore. I don't want to be with any other woman, Julie. And I certainly don't want you with any other man. I want us to be together."

He touched her face with both his hands, and she held her breath. Was he going to kiss her again?

God, please kiss me and make me forget about everything else.

"I have never felt this way about any other woman. Believe me, because I've tried. No one measures up to you." She was positive his eyes, those magnificent green crystals, held some sort of magic power. When he looked at her like he this—like she was the most precious thing in the world—she was lost. He owned her completely.

He brought his lips closer to hers and she held her breath.

She closed her eyes when his lips finally touched hers, gentle at first, but when her lips parted for a gasp of breath, his tongue slipped into her mouth. Her mind shut down and she let herself drown in his kiss.

She'd told him she had dreamed about his eyes for three months after they'd met, but it was a lie. She saw those bright green eyes—exciting and wondrous like the Northern Lights— every night when she closed her own to sleep. Josh was her friend, but Jason was like an anchor attached to her soul. He'd always been there for her, only she'd been too damn stubborn to admit it until now.

As Jason led her to his bed, she vowed to never turn her back on him again. He wasn't a frog or a toad. He'd always been her real Prince Charming, only she'd been too blind to see it.

———

JASON DIDN'T CATCH A WINK. HE WATCHED HIS woman sleeping in his bed with a sort of awe and reverence. He'd made love to Julie all night long, but he still didn't want to miss a thing. She finally passed out on him a little before dawn. He wanted to wake her again but thought against it as he took in her troubled, sleeping face.

He moved back the hair on her forehead to see the ugly wound from the car wreck. The stitches were still in but the bruising had faded. Even in slumber, she had dark circles under her eyes. She'd been through too much the past couple of days, so he let her rest. He needed some too, but his dad would have him up soon for a meeting in the home office downstairs. James kept copies of all documents, including the ones destroyed, and work must go on. King Construction had more than one project needing attention.

His thoughts were interrupted by the soft tone of the in-house intercom his family used in this monstrosity they called Home.

"Yeah," he answered quietly.

"Julie's gone, Jason," his mother said, panic dripping from each word. "I can't find her anywhere! Why would she leave?"

He sighed. "Mom, she's with me. Leave her alone this morning."

"What do you mean?" Now she was just playing coy. "I had a room all ready for her."

He wasn't in the mood for her games. "Mom. Knock it off, will you?"

The imp giggled on the other end. "I just wanted to be sure, honey." More serious now, she asked, "Is she okay, dear?"

"No, but she will be. I'll make sure of it." He stated it as a fact.

"That's my boy. Breakfast will be ready in an hour. Do you want me to have a tray sent to your room?"

"No, I have to meet with Dad soon."

"No you don't. Your father is as exhausted as the rest of us. He's had his team bring him what he needs for today. He said you needed a break too."

Jason relaxed back against his pillow. "Tell Dad I said thanks and will see him in a couple of hours. And yes, could you have a tray sent?"

"Of course, darling," He didn't miss the happiness in her voice as she put the handset back on the dock.

"What was all that about?" Julie mumbled.

He turned to face her so he could snuggle against her body. *Perfect fit.*

"Sleeping in a little while longer and having breakfast sent to my room."

"You're spoiled," she said as she wrapped her arms around his waist, her eyes still closed.

"Yes, I am." He rubbed her back in a circle until she fell back to sleep. He closed his eyes for what felt like three seconds when someone knocked on his door.

Groaning, he got out of bed and pulled on his jeans. He didn't bother to snap them. He opened the door to Josh, who stood there with a huge tray in his hands and a mischievous smirk on his face.

"Good morning, lover boy. Breakfast is served. Where's my favorite chef?" He tried to walk in and sneak a peek, the pervert.

Jason took the tray with one hand and pushed his little brother back into the hallway with the other. "Funny, asshole. Now get lost."

Josh only grinned before his face became sober. "Jarod got called to the hospital. Candy woke up."

Jason sighed. "That's good. Keep me posted on that front. Where's Charlie?"

"Not up yet. He's my next stop. Dad thinks we need to keep him busy today since he's not going to school. I agree. I know that kid, Jason. If we let him stew without giving him an outlet, he's gonna go ballistic. I've worked hard to help him keep his temper in check, and I'd hate for him to fall back on old, violent habits now."

"Agreed. What do you have in store for him?"

"Horse barn first, then some easy chores outside. If that doesn't work, we can always have a go at the heavy bag in the gym. He's a physical kid, so the more energy he burns off, the better he'll be."

"Good plan. Now beat it. I'm hungry." He smiled at his little brother before he shut the door in his face.

He took the food to the table and poured two cups of coffee. He made Julie's cup and waved it under her nose. She stirred a bit and then reached for it without opening her eyes. He pulled the coffee out of her reach.

She opened one eye. "Why are you messing with me at this unholy hour?"

"Because I love you?" he asked as he continued to keep the coffee out of her reach.

"More like because you're a jackass," she deadpanned.

He laughed and handed the cup to her.

"Dad's got everyone working from home today except the sheriff. You don't have to get up if you don't want to. You look very nice in my bed." He said, rubbing her cheek.

She reached up to touch her forehead and then her hair. "Oh, I bet I look like Miss America, huh?"

Joking and a sense of humor. All good signs. He let her drink her coffee, not wanting to upset the goddess before him.

She took a sip, let out a satisfied *ahhh* and declared, "Perfect."

"Yes, you are."

Her eyes lit up for him. "I meant the coffee, silly." She took another drink and then asked, "Aren't you going to eat?"

"Yes, just waiting for you. Shall I feed you in bed, or do you want to get dressed and eat at the table with me?"

He waited to see what she'd do. This was all new to him. He'd never slept overnight with a woman—had never wanted to. But this was Julie, and to him, it seemed natural for her to be here, in his room, with him in the morning. She was a little quiet, and he wondered what was buzzing around in her pretty head. Was she having second thoughts? Was it too much? Would she leave him?

God, he couldn't bear it if she left. He wouldn't go back to the way things were, with her ignoring him or treating him like crap. The more he thought about it, the more he started to sweat.

"I think I should eat something and then take a shower. But I'd rather you fed me in bed." The look she gave him was so heated he became uncomfortable in his unbuttoned jeans. She set her coffee on the nightstand and slid her hands up his chest. The naughty grin on her face told him everything he needed to know; she was staying, which was absolutely fine with him.

CHAPTER 18

Tattoo You

J ames King had summoned Jason downstairs for a meeting about fifteen minutes ago. Julie shook her head in disbelief, lingering in the shower as the hot water soothed her aching muscles.

What a difference a day makes.

She rinsed out the shampoo from her thick, long hair. Though the water remained hot she was still numb from all the revelations of the past twenty-four hours. Her world had turned upside down, for sure, but in a good way. Well, except for the hit and run... and Jason's house burning down... and that poor woman in the hospital.

And Charlie. God, she'd have to make it up to him somehow.

But Jason loves me.

Happy with the situation, she soaped up her loofa. Never in a million years would she believe Jason King could feel so right. Five years was a long time to be without a lover. Kinda like a Ritz cracker to a starving person, but that wasn't how it felt at all.

Jason felt like home.

Who would've thought she and Jason would be good together? But how should she act now? She took a few more swipes with the loofa and rinsed the suds from her body.

Shutting off the water she wrapped a towel around her head turban-style, grabbed a second fluffy towel from the rack and dried herself.

As she did she remembered Jason letting her examine all of his ink. Again, he surprised her. Every single one of his tattoos meant something to him. Billy's images had been picked out because he thought they made him look tough and held no personal meaning.

Each design on Jason's body (and oh what a body he had!) told a story of what he'd been like, or what he'd been thinking, at certain points in his life. Some were pretty and some were not, but they all had significance.

He was such a strong male.

And he claimed to love her.

She put the damp towel back on the rack to dry. Jason had fetched her things from the room his mother had prepared for her and she let out a heartfelt sigh at his thoughtfulness—before a it hit her...

Geez! Camille and James! What would they think of me now?

She closed her eyes and tried not to panic. No, it wasn't like her to sleep around, not like Jason.

She dismissed the disturbing thought right away because Jason never lied. His honor wouldn't allow it. He was many things but he'd never play with a woman's feelings.

She believed him, but... how did she feel in return? Did she even know?

Julie flipped her head down and waved the dryer over her wet hair.

In order to protect Charlie from her grief after their parents died Julie began locking her feelings deep inside. Billy had broken her heart at the same time, so maybe she hadn't only been protecting Charlie but also herself. Knowing what she did now about Billy made her sick, and angry. She'd wasted so much time on someone who obviously didn't love her back, not to mention the person had psychotic tendencies.

I'm such a fool.

Had it been foolish of her to sleep with Jason?

Ugh! She didn't know but that beautiful man made her feel things she'd never felt before; like being cherished.

Like a princess.

Billy had *never* made her feel special. On the contrary, he and his parents made sure she understood being with Billy was a privilege, and a temporary one at that. Oh, she understood everything now and it made her even more angry to have been so manipulated by those horrible people and her own immature desire to be loved.

She finished in the bathroom and made her way back into Jason's sitting room. He'd brought her bag in from the other bedroom as well. Apparently, he wanted her to stay in his suite. So typical of Jason to take charge of the situation and boss her around. However, instead of feeling railroaded by this gesture she felt wanted.

It stopped her cold as visions of the previous night flooded to the surface. She'd been examining a particularly interesting tattoo on his chest right above his heart...

. . .

"WHAT DOES THIS ONE MEAN?" SHE'D ASKED AS SHE leisurely outlined the beautiful, but exotic script above his left pectoral muscle.

He held her hand while she swirled her finger around and around the flowing lines. "My grandma DeeGee is Assyrian."

"Oh? Which grandma?" King didn't sound foreign to her.

"My mom's mother. We spent a lot of time with her when we were little. It's very important to her that she share her family's culture with us." She felt his emerald gaze while she continued her exploration.

"So what does it mean, silly?" Laying on his chest, she rested her chin on his sternum and bounced her eyes from his handsome face to his tattoo and back again.

He kept his left hand over hers, still caressing the ink while moving his right hand to her back where he drew soft circles around her spine, giving her goosebumps. After a beat he smoothed his right hand up her back and under her hair to grip her scalp, holding her in place.

With tenderness he looked into her eyes and said, "Ga kooli khayee libee eeli it deeyakh."

The words were both rough and enchanting. He spoke them with such passion to her, hypnotized by his voice speaking an exotic language.

"What does it mean?" she whispered.

Never taking his gaze from hers, he stroked her cheek with the backs of his fingers. He kissed her lips tenderly before saying against them, "For all my life my heart belongs to you."

"When did you get it?" she whispered.

His eyes welled with tears. "The day you became Charlie's guardian."

It was as if the earth shifted and everything became clear.

He really and truly loved her.

She slid up Jason's body and pressed her lips to his, getting lost in him once more...

RETURNING TO THE PRESENT, SHE CLEARED HER throat even though no one else was in the room. She wiped her eyes and cheeks dry and moved to her bag. With purpose and new optimism, she got dressed in order to face the day with a new and happy attitude.

At least, as happy as she could be with so much going on.

Oh, Julie, you are a silly, silly girl. You are not a princess and you still have a little brother who needs you.

Thinking of Charlie got her moving and all those unsettling thoughts disappeared as she focused on her brother and what he'd endured because of her childish association with a known psychopath. She had a lot to make up for and would make sure he stayed safe from now on.

Finally, she left Jason's suite to find out what everyone was doing.

She entered the smaller family kitchen first and found Camille at the stove stirring something in a big stock pot.

"Good morning, my sweet girl! How was your night?" Camille asked with a sly grin on her face.

Julie blushed from hair roots to big toes. "Wonderful," she said with a smile. She didn't want to embarrass either of them but Camille appeared happy about the situation, especially when she put the big spoon down and wrapped Julie in a warm, motherly embrace.

"Oh, my sweet girl. Don't be shy with me or embarrassed. I've been secretly rooting for Jason since Josh brought you home to meet us." Camille gave her another squeeze.

Wait, what?! Camille knew Jason's feelings?

"Really?" Julie asked, pulling a little away in order to look Camille in the eyes, the same bright green that graced Jason's handsome face.

"My dear, I know and love my boys. Oh, they think I'm just their overbearing mom but, as their mother, I know what's good for them. And you, Julie, are definitely good for my Jason." She hugged Julie again before returning to the stove and picked up the spoon to stir some more.

"Jason's my hellion, a true wild child. He was a lovable boy, don't get me wrong, but strong-willed. Jarod is the oldest but Jason has always been more of the leader. He tended to be more physical than the other two. James made sure to ingrain in all three of our boys the importance of right and wrong and for standing up for those who can't stand on their own. Thank God Jason understood what his father meant because with his size and crazy teen hormones his life could've gone in a different direction, especially since he was hanging out with that Billy." She spit Billy's name out as if it left a bad taste in her mouth.

Julie understood. "Jason had quite the reputation in school. I was afraid of him at first."

Camille agreed. "Yes. I can see how he would frighten you. However, when they came home that night, Jason acted funny. I couldn't put my finger on it until Josh told me what happened."

"You mean the fight and them getting kicked out of the arcade, right?"

"No. Fighting and getting kicked out of places was so normal I didn't even bat an eye," she laughed. "Jason had just met you, Julie. I could see it in his face. He'd been bitten by the love bug. The next morning all he talked about was you. He kept hounding Josh about what you liked, what classes you were taking, and did you have a boyfriend. When he found out Billy had swept you up right in front of his face my strong, confident son was crushed. It broke my heart."

Julie frowned. She remembered the time Charlie came home with a broken heart because a girl he crushed on had gone out with someone else. Offended on her brother's behalf, Julie didn't want to have anything to do with the girl, even though Charlie remained a part of their shared social group.

"You must've not liked me very much after that," she said.

"On the contrary, Julie. I knew your feelings for Billy were nothing more than a crush. Billy could be very charming, and like you said, you were afraid of Jason who can be intimidating. But Billy never fooled me and because he was involved with Jason and you, I tolerated his presence in my home on the few occasions he lowered himself to enter it… the little shit stain."

Julie coughed. Surely she'd misunderstood the last bit, it was said so low.

"Anyway, what I'm trying to say is I have known for a very long time that you and Jason were meant for each other. I'm glad it's finally happened so we can all move on and I can now focus on my other two sons."

And with that she put the lid on the stock pot and pulled Julie into the den.

CHAPTER 19

Dane

Jason was on the phone with his foreman when Julie and his mother walked into the den. Lord, she was even more beautiful now than she had been last night.

She's finally mine.

He winked at her and was rewarded with one of her shy smiles in return.

"The police have taken down the crime-scene tape from your office and cleaned up their mess. The security team your father sent over is still here reinstalling the cameras around the area. Will you be coming down to the site today?" his foreman asked.

"No, Dennis. Some things have developed here, so I won't be on site for the rest of the week. You can handle things until then. Just keep me posted on progress." Jason shoved his phone in his pocket and strolled over to Julie.

"Good afternoon, Jujyfruit. How was your shower?" He couldn't take his eyes off her, as she blushed prettily for him. This was going to be a great day.

"It was nice, thank you," she said quietly.

His mother had moved to kiss his father's cheek. They spoke quietly to one another at the executive desk near the window. His father's office was big enough for several conversations to take place without interrupting others. Jason admired the masculine space with mahogany bookshelves, a bank of filing cabinets, and a seating area with a sofa, love seat, and coffee table.

He ran his fingers across Julie's cheek to her forehead and frowned. The damn stitches reminded him not all was perfect in their world, even though she was a part of his life now. He hoped Jarod or Dane would have news this afternoon. Josh had said Candy was awake. Hopefully, she had the information they needed to rid Billy from their lives for good.

"What are you thinking about?" he asked her.

"I'm thinking what a difference a day makes."

"Good or bad?"

"Definitely good." She wrapped her arms around his waist and he held her in return kissing the top of her head, relieved she seemed happy. She hadn't told him exactly how she felt about him, but he wasn't going to complain. Later, when they were alone, they would talk things through. He wanted her to stay with him, but he was currently homeless, and she had a lot on her mind.

"Have you seen Charlie?" she asked. Then she crinkled her brow and said, "And where are Lauren and Josh?"

"Josh and Charlie are in the horse barn. Jarod and Lauren went down to the station," he said.

"I want them out; they're driving me crazy!" Charlie yelled as he burst into the house.

"All right, kid, calm down. Let me get the first-aid kit," Josh said, following close behind a raging Charlie.

"Oh my gosh, he's hurt!" Julie was out of his arms in a flash, his mom hot on her heels.

"Well, I guess we know where we rate," his dad chuckled.

"We'd better see what's going on. If I know Charlie, it sounds like he's still seeing red."

They followed the women into the utility room, where they found Charlie pacing and Josh rummaging through the cabinets.

"Mom! Where's the... Oh, there you are. We need the first-aid kit." Josh sounded a bit out of breath.

His mother retrieved the kit from one of the cupboards while Julie went to Charlie and quietly inspected him.

Obviously irritated, Charlie batted her hands away. "I'm fine, Sis, but I want these stupid stitches out. They're driving me nuts."

"So... what? You think Josh is going to cut them out of you? I don't think so. You need to be checked out by the doctor first, Charlie."

"Aw, come on! It's just a bunch of thread in my skin," he pointed out the obvious, "soaking up sweat and itching me like crazy. The doctor can look at my head later. Besides, Josh said we can't leave until we're safe." Charlie looked ready to take matters into his own hands, so Jason considered how to handle the situation. Removing stitches was no big deal, but he didn't want to cross Julie, either.

"Let me see your melon, kid." Jason gently inspected Charlie's wound.

"Here's the nippers, Jason." He took the scissors from Josh and glanced at Julie. Her forehead was kissably scrunched up again. He fought the urge to take her back into his arms.

"Have you removed stitches before?" she asked.

"Yeah. It's not a big deal, Jujyfruit, and Charlie will feel better without them. The wound looks healthy and closed, so he should be fine." With care, he used the scissors and a pair of tweezers to cut and then carefully remove each stitch. Charlie didn't move a muscle, trusting Jason to fix him up.

When he was done, his mom handed him a cotton ball with antiseptic ointment on it and a couple of butterfly bandages.

"Leave those on until tomorrow, Charlie. Just to be on the safe side." Jason put the scissors and tweezers back in the kit and watched Julie as she inspected her brother's forehead in her typical concerned fashion.

She'll make a wonderful mother someday.

Julie interrupted his uncharacteristically domestic thoughts, asking Charlie, "What have you been doing today?"

"Josh and I went out to the barn and did chores; then we hit the gym." Charlie turned to look at James. "The new gym is fantastic! Josh and I put on boxing gloves and punched the heavy bag. I think between all the sweat and the hay from the barn, it made my head itch like crazy. I couldn't stand it any longer." Charlie smiled with chagrin at everyone. "I'm sorry I freaked out."

"Well, let's all go in and have a bite to eat, shall we?" Camille led the way back inside.

Jason was surprised when she said, "Julie, I talked to some friends about having you cater their party next month. Are you sure you're interested in giving catering a go? They've already enlisted me to help with the décor for their event."

Julie's going into business with my mother? Why didn't she tell me?

They followed Camille into the family kitchen. She'd prepared Jason's favorite, minestrone soup and some sandwiches. As Jason dug into his soup, angry voices issued from the utility room. Everyone at the table turned to listen to the argument taking place between Jarod and Lauren.

"You might be my boss at work, Jarod, but you are not my anything after hours! You have no right to dictate to me where I can go on my own time!"

"Calm down, Lauren."

"I will NOT calm down. I'm getting sick and tired of you ignoring me except when you feel like paying attention, and that usually means you want to dictate how I should live my life! I'm sick of it!"

Lauren burst through the kitchen door and came to a dead stop. Obvious embarrassment etched her face at being overheard by everyone.

Jarod, close on her heels, stopped as well at the sight of his family gathered around the table. Schooling his features, he announced, "Oh good, you're all here. I have news."

He gestured for Lauren to sit with the rest of the family. She glared at him but didn't argue further, finding an empty seat at the table.

Jason had a hard time containing his mirth.

"Let me get you some plates," his mother said.

"I can't stay, Mom. I'm needed back at the station."

"Well, maybe *I'm* hungry, you bossy bastard," Lauren mumbled as she got up to help their mother.

Jarod must've really pissed her off this time. Jason chuckled then groaned when Julie's pointy elbow jabbed him in the rib.

"Ow." He gave her a questioning look.

"Stop making fun of Lauren," she said quietly but not unkindly. She rubbed his sore rib for him.

"If everyone is through messing around, I'd like to hear what the sheriff has to say."

James gave everyone the stink eye.

"Did the girl at the hospital give her statement?" Charlie's question interrupted everyone. Apparently, he was just as impatient as Jason's dad.

Jarod placed a hand on Charlie's shoulder. "She's in and out. She hasn't been awake enough to give a statement."

Charlie groaned out loud, as did the rest of the table.

"But something interesting happened in Julie's neighborhood." Jarod-the-drama-King, paused for effect.

Jason rolled his eyes.

Finally, Jarod continued. "Dad, have you spoken to Dane today?" He gave good cop face to their father.

"Early this morning. He said since the girl wasn't alert enough to make a statement, he planned to do a little recon at Julie's house. I haven't spoken to him for hours. I assumed he was on stakeout. What's happened?"

Jarod raised his eyebrow at the news.

Jason had no clue where this was going. He could feel tension radiating from Julie, and he didn't like it at all. "Get on with it, Jarod. You're starting to piss me off. I don't feel like being arrested for assaulting an officer, even if he is my big brother and deserves a good pounding."

Julie pressed in against him. He put his arm around her shoulders, but as soon as he did, she sat up straighter and said, "Yes, Jarod. We're all in suspense here. Spit it out." Her adorable chin jutted out in command.

That's my girl.

"Dane's been in an accident," Jarod stated.

Everyone spoke at once.

"What's happened to him?"

"Is he all right?"

"I thought he was an accomplished driver?" Jason smirked.

His dad gave him a glare. "Of course, he's an accomplished driver. I wouldn't have hired him otherwise!"

"Calm down, Dad. I didn't mean anything by it. It's just odd Dane would be in an accident."

"If you all would shut up, I'll continue with my story." Jarod shook his head in frustration. "It seems Dane was, indeed, staking out Julie's house. He was parked around the corner from my deputy's squad car, evidently watching from a different vantage point. My team had seen nothing all night. The house was sound. However, by the time Dane got into position early this morning, he witnessed three men climbing out of a black pickup truck matching the description of the vehicle that hit Julie on Saturday."

"You're kidding. We got the guys?" Josh asked.

"Yes, we got the guys but only because Dane decided to ram his car into their truck."

"What? Why didn't he call it in?" His dad looked puzzled.

"Because by the time his call would've been transferred to the officers on scene, Julie's house would've been well on its way to looking like your house, Jason—a pile of ash."

"What?" Julie asked.

"They had six gas cans filled to the brim with fuel. They planned to climb the back fences behind your house in order to gain access and start the fire. Dane decided a fender bender would disable their vehicle long enough to give my officers around the block time to arrive. After seeing the gas cans, the officers took them into custody."

"Have you spoken with any of them? Who are they?" Jason wanted this bullshit over with so he and Julie could move on with their lives.

"They've all clammed up. I don't want to give you names yet, but I need you, Julie and Josh, to come down to the station to look at a lineup. I want to know if they're the same assholes who attacked Julie last week. If they are, we can add assault and attempted assault to their charges. I should have them ready for you this afternoon. They're still being processed. Dad, you might need to give Dane a ride home as well. He hit their truck pretty hard."

"Jarod, honey, please sit down and eat something before you go." His mom had put a place setting right next to Lauren's at the table.

Lauren didn't look pleased at sitting next to the sheriff. Things must not be going well for her. Jarod could be a stubborn ass. It was too bad his ex-wife did a number on him. It would take years for him to trust a woman again, but Lauren was one tough cookie. Just maybe, if she stuck to her guns, she could take on his shrewish brother.

Grinning at himself, Jason helped Julie out of the bench seat.

"What's so funny?" she asked, giving him her cute, puzzled face.

"I'll tell you later. Let's get down to the station."

"I'm coming with you guys. I'm not riding in the same vehicle with that jackass," Lauren huffed as she followed them to the door.

Jason laughed and said, "Come on then, Sassy Pants." At her shocked expression, he completely lost it and opened the door for them both.

Dirt Bags

"All right, spill it, Lauren." Julie flipped around to face her BFF who sat in the backseat.

Lauren glanced at the back of Jason's head before giving Julie the not-in-front-of-the-enemy glare.

"He won't say anything to Jarod, will you, Jason?"

She could see the dimple in his right cheek as he stared out the windshield while he drove them to the station. "Jason?" She gave him her best behave-yourself-or-you'll-be-in-trouble face. It only made him laugh out loud, so she smacked him on the shoulder. Not too hard, though.

"Okay, okay! No need to get all violent on me, Jujyfruit." He looked at Lauren in the rearview mirror. "I won't say anything to him, cross my heart. Besides, I'm curious myself. What is going on with you two?"

With a huff she said, "There is no 'you two' because he's a stubborn ass who doesn't know what he wants."

Jason asked, "Then why did he bring you to the house today?"

Lauren flopped back in her seat and groaned. "I don't

know, Jason. One minute I'm opening the door to my car, and the next he's got me by the arm and putting me in his cruiser. In the backseat," she stressed the last.

Affronted for her friend, Julie said, "What?!"

Jason chuckled, "You're kidding."

"No, I'm not kidding, Jason King!"

Still laughing, he questioned, "Why would he put you in the backseat?"

All Julie could think was Jarod must have a death wish. Putting Lauren in the backseat of his cruiser was tantamount to starting a war.

"He said it wasn't safe for me to be out by myself while Billy was still lurking around, and then proceeded to harass me about being more prepared the whole way to your house. I'm never speaking to him again," she declared.

Julie studied her friend closely. Lauren had been crushing on Jarod since they met but the age difference had been a little too big at the time. Besides, Jarod had had a steady girlfriend who he later married, only to end in a bad divorce. No one liked to talk about it.

"I'd say give him time, Lauren, but it's been years. Maybe it's time for you to throw in the towel?" Julie was sick of her friend being in constant turmoil over that particular King.

"Maybe you're right." Lauren's small voice tugged at Julie's heart. She knew all too well what a broken heart felt like. She looked at Jason and wondered if *he* would break her heart. She was afraid of where their relationship was heading, but she shoved the thought away... for now.

She had other problems at the moment.

Jason pulled into the sheriff's station and found a parking spot in front. Lauren opened her door, but Jason grabbed it and helped her out.

Julie hopped out in time to hear him say to her best friend, "Don't give up on him, Lauren. If anyone can tame him, it's you." Then he turned and pulled Julie into his side, his arm around her shoulders.

Julie smiled up at him and whispered, "Thank you."

Her friend looked as if she were going to break down. "Come on, Lauren." Julie put her hand out to her friend, glad Lauren took it and held tight. There were tears in her eyes.

Men. Sometimes they plain ol' sucked.

Jason opened the station door for them. Surprising Julie, Lauren hugged Jason before she hugged Julie. "I'm heading to my desk. I'll see you later tonight as I have been summoned to stay the rest of the weekend." She winked and sashayed off to parts unknown. Julie felt better about her friend's emotional state. Lauren was never down for long, that was for sure.

They waited in the vestibule of the station, which doubled as a waiting room. Red plastic chairs ran in two rows and a magazine rack hung on the wall. Just as they seated themselves, Josh and Jarod came out of the same door Lauren had entered a few minutes before.

"You're up, Jason." Jarod gestured to follow him down the hallway. Josh took the vacated seat next to Julie.

Surprised, she asked, "You've already seen the lineup?"

"Yup." Josh gave her his playboy grin. She hooked her arm through his elbow and hugged her dear friend to her and he squeeze her back. Jason's departure had left her feeling bereft.

Josh had always been her friend. She was so thankful he was in her life. Without him she would never have known Camille, James, Jarod, or Jason. They were all so important to her. She could never repay them for their help with Charlie. All because Josh wanted to compete with his brother and have two girlfriends. Thinking about it helped take her mind off of what she was about to do until…

"Hey, are you ready for this?" Josh asked.

"Sure." She waited a beat before asking, "Are they in there? Those men from the construction site?"

"Jarod asked me not to say anything so he could get an honest identification out of you." He was very serious. "But yes, it's the same men. I won't tell you where they're standing or what they're wearing, though. Will you be okay seeing them again? We can stay with you if you want."

"Yeah. That would be good." She was starting to feel a little nauseated. She didn't know how she was going to react to seeing those creeps. Fear and anxiety spiked in her chest.

The door opened and Jarod called her back. Jason wasn't with him. She kept her arm in the crook of Josh's elbow while they followed Jarod to the viewing room.

Two people waited: Jason and another man in an expensive suit with a file folder and briefcase. Jason quickly retrieved her from Josh's care.

"How're you holding up?"

"Not sure. They can't see us, can they?" she asked Jarod. There was a good possibility she might throw-up as she looked through the window to see the men standing in the next room.

"No, this is one-way glass and this room is soundproof. We can hear them if you need to identify by voice. Do you need to hear them?"

"No." She swallowed, shaking her head.

"All right then, Julie. Do you recognize any of these men?" Jarod formally asked in full cop mode; she had a feeling it was more for Mr. Sharp Suit than it was for her.

She looked at the men in the lineup. The room was big, and twelve men stood underneath numbers.

"Just say the number above the head of the man or men you recognize."

"Numbers two, eight, and eleven."

"And where do you recognize these men from?" This from Mr. Sharp Suit.

She cleared her throat and tried to act confident when in reality she was shaking in her boots. "They harassed me at my business, Cafe Armstrong, last week and got into a fight with Jason and Josh. Jason banned them from the construction site."

Sharp Suit smiled like a shark, all super-white teeth and no true emotion.

"Thank you, Miss Armstrong. You've been very helpful." With a click of his briefcase, Mr. Sharp Suit exited the room.

"Who was that?"

"He's from the District Attorney's office. Don't worry, you did great." Jarod gave her an awkward hug then turned to leave the room. They followed him out.

"So who are those assholes?" Josh asked, dripping with exasperation.

"Raymond Hicks, Gerald Brown, and Sean Davis. Three nobodies who lawyered up with the same firm that's on retainer with Billy's father."

"Shut the front door!"

Julie giggled. Josh had been using that turn of phrase for years. The brothers all had potty mouths, but they tried to tone it down when they were around her.

"Seriously? How do you know that?" Jason asked.

"Because that little prick in a suit who just left told me so," he said, jerking a thumb over his shoulder. "Apparently, he went up against their attorney in court when Billy's dad was charged with fraud. Go figure." Jarod smirked.

"What happens next?" Julie asked.

"We wait. For now, they'll be in holding until their arraignment or someone bails them out. If that happens, I'll let everyone know."

"What about Candy?" Jason asked.

"I've sent their mug shots to the hospital. As soon as she wakes, my guys will have her look at them. If she can make a positive I.D., then we can charge them for what they did to her, along with the assault charges pressed by you and Josh, harassment, and conspiracy to commit arson. Of course, we'll have to prove the conspiracy charge since Dane jumped the gun and stopped them before we could grab them on your property." Jarod shook his head in disgust.

She hadn't thought about that. While it was great they'd made the arrests, it would be difficult to prove they were trying to burn her house down if they were only caught in the neighborhood and not on her property. Crap.

"But I've got deputies showing mug shots to Jason's neighbors. Hopefully, some of them will remember seeing them when your house burned down. The truck they were picked up in matches the vehicle seen in your driveway. If we can find a witness to I.D. them, we can add arson to the list of charges." Shrugging his shoulders, he repeated, "Right now, all we can do is wait."

They didn't want to keep Jarod from his work, and he had gotten all he needed from them. Jason escorted her out of the building to his truck. To Julie's surprise, Josh's truck was a row over from them.

"How did you get to the station before us?" she asked him.

He smiled and said, "Shortcut, and I followed the sheriff with his lights on. Besides that, Jason drives like a grandma." He laughed and got into his truck.

Jason flipped him off before opening her door to help her into his pickup. Climbing into the driver's seat, he asked, "Where to, Jujyfruit?" as he put the key in the ignition.

She had no clue. Floundering for something to say, she shrugged her shoulders. "The rest of my day is open. Any suggestions?"

He started the truck. "I might know a place."

SHE DIDN'T KNOW HOW TO ACT AROUND HIM AFTER last night. Her feelings for him were moving like a roller coaster at top speed with dips and turns which left her tummy in chaos and her mind a confused mess.

Until two weeks ago, she felt nothing but contempt for this man, spending most of her time thinking of ways to avoid him. She'd wasted five years wallowing in loneliness and bitter heartache for the wrong man.

She could only blame herself. Josh had repeatedly tried to tell her Billy was no good but, in her stubbornness, she'd refused to believe him on the grounds that Josh's attitude toward Billy was out of respect and loyalty to his brother.

She wished she'd listened to her friend.

Making love to Jason was like lifting off a blindfold. Never before had she felt so cherished. He'd taken his time touching every part of her body, only to follow those magic hands with tender kisses and gentle words. He made sure to fulfill her needs before he allowed himself his own release; then he'd start the whole process over again. Her body tingled at the memory of it all.

She'd been a virgin when she met Billy, but if last night was anything to go on, she was certain her whole perspective on sex had been based on a faulty foundation. She'd been living under the assumption a woman was lucky to enjoy herself during sex. She'd never understood all the magazines and social media sites which talked about how to be a better lover in bed. Why would she want to be better at something that wasn't all that great to begin with?

Now she was confused but happy to know an intimate relationship with a man could be wonderful. She was also angry she'd been lied to and felt stupid she'd wasted five long years pining for a cretin who'd never loved her while her Prince Charming had been in front of her all along.

In fact, the whole royal family had kept watch over them from the moment her parents had died.

She glanced over at Jason as he drove his truck to destinations unknown. He reached for her hand and brought it to his lips. He kissed the backs of her fingers gently, all without taking his eyes off the road ahead. He kept her hand in his but on his thigh while he drove one-handed.

His forehead crinkled. When he turned to her, she saw uncertainty in his eyes, those beautiful emerald gems which had haunted her dreams since the day she met him.

What in the world was wrong with her? This awkwardness needed to stop.

"Where are you taking me?" She smiled with genuine curiosity.

Speaking words aloud helped her to dispel the weird shyness that had overcome her since leaving the sheriff's station. Jason smiled and kissed her knuckles again before returning her hand to her lap.

"I'm taking you someplace special." He frowned and then clarified, "Well, it's someplace special to me, but I really hope you like it, too."

He turned the truck into a rough driveway, where a gate was hidden in the fence lining a big field. She realized they were on the opposite side of his parents' property on a private road. When he stopped in front of the gate, she leaned across the console and took hold of his face.

"I need a kiss."

She smiled at his surprised expression but sighed when, with exquisite care, he caressed her face before his lips met hers in a soul-searing kiss that ignited her libido. She couldn't get close enough to him. Unfortunately, they were confined by the console and steering wheel.

He broke the kiss by whispering her name, "Julie. Julie." He caressed her face with gentle hands. He pulled back from her as she gazed up at him. "Let's take a walk."

She smiled. "Sounds nice."

Her mouth watered at the sight of him getting out of the cab to open the gate. He got back in, drove the truck through the opening, and then stopped to close the gate again.

When he returned to the cab, he put the truck in gear and explained, "I used to come out here when I was a teen. There's a high spot up this dirt road through the trees. It has a great view of the sunset. I want you to see it."

The land began to flatten out as they rose to higher ground. There was an old log that had been trimmed up and served as a parking block. He pulled up to the log and cut the engine.

"Don't get out until I come around to open your door, okay?"

"Sure." He looked so serious and sincere that she wouldn't deny him his chivalry.

Her unlikely Prince Charming came around to her side of the truck. She remembered he kept his small gun in an ankle holster above his black lace-up boot under his pant leg. If she didn't know it was there, she wouldn't notice it at all; she could just make out the slight outline if she squinted. His jeans were worn out in all the right places, and it made her breath speed up. His t-shirt was bright white, tucked into those awesome jeans, and outlined every muscle in his upper body except for his tattooed arms, which were exposed in the short sleeves.

She used to think all that ink made him look dangerous. But now that he'd explained what each image was and why he had it permanently imprinted on his body, they collectively became an open picture book of his life, keeping no secrets hidden. They described his faith, his desires, his values; and one even described how much she meant to him. Oh, how she loved that tattoo.

He took her hand, helping her out of the tall cab of his truck. When he closed the door, he took her in his arms and kissed her breath away. All she could do was cling to him until he let up and smiled.

"This is what I wanted to show you." They faced what looked like a camp site complete with a fire pit surrounded by stones and wooden camp chairs in the Adirondack style. A pile of wood ready to burn stood at the ready. A small picnic table, which looked homemade, sat on the other side of the chairs. But as he turned her in the opposite direction, she froze at the sight before her.

From this vantage point, she could see the entire town below and the mountains on the other side. Some of the trees were beginning to turn colors a bit early in the higher ground —just some yellowing at the tips of their leaves, letting the world know summer was at an end and fall would be here soon. The nights had already begun to dip into the high forties, giving the night air a brisk feel. The sun was beginning to set now, and the sky turned to a myriad of pinks, purples, and blues.

It took her breath away.

"What is this place?" she asked with wonder, still gaping at the gorgeous vista.

"This is my spot," he said simply. "My parents sectioned off the property in three places for me and my brothers. It's where they want us to build homes for ourselves."

"Your parents want to subdivide?"

"Only to their children," he said with a smile. "They're hoping if we all settle here, their future grandkids will only be a stone's throw away."

Amused, she thought, *That sounds like something Camille would say.*

"Well, it's very beautiful up here." She put her arms around his waist because she needed to touch him. "This spot is perfect for a home. Will you start something now that your home was burned down?"

"That house wasn't my home, Jujyfruit. It was an investment, remember?"

"But all of your things are destroyed... your clothes, your personal mementos, photographs..."

He interrupted her, "You were never inside it, so you don't know this; I didn't really 'live' there. I stayed there, but there was nothing in the house that can't be replaced. All my valuables are either at the bank, in a safe deposit box, or at my parents' house. You saw my room last night. Any, mementos, as you say, are there."

She thought about it for a minute. No, she hadn't ever been to his house because she'd had no reason to go there. She didn't think Charlie had ever been there either, because most of their time together had been spent on sports or at the

King Estate. She would have to ask Charlie about it to be sure.

She shook her head. "That doesn't answer my question, though. Will you build here now?" She wondered what type of home he'd build for himself in such a place; would it be a simple structure so as not to take away from the landscape, or a mansion like his father's?

He tightened his grip on her waist and whispered in her ear, "Well, we'll have to see what the future brings, right?"

"That sounds cryptic," she laughed.

Squeezing her tighter, he answered softly, "I haven't been this happy in a very long time, if ever. You make me feel this way, Julie." He kissed her temple, giving her that cherished feeling again and filling her eyes with tears. She swallowed the lump in her throat. Again, her awkward shyness pulled at her psyche.

Why was this so hard? Was it because she didn't know how to feel or because no one had ever said such a thing to her before?

"Why do I make you happy?" she whispered.

"Because you are all I've ever wanted, Julie. I don't know if it's human chemistry or divine providence. After last night, I am absolutely certain you were made for me. There is no other woman who compares to you, and if I build here, I want it to be with you."

Turning in his arms so she could look him in his beautiful face, she let her tears flow. She finally realized he was her everything, and she didn't want to hold back any longer. Just as she was about to speak her heart, a familiar laugh came from behind them.

Billy stood in the campsite.

"Well, Jason, looks like you finally stole my girl."

CHAPTER 21

Demented

How the hell did he find us?

"What are you doing here, Billy?" Jason remained quiet and calm on the outside, not wanting to spook Julie. He knew Billy too well. Sociopaths lived off people's fears to feed their own ego.

He stood there looking smug, but Jason knew Billy never came unprepared. He guessed Billy either had backup hidden somewhere in the trees or he carried a weapon. Either way, Jason was ready for whatever he had planned. No way would he let Billy hurt Julie.

Billy stared at them for a moment, his head cocked to the side in that way he had, as if he were assessing the best way to corner his prey—which was exactly what he was doing.

Jason kept his heart rate down, his breathing regulated, prepared for anything.

Billy's lips moved into a self-satisfied half smile which didn't reach his eyes. "I just wanted to make sure you were doing all right, old friend. I mean, we are old friends, aren't we?"

"No, Billy, we're not. We haven't been friends for a very long time," Jason said with complete honesty.

"That's right, you hypocrite. You didn't like my extracurricular activities. What's the matter, Jason? Did I cut into your pussy stash? Well, it certainly looks like you've returned the favor though, haven't you?" He sneered at Julie.

Julie gasped behind him and her fingers dug into the waistband of his jeans. He fought his instinct to knock Billy's teeth out, refusing to take Billy's bait. However, not knowing what the prick had up his sleeve, Jason maintained eye contact, preparing for the inevitable attack.

"Don't you speak to me that way, you pathetic excuse for a man!" Julie said from behind them, startling Jason.

He wasn't sure if playing the woman scorned was a good idea, especially with the maniacal look in Billy's eyes. Jason didn't budge from the protective stance he had in front of her, though. If Billy wanted a fight, he would get one, but not until Julie was out of the way.

"Ah, the love of my life speaks. Well, honey bunches, soon you'll see how real this man can get. Even though you've sullied yourself with Jason, I'm willing to take you to my bed."

Every muscle in Jason's body tensed. All he wanted to do was pummel this asshole until he bled. He gritted his teeth and growled, "You won't be touching her ever again, Billy. Leave her out of it. This is between you and me."

"Maybe, Jason, but she's still a part of it, isn't she?"

Unbelievably, Jason's cell phone began to ring.

Billy laughed. "Go ahead, answer it."

Never taking his eyes off Billy, he dug the phone out of his pocket and slid his thumb across the screen.

"Hello?"

"Christina Mason just gave her statement. There's a warrant out for Billy's arrest," Jarod said without preamble.

And that's why Billy has flipped his lid. Great. He has nothing to lose.

Storing that information for later, Jason answered calmly, "That's good. When will they pick him up?" Jason watched Billy's oily smile and knew Billy was cornered.

"My boys are on their way to his last known address, which is his father's house."

"They won't find him there."

"Why's that?"

"Because he's standing in front of me at the campsite."

Jason didn't hear anything for a few seconds before Jarod said, "On my way," and hung up. He calmly returned his phone to his pocket.

Billy's sick smile grew wider. "Well? Is big brother bringing the calvary?"

"Seems so," Jason said, still maintaining eye contact with Billy.

Julie kept a death grip on his waistband while she whispered, "What's going on?"

Billy's eyes flashed as he said, "Yeah, Jason. Tell us the sheriff's good news."

Jason didn't want to play this game; he wanted it over with. He hoped Jarod arrived before the fight occurred because the look in Billy's eye told him that was exactly what he had come here for. And Jason was itching to fulfill that need.

"Jason?" Julie whispered. Her shaking voice reminded him she was the person he'd fight for, the one he had to protect. He needed to remember she was the least confrontational person he'd ever met and didn't understand what was happening. He had to play this smart.

So he opted to keep the dipshit with the sly smirk on his face talking.

"You first, Billy. Why would Jarod issue a warrant for your arrest?" Jason thought he might turn the tables if Billy lost his cool.

"Maybe because you guys have always hated me, always been jealous that you just don't come up to scratch?" A vein throbbed on the side of Billy's temple. His whole body shook.

Steady—it's only a matter of time before he breaks.

"That's not a reason for an arrest warrant," Jason said quietly. Shaking his head from side to side, he continued, "No, I think you've been caught red-handed, Billy. Tell Julie how you know Christina Mason."

"Who?" Billy truly looked like he didn't know the name.

"Candy? Does that ring a bell?" *You asshole.*

Billy's expression went slack for a split second before he answered, "She's one of my favorites." Billy looked at Julie and smiled. "She'll do anything I ask her to."

"Then why beat her up?"

"Because some people need a reminder to keep their big mouth shut."

"How could you?" Julie asked with complete disgust in her voice.

His face split into a maniacal smile again, and a chill ran down Jason's back. "Oh, sweetheart, you have no idea what I can do. But don't worry. I'll make sure you enjoy everything I have to share later." He winked at her.

Jason's muscles bunched up as Raymond Hicks, Gerald Brown, and Sean Davis, the men they'd identified at the station, stepped out of a van. Jason grimaced over not hearing the vehicle approach.

"'Bout time you guys showed up, Hicks," Billy said amicably to his posse. "No trouble getting out?"

"Your dad's lawyer came through just like you said he would."

Billy smiled and said, "Good." Then he looked at Julie. "Get in the van, sugar."

"No."

"You can either get in the van, or you can watch us have some fun with Jason." Billy drew his knife at the same time his goons moved in closer.

Jason pushed Julie behind him, giving himself some space. He assessed every man there before he whispered to her, "When there's an opening, I want you to run, and don't stop until you're safe."

Her eyes dropped to his ankle briefly. He hoped she wouldn't give anything away to the men. Wearing an ankle holster alleviated the worry of someone disarming him while he threw punches, but it's a difficult draw; he had to be down already in order to surprise an adversary when he retrieved it. However, he had practiced the draw for hours, and he'd already fought these dicks before; none of them presented a real challenge, even with the knives. He may not need to draw at all.

"What is this all about, Billy? This is ridiculous!" Julie shouted.

"It's about a little payback and a whole lot of silence, sweetheart. Now, get that perfect ass of yours in the van!" Spit flew from his lips as he screamed.

Jason tried to position himself so she could run around them, but as the men began to close the circle, she lost her chance to flee. He was going to have to keep all of them busy if he wanted Julie out of the melee.

"You're not making any sense, Billy. Payback for what?

Silence about what? You haven't been around in years. What could we have possibly done to you?"

Jason knew she was stalling. She kept Billy's attention on her so Jason could lure the other three away.

"Don't play coy with me, Julie. You know what happened to your parents. That's why you had Candy investigated. And that's why you're going to get in that van!"

She sucked in a breath before she said, "My parents? What about my parents?"

"Shut up and get the van. Charlie's waiting for you."

"No!"

As Julie ran to the van, the goons moved in on Jason. He heard Billy's snort of disgust. "So easy," before a fist hit Jason in the face.

Julie ran as fast as she could to the van. She didn't want to leave Jason, but if Billy had somehow gotten Charlie, she had to know if her brother was okay. Before she could reach the door handle, rough hands spun her around. Ice-blue, empty eyes stared into her face.

"I changed my mind, you traitorous whore. I want you to watch Jason get what he deserves." Billy flipped her back around as the two smaller men held Jason's arms and the big one, Raymond Hicks, punched him in the stomach. She watched in horror as Jason bent at the waist on impact from the huge man's fist.

"STOP IT!" she screamed, but it only made Billy laugh.

Her mind swam. She didn't know how to help Jason, and she desperately needed to know if Charlie was dead or alive.

"They won't stop 'til I say so. Don't worry, though; they know to leave enough for me to finish him off."

She wasn't going to acknowledge the threat against Jason, which is what Billy wanted. However, she couldn't stop the cold dread seeping into her voice. "Where's Charlie?"

"I told you, he's in the van. You'll see him in a minute. We're almost done here."

Just when Julie didn't think she could stand one more minute of this, one of Jason's shorter captors stumbled to the ground, releasing his hold. In the next instant, Jason shoved the big man far enough away for him to punch a fist into the other man's temple, knocking him out cold. The man who'd stumbled writhed and screamed on the ground, holding his kneecap.

"That son of a bitch was always fun to watch in a fight," Billy chuckled in her ear. His hold barely allowed her to breathe as he yelled encouragement to his goons. "Watch him, Hicks. You don't want him to connect with that left."

Julie readjusted herself, trying to loosen Billy's hold on her, but his grip only tightened as he whispered in her ear, "Don't move, Julie, or I'll remove your kidney."

She felt the tip of his blade in her back and stilled.

"That's better, sweetheart," he whispered, "I forgot how good you feel." He chuckled when she gagged at his nuzzling of her neck.

Her eyes welled as Jason's fight escalated. Round and round they went; Hicks had finally drawn his knife, and Jason had a couple of defensive wounds. Blood covered the tattoos on his forearms. She wasn't sure why he hadn't shot the monster with his pistol.

As the bruiser went for Jason's throat, he grabbed the man's wrist with lightning speed. Jason brutally twisted his arm at an inhuman angle. She heard the snap of bone as the knife fell to the ground. Hicks's arm dangled, useless, while he screamed bloody murder. Jason took the opportunity to shove a fist into the guy's mouth to shut him up. With his infamous speed, Jason repeated the process until Raymond Hicks was nothing but a bloody heap on the ground.

Jason stood up and turned to Billy.

"It's over. Let her go."

Julie felt Billy's body shaking, but his voice was as slick as oil. "I can't. She's coming with me. And her brother."

Jason started toward them when Julie felt a sharp pain in her back. "Augh!"

"Julie!" She heard him say, but her eyes were closed in pain.

"Let her go, shit for brains! It's me you want. If you're a man, you'll let her go, Billy!" Jason shouted.

"Why? So you can hand me over to your brother? No, I'm not going to jail. If it weren't for you, I'd be where I should be, living the good life. But you had to ruin everything!" he screamed in the high-pitched tone of a man who had lost his mind and had nothing left.

From behind them, Jarod said, "Let Julie go, Billy. You're surrounded."

She felt the sharp stab of the knife in her back, and warm liquid dripped down her pant leg. "Shut up or I swear I'll kill her!"

Excruciating pain made her head spin. Billy kept pulling her closer and forcing the point deeper. She needed to hear Billy's confession before she passed out. Taking a deep breath, she asked, "What happened that night, Billy? Tell me, please." She hoped if she seemed weak, which she was, his delusion of grandeur would cause him to bestow the information on her.

Before he could answer, Jarod spoke up instead. "He had to

leave before we put the pieces together about the hit and run. Isn't that right?"

Billy shifted them around so Jarod and Jason were in front of them. Jason had drawn his weapon, mirroring Jarod. She could hear the crunch of more vehicles coming up the road. This was now a no-win situation for Billy, and she was terrified she'd lose a kidney before Jarod's deputies could make the arrest.

CHAPTER 22
Ambulance

Relieved the troops had arrived, Jason focused his attention on the knife currently tearing through Julie's flesh.

He should've disarmed Billy first before taking out the other losers. They'd been no match for him, and he had only allowed them to capture him so Julie could get away. Jason wasn't sure if Charlie was in the van or not, so his only priority now was to see Julie to safety.

A confession out of Billy would be nice. He wanted the bastard talking before Jarod let him beat the shit out of him.

"What's in the statement, Jarod?"

"In a nutshell, she claims she was with Billy the night he ran a vehicle off the road and into a ditch. She claims she hadn't realized anyone had been hurt because Billy left the scene. She also claims she begged to go back and help whoever had crashed, but Billy was adamant they were fine. Billy beat her up when she tried to talk him into turning himself in after hearing about the Armstrongs' deaths on the news."

Jason watched Billy tighten his grip on Julie. Her eyelids were scrunched up, pain marring her beautiful face.

This has to end. Now.

The other officers had arrived, and Josh and his father had just pulled in.

He called out to them, "Check the van! He claims Charlie is inside!"

They didn't act surprised but relieved, which had the hair on the back of Jason's neck standing on end. He hoped to God the kid wasn't in that van.

He turned to Billy. "It's over, but I can see you're going to play this out to the bitter end. So let's get to it, shall we? I'll put down the gun, you let go of Julie, and then you and I can finish this once and for all."

Jason knew the moment when Billy let the idea sink into his demented head. They both knew in a face-off, Jason was a far better fighter. He was banking on Billy's ego to win out.

Billy sneered, "Yeah right. Like Jarod will go along with that?" His wild eyes tried to keep everyone in his line of sight, jerking Julie with him every direction he turned. Jason wanted to act now but was afraid Billy would jam his knife all the way home. So he sweetened the deal.

"I'll even let you keep your knife."

"What about them? You think I believe they're just gonna let us fight it out? No, as soon as I let her go, they'll take me down."

As much as Jason would love for that scenario to play out, Billy wouldn't let her go if he thought that was the plan. Too much blood ran down her legs. They were running out of time.

"Jarod, tell your men to back off, will you?" he asked as calmly as he could through his gritted teeth.

Jarod seemed to think about it before he ordered, "Stand down."

"Well? What do you say, asshole? Are we going to do this or are you just gonna to be a bitch?" Jason asked as he put his gun at his feet.

Billy's eyes flared and roamed the area. "Why not?"

Before Jason could fully stand up, Billy flung Julie into him and then charged them both with his knife. Jason had been expecting the move, so he quickly brought Julie to the ground and rolled her in Jarod's direction while kicking out at Billy's feet. The move brought Billy to the ground but the bastard gained his feet again in a flash.

Now that Julie was no longer being threatened, Jason could concentrate on his prey. He and Billy circled each other, gauging the best plan of attack. Jason followed Billy's eyes as they swept the area. From his peripheral vision, Jason could see Hicks, Brown, and Davis had been either taken into custody or put in an ambulance. Billy would find no help from his posse.

"It's just you and me this time, Billy. What are you going to do about it, huh?" he taunted.

With a growl of anger, Billy lunged with the knife. Jason kicked out with his steel-toed boot and removed the problem; the knife sailed out of Billy's hand, leaving him to rely on his fists which were no match for Jason's.

Billy screamed as he tackled Jason at the waist. Jason used the momentum to flip Billy over his head so that he landed on his back. Not wasting any time, Jason pulled his elbow back and went to town with his fists. It seemed he'd only just begun to rearrange Billy's face when rough hands pulled him off Billy.

His father said, "That's enough, son. He's done."

Jarod rolled Billy over onto his stomach and cuffed his wrists.

"Where's Julie?"

"With Charlie in the ambulance."

All the blood drained from his head as he looked at his father while James ushered him to Jason's pickup. "Gimme your keys, and I'll tell you while we drive." James held out his hand for the keys.

Jason shook his head, adrenaline still flooding his system. "You talk; I'll drive, Dad." No way was Jason going to sit still in his own truck—again—while someone else drove him to the hospital.

With a huff, his father got into the passenger seat. Jason climbed in and started the engine.

"Where'd Josh go?"

"Followed the ambulance. We found the kid bound, gagged, and unconscious. Charlie's face is in pretty bad shape." His father's voice cracked as he explained Charlie's condition.

"How the hell did they get him?" Jason couldn't believe Charlie would have left the grounds. Damn it, he was too smart for that.

"Josh had been keeping him pretty busy all morning in the stables and then in the new gym. After everyone left with Jarod, he asked if he could saddle one of the horses and ride the fence line.

"I figured as long as he stayed on the property, he'd be fine. Josh agreed Charlie needed a bit of alone time to clear his head." His voice cracked again when he said, "We won't know the details until he wakes up," he trailed off, probably not wanting Jason to hear him cry.

"He was still out when they took him to the hospital?" Jason's heart beat faster with fear for the kid. His anger amped up again. He wished those scumbags were free so he could beat their asses all over again.

"Is Julie in the same ambulance as Charlie?"

His father huffed an irritated breath. "She wouldn't hear it any other way, Jason. That woman is one fierce and protective sister." His voice was full of admiration.

"How did her wound look?"

"The tech put some packing on it when he determined it was deep enough for stitching but not bad enough for surgery. They'll sew it up at the hospital."

They arrived at the emergency room in fifteen minutes and it took another five to find Julie. However, they couldn't get past the nurses' station, where the nurses said they couldn't go into the examination room because they weren't Julie's family.

Not yet. But soon she will very much be a part of my family.

Frustrated, Jason began to throw a fit until his mother showed up and explained to the charge nurse that they were, in fact, Camille and James King, benefactors of the new trauma center, and she didn't want to have to bother the hospital chief in order to see Julie, who, she explained, "is like a daughter to me."

They were immediately granted full access, God bless her. Unfortunately, his mother also demanded Jason be triaged before he did anything else. When Camille was satisfied his injuries were minor and had been treated properly, she located where Julie and Charlie were being treated.

Jason found Julie lying on her stomach complaining to the doctor that he needed to speed things up.

"What's taking so long? I wanna find out about my brother's condition! He's all I have!"

Rushing to her side, Jason said, "Calm down, Jujyfruit. Mom's checking on Charlie right now."

Her eyes filled with tears and her bottom lip began to

quiver. The ordeal left her an emotional wreck, and she was the most beautiful creature he'd ever laid eyes upon.

Oh yeah. I'm definitely keeping her.

"Jason," she whispered. "I was so scared for you."

She reached for his hand. He took it and smoothed the back of his fingers down her face.

"I'm almost done here. Then you can check on your brother, Miss Armstrong," the doctor said.

"Thank you," she said in a small voice.

Jason watched the doctor carefully sew up the wound. She'd have a two-inch scar right over her kidney. Again his temper rose, seeing Billy's knife in her back, the blood... it took everything he had to calm himself down again.

He heard the doctor chuckle when he asked, "Squeamish?"

Not wanting to upset Julie further, he only shrugged and said, "Something like that." Then he bent down and kissed Julie's sweet lips.

<hr>

WHEN JASON HELPED HER OFF THE TABLE AND OUT OF the exam room, all she could focus on was finding Charlie. She couldn't keep her tears at bay as she remembered him on that gurney in the ambulance. He had a black eye and blood had oozed from a crack in his lip. His cheeks were swollen, knuckles torn and scabbing. He'd tried to fight them off.

He'd been recovering from a concussion sustained two weeks ago and now this.

Why won't he wake up? she'd wondered in a panic as they'd shared the ambulance.

Jason kept his arm around her shoulders, guiding her down the hallway to where James paced outside of another exam room. He smiled at them and said, "We've been waiting for you. Charlie's awake. Camille and Josh are with him now while the doctor goes over his injuries."

Relief flooded her body to the point that her knees weakened, but Jason, her Prince Charming, was there to steady her. He ushered her into Charlie's exam bay.

"...and I don't want you to exert yourself in any way until I can see you in a week. There's no fracture to your orbital socket, but a second concussion is a worry," the doctor was explaining.

"I know. I was taking it easy until that creep jumped me," Charlie said as he looked up to see Julie. His eyes welled up, but a relieved smile crept onto his face. "Oh God, Julie! I thought you might be dead!"

She rushed over to him and hugged him, relieved he was going to be all right.

The doctor continued his long laundry list of dos and don'ts for the next couple of weeks. He reminded her to call his office to schedule another appointment. She was surprised he hadn't mentioned the absence of stitches from his forehead. Thank goodness. She didn't think she would be able to stand any criticism at this point.

"When can we go home?" she asked as she wiped her eyes.

"I'll start his discharge papers." The doctor left the room to be replaced by Jarod, cop face in place.

"How're you doing, Charlie?" he asked.

Julie didn't like his tone of voice, but then, that was Jarod when he was acting in the capacity of sheriff.

"I've been better. It was Billy who hit me. I don't really remember anything else until I got here."

"Billy acted alone?"

"Yeah. He drove some creepy van. I didn't realize it was him until it was too late."

She felt Jason's hand on her head and neck. It was like he couldn't stop touching her, and she didn't want him to, either.

Josh said, "How did he get you off the horse?"

"He didn't. I'd ridden her hard, and we were out pretty far, so I decided to dismount and walk both of us, letting the mare graze by the fence line. I needed to clear my head and think, ya know?"

He closed his eyes for a minute as Julie squeezed his hand. "Take all the time you need, Charlie."

Sighing, he continued, "I saw the van on the other side of the fence near the road but didn't think much about it because I was behind the tree line, and it seemed to be abandoned. Billy hid in the trees. I don't know if it was just dumb luck I was there for him to find or what, but he jumped me. When the horse startled, I let her go, hoping she'd find her way back to the barn quickly so you'd know something was wrong." He looked at Josh, who was pacing the room.

"Good thinking, kid," Josh whispered, clearly agitated by the whole story.

Jarod said nothing but seemed to be playing things out in his head. He could be very cold at times, and she wondered what Lauren saw in him.

Josh stopped pacing and said, "When the mare came thundering into the barn alone, my heart nearly stopped. I didn't know if you'd fallen off and been hurt or what."

"I'm sorry, Josh. I didn't have my cell phone, but it wouldn't have done much good anyway. The bastard had me pinned to the ground before I knew what was what and started punching."

Julie shuddered with fear and anger as he told the story. She heard Jason inhale and exhale, something she knew he did when he was trying to keep his cool.

Josh punched the wall.

"That's enough, Josh," Camille said. "He's here, he's safe, and that *Billy*," she said with distaste, "is going to jail where he belongs. Your brother will make sure he stays there. Won't you, Jarod?"

"Yes, ma'am. That's just what I plan on doing."

Josh rubbed his sore knuckles and gave Jarod a meaningful look. "You'd better. Because if I ever see him on the street..." He trailed off, shaking his head, and began pacing again.

It was hard for Julie to see this fun-loving, playboy brother so upset on top of everything else she'd witnessed today.

Jason kept rubbing her back. "So Billy had the van first," he mused. "How did he deliver the van to his buddies at the jail? Charlie was in the van the whole time." He muttered the last in contemplation.

Julie didn't understand how that could have happened either. She looked at her brother with concern. Why had Charlie been out for so long?

The nurse came in with his discharge papers and began to hand them to Camille.

"Excuse me. Those belong to me," Julie said with a sigh. She had no clue where she was going to find the money for all of the medical bills piling up, but she refused to let it get her down.

"Sorry," the nurse said and handed her the papers. As she went over the forms, Julie could feel Jason's every move next to her; he refused to leave her side. Camille helped Charlie put his shoes on; bending over most likely hurt his head. When Julie was done signing her life away, she handed the forms back to the nurse and looked up at Jason. He smiled and kissed her. He had dried blood and bandages all over his arms.

"Are you all right?" she asked him. "You've got some pretty deep cuts."

"I'm fine now that I know you're safe, Jujyfruit." He kissed her forehead again and kept her in his arms all the way out of the hospital.

Jarod left the hospital to finish processing Billy.

There were three vehicles at the hospital, so Julie and Charlie rode with Jason; Josh followed in his own vehicle. James drove Camille's car, leading them all back to their large home.

Julie was exhausted and her back hurt as the numbing agent began wearing off. Every bump in the road aggravated the stab wound. She turned to see Charlie's eyes closing in the back seat. "Don't go to sleep, okay, Charlie?"

"I know. I'm super tired, though. I can't seem to keep my eyes open." He sat up straighter and rolled his window down to let in some fresh air.

Jason reached over and took her hand, slowly bringing her knuckles to his lips for a tender kiss, all while keeping his eyes on the road. She noted the bruising on his face and the bandages on his arms. His shirt was filthy, too, and covered in dried blood. Charlie's shirt wasn't any better. Then she remembered Billy had shoved his knife through her shirt and how the warm wetness had run down her back and into her jeans. She chuckled to herself in an obvious moment of delirium.

"At least we all match," she said to no one in particular.

"Huh?" came from the back seat, which made her chuckle in earnest. Jason jerked his attention to her before returning his gaze to the road in front of him.

"Are you all right?" he asked, which startled a guffaw out of her. No, she was probably having a nervous breakdown. At least she thought it was funny.

As they all parked their vehicles in and around James and Camille's garage, Julie's bout of the giggles had subsided and her back seriously hurt at this point. Getting out of the truck was as much fun as a head cold in the summer.

When they got to Jason's room, she noted it had been cleaned since she'd left it this morning. Two sets of clothes had been laid out on the bed for them: black jeans and a t-shirt for Jason, her yoga pants and a loose blouse for her.

"I'm going to start the shower," he said as he walked into the bathroom.

She sat down on the bed but immediately stood up when the stiffness of her jeans reminded her of all the dried blood. She was too tired to care about anything except getting clean, so she began to strip.

"Let me help you, babe," he said as returned from the bathroom. He'd taken off his shirt, and the snap to his jeans was undone. She couldn't take her eyes off him. He was so handsome, so strong and so... hers. She took a deep breath and let it out as his hands began to lift her shirt.

"My stitches need to stay dry," she whimpered in frustration, which ticked her off. She hated being weak in front of him because he was so strong.

"I know, Jujyfruit. Don't worry about that part. I'll take care of you."

He kissed her cheek and then her lips before he gently pulled her shirt over her head. She hated the bruises on his face —how those horrible men had put their fists to him and marked him. She put her hands on his chest and traced her fingers around the tattoo over his heart, the one about her. She leaned her forehead on his chest. He smelled so good, even after today's fight—his soap, his sweat—him. She loved the way he smelled, the way he felt, and the way he looked at her.

She loved him.

He kissed her hair and then brushed her hands away from his body before he bent down to one knee in front of her. He took her hands and placed them on his shoulders. "Hold on while I get you out of these nasty jeans."

She toed off her shoes. Her jeans were covered in crusty, dried blood which made them stiff and gross. As he peeled them off, she was itchy all over and ached everywhere. Her head hung down as he pulled both her jeans and panties down her legs to the floor.

"Step," he said softly.

She stepped out of her clothes. He held onto her naked hips and pressed a sweet kiss to her belly. She smiled to herself as she moved her hands from his shoulders to his soft, cool hair. He looked up at her with such love in those beautiful, haunting eyes that it took her breath away. He kissed his way up her torso to her breasts, kissing each one through the material of her bra before reaching around her to unhook it. He was kissing her softly and tenderly when he took it off her body. She stood there naked, not at all self-conscious as he smoothed the hair from her face and kissed her forehead, eyes, and cheeks before placing a chaste kiss on her lips. She felt worshipped and cared for, and it brought those damn tears back to her eyes with a vengeance.

Never taking his eyes from hers, he whispered, "I love you so much it hurts. I don't know what I would've done if I'd lost you today." His chest rose and fell as he gained control over his emotions.

Her emotions were a train wreck.

As the tears continued to pour down her cheeks she

reached up, wincing at the pain shooting from her wound and up her back. Ignoring it, she grabbed his face to bring his lips to hers. Before she kissed him, she admitted, "I love you too."

She felt all of his muscles bunch up as he growled and hugged her close. She had her hands on the side of his head, her thumbs brushing the tears from his cheeks.

Jason is crying! she thought with awe. It made her more voracious for his touch and his kiss.

"I never thought I would hear you say that," he choked out. Between kisses he said, "God, I love you so much." He gently picked her up and carried her to the bathroom.

CHAPTER 23

Princess

His heart swelled in his chest. He thought he might be in shock.

Julie loves me.

He'd never thought he would ever be with her like this, to care for her in this intimate way, and now here she was in his arms, bloody and bruised, just as he was. He'd love her, but not tonight. Now that Billy was out of their lives forever, they could move forward... together.

But first he had to make sure her new stitches didn't get wet.

Jason carried the woman he loved into the bathroom and set her in the tub, out of the spray. "Do you trust me?"

"Of course." She looked affronted he would ask her such a thing, and it made him smile.

He kissed the bridge of her nose. "Mom had someone set out plastic wrap and medical tape. I'm going to wash you down with a washcloth before you get into the spray."

She scrunched her face up in that adorable way. He smiled

when she shrugged and stayed where she was. She looked too tired to care anyway.

He wet the washcloth and began to scrub her flesh of the dried blood, careful not to pull at the skin around her wound. She winced so he eased up in his ministrations. He took a soft towel and dried her before picking up the plastic wrap and tape. He thought about cutting off a square and taping it around the bandage, but that wouldn't work.

"Don't you dare laugh at me, Jujyfruit," he chuckled as he wrapped the plastic all the way around her torso.

She tried not to smile but he caught it and she giggled.

"I told you not to laugh," he said in a stern voice, but he was unable to hold back his own laughter. "Hold still while I tape the wrap in the back so water doesn't seep underneath. I'm not going to keep you in the spray too long, only enough to wash all this crud off."

He stood and admired his handiwork. Satisfied her wound would stay dry, he stripped out of his own filthy pants and got into the tub with her. She was weak, so he had to make this fast, more clinical than romantic, but being this close to her stirred him.

And she loves me.

Tenderly, he washed her hair. "Close your eyes." He rinsed her hair out and then covered her with his body wash. He turned her under the spray again and said, "All done."

"Your turn."

She surprised him by snatching up the body wash. She put some on the washcloth and began to clean every inch of him. Her touch nearly killed him. He gritted his teeth and let her have full rein. She carefully washed the blood and dirt from his face.

"Close your eyes," she repeated his words back to him.

When she was finished, she pushed him gently into the spray and he rinsed off. When the suds were gone he turned the water off and reached for a towel. He wrapped it around her, then quickly dried himself and wrapped his own towel around his waist. He scooped her up as she began to droop.

Because he couldn't stop himself, he kissed her sweet lips while he carried her out of the bathroom and to his bed. When he sat her down, he realized water dripped everywhere from her hair.

Damn it! Some caretaker I am!

The very last thing she needed right now was a case of pneumonia. He snatched the towel from around his waist and gently toweled off the excess water from her beautiful locks. Then he carefully peeled the plastic from her waist finding her bandage underneath perfectly dry. She closed her eyes and her shoulders began to relax. "Let me grab the comb." He began to stand up when she grabbed his arm.

"No, it'll be fine. Don't leave me."

"Never." He kissed her forehead. As her eyes closed now, he tucked her into his bed and then got in beside her. He gathered her close to him, spooning behind her so her wound wouldn't be disturbed. "How's your back?"

"It hurts, but I think the painkillers are kicking in because I'm so tired."

Her body relaxed in his arms as he nuzzled her neck and settled in for a long night's sleep together.

"I love you, Jason." The words sang in his ears like a lullaby before he nodded off to oblivion.

<u>NOT THE END BUT A NEW BEGINNING</u>

. . .

"Mornin', Julie. I'll have a granola cup and a coffee, please."

"Here you go, Dennis." Julie smiled as she handed him his breakfast. The early morning sunlight caught the many facets of her diamond engagement ring, a princess cut, of course.

She sighed happily and served the next customer.

It had only been a month since Billy's arrest. Things were far from back to normal, as Jarod had reopened the investigation into her parents' deaths. They'd also discovered not only had Charlie suffered another concussion, but Billy had drugged him to keep him from escaping while he attempted to kidnap Julie. The mystery of the car switch was actually no mystery at all. After he dropped the van off at the jail for his buddies to drive, Billy had stolen a car from the lot—one more charge to add to his list of crimes.

The trial was set to take place in a few months. Candy had promised to testify against Billy. There'd been some grumblings about his attorney wanting to claim mental instability, but Jarod thought too many of Billy's plans had been premeditated for it to hold up.

Julie hoped he was right.

Jason wouldn't let her move back into her house, so they were still at his parents' home. They would stay there until their house was built on the parcel James had given him. It wouldn't be finished for quite some time, as Jason was still busy with the strip mall. There was now a wedding to plan and Billy's upcoming trial. But she could wait.

Camille insisted on coordinating the wedding; there would be no other for her son. Since he was marrying "the daughter of my heart," as she had said to Julie with tears in her eyes, Camille wanted to do it up big. Julie was relieved to have such a huge responsibility taken off her hands. All she really cared about was Jason. How they were married didn't matter to her one bit, as long he showed up on her wedding day.

Charlie loved staying with the Kings; Camille mothered him like crazy, and James fulfilled the all-important fatherly role Charlie craved. He took an interest in everything Charlie did. It was nice to have family again.

"What are you thinking about, Jujyfruit?" Jason's beautiful green eyes were shining up at her from the order window. She loved it when he called her that, knowing it was an endearment that held special meaning for him.

"I'm thinking about how nice it is to have family again."

His smile was shy but bright. "You always had a family, Julie. You just didn't want to acknowledge it."

She smiled down at him while she handed him his breakfast. "I couldn't acknowledge what was right in front of me. All those years searching for Prince Charming, and you were here all along. I must be the dumbest woman on earth."

"Princess, you were under an evil spell. All you needed was a kiss from the right frog."

Hey friends,

Welcome to the new *Trouble In Timbisha Township* series.

Thank you so much for reading *Jason's Princess: A King Brothers Story - Fourth Edition*, and the first book in the new series. When I began this saga a decade ago, I had no idea where it would lead. It's had many faces, been released different ways and, finally, it's all mine.

Jason, Jarod, and Josh are the original stories in the series and I thought I'd stop with a trilogy but other characters from Timbisha Township demanded to have their own stories told. I can't wait to share them with you.

A Sister's Love is Charlie's short prequel found at the end of this book.

Thank you, again, from the bottom of my heart for reading *Jason's Princess*. If you're around on social media, please don't be a stranger! I'd love to hear from you.

Sincerely,
Elise

Instagram Elise Manion
www.elisemanion.com
or visit my free Substack newsletter *Happy Distractions*.

A Sister's Love

FROM 12-YEAR-OLD CHARLIE'S PERSPECTIVE

COURTHOUSE

Charlie Armstrong lay on his bed backward, bouncing a tennis ball on the wall above his headboard and then off the ceiling. He aimed for the remnants of a dead spider he'd squashed two weeks before but hadn't gotten around to cleaning off yet.

Maybe it'll disappear if I hit it hard enough.

He threw the ball harder. *Bah-Bonk!*

Turning the ball in his hand, he found no spider juice on the fuzz. He sighed and took aim again. He'd been chucking the ball all morning for lack of anything better to do. Timbisha Township Middle School had given him a week off for mandatory bereavement. His parents were dead. Like he had a choice *not* to be sad.

The funeral replayed over and over in his mind, his stoic sister shaking hands with the vultures who'd come to gawk at the new orphans, Julie smiling sadly and thanking them for coming.

Thanked them. Geez, what bull.

The gawkers had only come to gossip and to speculate what would become of him now. Timbisha Township was small and small town folks talked nonstop, making judgements about people and the unfortunate circumstances which befell them. But they didn't know what horrible "circumstance" Charlie had witnessed, or that his parents may have died because of what he'd seen.

He squeezed his eyes shut, trying to remove the awful images from his mind. He was afraid to go there, to picture it again, or to hear that filthy pig ask him if he wanted a "piece" of the girl too. Billy's laugh haunted his dreams but his threat to kill Charlie's family if he breathed a word of what happened still rang out loud and clear. No, Charlie hadn't told a soul Billy had raped that girl, but his parents were dead anyway, killed in a freak car accident. Though Billy had left town abruptly, Charlie had no proof of either crime, but he wouldn't risk losing his sister. He'd take his secret to the grave to keep her safe, even if she was an idiot for dating the bastard.

"Charlie, it's time to go." Julie stood in the doorway leaning on the jamb, her arms wrapped around herself and a bleak smile on her face. Her cheeks were blotchy from crying again. Thankfully, she wasn't a wailer or he'd go insane.

"Where are we going again?" he asked without missing a bounce off the wall and ceiling.

"We have to meet with Child Protective Services."

Bah-Bonk. Bah-Bonk. "Why?"

Julie sighed. "We've gone over this, Charlie. You're a minor with no legal guardian."

"So?" *Bah-Bonk. Bah-Bonk.*

"So, Mom and Dad didn't leave instructions on who should take care of you if something were to happen to them."

"Something DID happen to them." Charlie threw the ball with more force.

"Yes, and that means the state needs to know you have a home to live in or you'll go to foster care."

Charlie caught the ball and sat up. "Like hell. I'm not living with a bunch of strangers, Julie!" His heart raced. He felt the awful pressure in his head, the burning in his eyes.

He wouldn't cry.

He. Wouldn't.

She stepped into his room now, hands raised as if to quiet a frightened animal. "I won't let them take you, bubba. Just calm down."

"Calm down? You just said I was going to foster care and you want me to calm down? They can't take me from my home. I won't go, Julie. I WON'T GO!" He was standing and didn't remember getting to his feet. He threw the ball over her head into the hallway where it ricocheted off the walls and into the kitchen.

"Charlie, quit yelling and put your shoes on so we can go. Throwing a fit and being late will make things worse for us." A tear spilled down her cheek before she turned on her heel and left his bedroom.

He quickly tied his shoe laces and grabbed his zip-up hoodie. Then he found Julie in the living room looking through her purse for her keys. Impatient, he walked outside and waited by the car. When she finally clicked the fob to unlock the doors he scrambled inside and out of the cold air.

"Foster care, my ass," he mumbled as he stared out the window at their small front yard. Dead petunias still decorated the ring around the tree. He'd planted them with his mom last June. Now there was nothing left but brown stems and twigs they hadn't gotten around to digging up yet.

They rode in silence the short distance to the Timbisha County Court House. Deputy Jarod King was standing in front when they arrived.

"What's Jarod doing here?"

Julie's eyebrows scrunched up. "I don't know, Charlie. I guess we better get out and see what's what, huh?"

Charlie took a deep breath before climbing out into the frigid sunshine. His breath billowed out in a cloud while the stinging cold bit into his fingertips. He slammed the door too hard, ignoring his sister's warning glare, and shoved his hands into the front pocket of his hoodie.

Jarod walked over to them. His uniform shirt stretched over his massive chest, and the bulletproof vest underneath made him seem bigger than usual. Charlie stood taller and met the oldest King's piecing blue eyes before Jarod placed a firm hand on Charlie's shoulder.

"How ya holding up, kid?"

Charlie just shrugged. What could he say?

Life sucks ass.

"Mom and Dad are inside, along with Josh and Jason. We're here to offer our support and to provide a character reference for you, Julie. Do you have your proposal with you?"

"Yes."

"Good, Judge Cook will want to know how you plan to provide for Charlie. Honestly, I think it's superb."

Charlie glanced at his sister but she steadfastly looked at the courthouse. "I hope this works," she said as she led them to the front doors.

GUARDIANSHIP

She hoped what worked?

Charlie followed his sister inside the old building. It smelled like time and history, neither of which was good.

As promised, the entire King family waited for them. Josh, the youngest brother, was one of Julie's best friends. Charlie didn't know much about the rest of the family but they all had friendly faces that seemed to be genuine, unlike the funeral goers the other day.

"Charlie, these are my parents, James and Camille King," Josh said.

Josh and Jarod resembled their father. Mr. King was big, with piercing blue eyes and gray around his temples. All three of them looked formidable, commanding respect with their very presence.

Camille King was the opposite. She had a great smile and the most beautiful green eyes Charlie had ever seen, until he was introduced to Jason, who wasn't beautiful. He was huge and covered in tattoos. He winked at Charlie before those emerald-like eyes glared at Julie.

Charlie wondered about it for five seconds before he realized he didn't care if Jason liked Julie or not.

He just wanted this day to be over with.

He wanted to know what was going to happen to him.

Charlie tasted blood, not realizing he'd been chewing on his lip. He wiped it on his sleeve hoping no one noticed, but since he'd already established life sucked right now, Mrs. King immediately stepped in front of him and handed him a tissue from her purse.

"Hold it just so and it should stop bleeding, dear." Her

smile was comforting and he scrounged up a brief smile in return.

"Thank you, Mrs. King," he mumbled.

"Call me Camille, Charlie. It's a pleasure to finally meet you."

He was about to ask what she meant when they were called into the judges chambers.

Judge Cook came around a huge wooden desk which was crammed into the small office and offered a hand to Mr. King, uttering quiet words before he addressed the room.

"My apologies for the small space. I didn't count on James bringing his entire brood with him today." He smiled briefly before clearing his throat. "Miss Armstrong, this informal meeting is to determine guardianship of your brother, Charlie Armstrong. I understand you have a plan you'd like to present to the court. Before doing so, I'm offering to hear it prior to making a formal decision in the event it would need to be revised. I believe family should stick together if possible. Charlie?"

Charlie sat straighter in his chair answering, "Yessir." He hated being the center of attention and now everyone stared at him. Sweat dripped down his back under the hoodie and he swallowed the panic crawling up his neck.

"Before we go any further, I need to know if you are willing to live with your sister or if you wish to live somewhere else."

He turned to Julie who flipped through the papers on her lap. Did he want to live with her? She'd dated Billy, brought him to their home and now their parents were dead. But, what choice did he have? He didn't want to move from Timbisha Township, and he really didn't want to live with strangers.

He felt a strong hand settle on his shoulder giving him a

comforting squeeze. He glanced back and up, straight into Jason's knowing green eyes.

"Come on, kid. Answer Judge Cook honestly."

Charlie turned back to the judge. "Well, sir, I don't want to move to Reno and live in a dorm with my sister. I want to stay here in Timbisha Township."

"I see," Judge Cook said. "Julie, do you intend to move Charlie to Reno?"

"No, Your Honor, I do not. I intend to stay in Timbisha Township until Charlie graduates from high school, sir."

Charlie turned to her. "But what about college? You're almost done, Julie."

"I can always finish later," she said with a sad smile.

"But..."

Judge Cook cleared his throat.

"I will ask you one more time, Charlie. Would you like to stay here in Timbisha Township, in your home, and be raised by your sister?"

"Yessir."

"May I see your proposal then, Miss Armstrong?"

Julie handed her papers to the judge. The room remained silent while Judge Cook thumbed through them. Charlie's lip stung as he bit through it again.

"Have you purchased the vehicle for your business yet, Miss Armstrong?"

"No, Your Honor, but I have one on hold until the custody of my brother is settled, sir."

"And what of a customer base? Do you think there is a need in Timbisha Township for a food truck operator?"

Food truck?

Charlie stared at her in disbelief.

"Judge Cook, I can testify that a mobile restaurant would

be most welcome at my worksites. My crews are large and their appetites larger. They should provide an adequate starting point for Julie's business," Jason said, his hand still on Charlie's shoulder. When he said Julie's name, he gently squeezed Charlie one more time.

Judge Cook glanced at Mr. King, who nodded. He seemed to think it over for a bit before he finally put all of the paperwork together and handed it back to Julie.

"Miss Armstrong, you're willingness to drop everything, withdraw from school, and jump into a new business for the sole purpose of caring for your younger brother is admirable. I wish more twenty-year-olds were like you. However, I do have some reservations on the success of your business venture, along with your ability to care for your brother. If guardianship is granted you will, in essence, be his parent. Do you understand the demands that responsibility will put on you?"

"I can't understand because I'm not a mother. But I am a sister and I'll do anything to keep Charlie with me. I promise to make sure he grows up healthy, happy, and that he graduates from high school, sir. It's what my parents would've wanted."

She took a shaky breath and Charlie realized his fate rested with his sister's ability to take care of him.

Judge Cook looked around the room. "Can any of you gathered here think of a reason why I should not grant Miss Armstrong temporary guardianship over her brother, Charlie Armstrong?"

Charlie held his breath for what seemed like forever but no one said a word.

"I can't either," Judge Cook said. "If you'll wait just a few more moments, I'll get a court reporter in here and we'll do this all right and tight. I'm granting you temporary guardianship for one year contingent on your ability to provide for your brother, and with evaluations every six weeks. Does that sound fair?"

"Yessir," Charlie said at the same time as his sister.

DIRTY PICTURE

The judge had admonished Charlie to continue getting good grades in school, mind his sister as if she were his mother (yeah right), and stay out of trouble. If Charlie couldn't comply with those three rules, permanent custody could go to someone else.

He'd always liked school and his grades were near perfect. His only challenge now would be keeping his temper reigned in. There were times when he got so mad he couldn't control himself. He wanted to break everything he owned and run away.

By Monday he was glad to get out of the house. "Do you want me to drive you to school?" Julie asked while she put away the breakfast pans.

"Nah, I'm good with the bus. What are you doing today?" He honestly didn't care what she did but he asked out of politeness since she'd made his favorite breakfast—cinnamon pancakes and eggs. She almost had them tasting like Mom's.

"I need to finalize things for the food truck. Do you want to see a picture?" she asked, suddenly excited.

Charlie wiped his mouth and got off the barstool. "Can't. I need to get my books and head out to the bus stop." He hurried to his bedroom to get his things. Out of habit he went to the empty turtle terrarium sitting on his dresser. Trevor died a week before his parents' accident. He shook off the grief and gathered his things, placed them into his backpack and hauled ass out of the house.

He pulled the hood over his head to keep the January cold

off his ears and half jogged to the bus stop where Marco was kicking a Hacky Sack while McKayla and Hailey huddled together watching something on Hailey's phone. Dillon and Ryan were eyeballing the girls, who pretended not to notice.

"How'd court go?" Marco asked while juggling the sack with his feet.

"Okay, I guess."

Marco stopped what he was doing to stare at Charlie. "I texted you last night. How come you didn't text back?"

"Dude, I just didn't want to talk about any of it, all right?"

Marco shrugged. "Fine. Be a bitch."

Charlie grinned. "Yeah, screw you too."

They'd been best friends since forever and been through a lot together. When Marco's parents went through their divorce, he had practically lived with Charlie until the fighting stopped. When Scott Miller decided to pick on Marco for no good reason, together they'd put a stop to that shit.

Scott wasn't a bully anymore.

The Hacky Sack hit Charlie in the chest. He put his things down and kicked it around with Marco until the bus showed up.

They followed Hailey and McKayla onto the bus. The girls sat in front of them, their noses still glued to the phone. They giggled every now and then before the driver pulled away from the stop.

"How do they walk without looking where they're going?" Marco asked loud enough for the girls to hear.

"Because girls rock, Marco." Hailey sighed, not taking her eyes off the tiny screen.

Charlie laughed until he noticed Dillon taking a picture of Hailey with his phone from across the aisle. Charlie narrowed his eyes when an alert appeared on his own phone. He opened up the Snapchat app and found the picture of Hailey that Dillon had just taken, with her blouse gaping open and focused in on the pink bra beneath.

Dillon hadn't just sent the Snap to Charlie, but also to his Story within the app which meant everyone in Dillon's contacts could view it for the next twenty-four hours. Dillon now wore a villainous smirk.

"Hailey," Charlie said loudly. "Button your shirt."

She gasped and looked down. "Oh no," she squeaked before zipping up her jacket. "The button popped off." She fumbled with her clothing before she turned to glare at him. "How could you know that, Charlie? You're sitting behind me."

He didn't bother answering. He was too busy staring down Dillon. "Delete it, asshole."

"Screw you, Armstrong. If I'd known you were such a pussy, I wouldn't have alerted you."

"Take it down before I make you." Charlie had been itching to punch something for a week and Dillon's face would do just fine.

Whistles and jeers directed at Hailey now filled the bus. Everyone had seen the photo. Hailey began to cry, ratcheting up Charlie's ever-boiling anger.

"Decide now, Dillon. Take it down or I take you down," Charlie seethed. He stood up and Dillon got to his feet to face him.

The bus had grown quiet but Charlie didn't care. Dillon was a douche bag for posting the picture and Charlie had had enough of douche bags to last a lifetime.

"What's going on back there?" The bus driver asked, glaring at them in the rearview mirror.

Dillon broke eye contact first. "Nothin'. It's all good," he said before sitting back down in his seat.

"Is it?" Charlie narrowed his eyes.

"Yeah man. It was just a joke." Dillon held up his phone. "It's gone. Chill out, will ya?"

Charlie sat down and didn't say anything until they pulled into the school grounds.

"Thanks, Charlie," Hailey said quietly before she scurried off the bus, head down followed closely by McKayla.

"Think Dillon's gonna need a lesson anyway?" Marco asked as they followed Dillon and Ryan off the bus.

"Probably," he said with disgust while making his way to the first class of the day.

JASON

By the end of the week Charlie was twiddling his thumbs with extra time. Without Billy there to steal his homework and "accidentally" destroy it, staying caught up was a breeze. However, the more time he had on his hands, the more he thought about his parents. He missed them terribly. Julie was her normal annoying self, thinking only about her stupid food truck business.

It was Saturday morning and the heavenly aroma of coffee and bacon floated underneath his bedroom door to tickle his nostrils, triggering a gnawing ache in his belly. His sister had made breakfast every morning since the funeral and his body was getting used to her cooking, even looking forward to it. She still didn't have the cinnamon pancakes right but, damn, the bacon had been perfect three days in a row. Another loud grumble from his stomach had him swinging his feet off the bed and onto the floor.

He stretched and yawned his way into the bathroom. He did what he needed to do, washed his hands and brushed his teeth. He contemplated popping a ginormous pimple forming under his left nostril but it wasn't ready yet. It would hurt like a bitch anyway and he wasn't up for self-induced pain this morning.

Lauren Lockwood's voice drifted to his ears from the kitchen. Charlie stopped in his tracks and looked down at himself. He'd had a secret crush on Lauren for a while. She was beautiful and funny, and every time she smiled at him it did something to his body which would be entirely noticeable in his boxers. He spun on his heel, went back to his bedroom and got dressed. He took one more look in the bathroom mirror, sucked in a breath, and popped the annoying zit under his nose. As he feared, it wasn't ready but he got most of it—and two watery eyes for his effort. He wiped the tears away, did a quick check to make sure the stupid thing wasn't bleeding, and hurried into the kitchen.

Lauren sat on a barstool at the small counter with Josh and Jason. Josh was always over but to Charlie's knowledge, Jason had never been over before. Julie dished out eggs and bacon. There was an empty seat between Josh and Lauren, so Charlie took it.

God, she smelled as good as the bacon.

"Good morning, sleepyhead!" She gave Charlie's hair a tussle. Her fingernails scraped his scalp sending tingles all the way down his body.

Yep, good thing I changed my clothes.

"G'morning. What are you guys doing here so early?"

"Helping your sister pick up her new food truck." Josh scooped some eggs into his mouth. "We're gonna need your help."

Since Charlie couldn't give a crap about her stupid truck he'd need to come up with an excuse not to go. He chewed his bacon slowly, giving himself time to think. "I've got plans with Marco today." It was a partial truth. They'd planned to meet up at some point.

He expected Julie to say it was fine, like she always did, but instead an awkward silence grew. He began to squirm, but he also refused to be bullied into something he didn't want to do, and doing anything with Julie made the list.

A low conversation began around him, mostly involving the new business. By the time the last bite of breakfast made its way to his stomach, the urge to escape the house was unbearable.

"Yeah, I'm outta here," he mumbled before shoving his plate away and sliding off his stool. He skittered down the hallway to his room, but not before he heard Julie sniffle. He refused to acknowledge her while he put his phone in his pocket.

"What are your plans with Marco?" Jason filled up his doorway, brightly-colored tattooed arms crossed over his massive chest. His intimidating green gaze penetrated Charlie's skull, amping up the anger that was never far away.

He thought about making up some bullshit story but something in Jason's stare gave Charlie pause about lying. Carefully, he admitted, "I'm not sure yet."

"So, you could meet up with your buddy later."

Charlie heard the command and didn't like it one bit. Still, he remained careful. "I guess," he said as he shrugged into his hoodie. "But I'm not gonna." He tried to leave the room but the behemoth blocked his exit.

"Tell ya what, Charlie. Today, I'll give you a pass since you seem out of sorts. Use your time wisely with Marco because I'll be checking in on you from now on. Understand?"

"Just who the hell do you think you are?" Charlie shook with anger at the nerve of this guy.

"I'm the one who's going to make sure you do what is expected of you by your sister and Judge Cook," Jason stated without blinking.

Charlie glared back at the giant. Was this guy for real? "Why the hell do you care?" he asked belligerently.

"It doesn't matter," Jason said quietly before leaning into Charlie's face. "Just know that I do." With that he backed up and let Charlie through the doorway.

Hot rage filled him up, making his heart pound. He needed to get out of the house before he lost it. He shoved passed Jason, who barely moved, rushed down the hall and passed the kitchen without saying goodbye.

Slamming the front door sure felt good.

FIGHT

The weeks passed by in tortured slowness while Charlie continued to ignore his sister. She hadn't cared about him when his parents were alive, so why the hell would she care about him now? She'd let her boyfriend plague him day and night with his stupid games, only to defend the piece of garbage when Charlie complained. Julie was an idiot. Sometimes he couldn't stand to look at her face.

Despite Jason's warning, Charlie hadn't seen much of the guy. He'd seen plenty of Josh and Lauren, though, who were over almost every weekend helping Julie with her storage issues for the food truck business. They'd turned the single car garage into a make-shift food pantry. They'd drive back to Timbisha

Township from Reno where they attended school. Julie was supposed to be with them but she'd given up school to start this harebrained scheme.

No, she'd dropped out of college to take care of you, asshole.

The thought hit Charlie like a hammer making him suck in a breath, the same way Dillon's fist sucker-punched him in the gut that morning. Dillon ambushed him during passing on their way to second period. Charlie had doubled over, giving Dillon an opening for another punch, this time to Charlie's chin. Good thing Dillon was a skinny prick or it could've been all over for Charlie.

The look on Dillon's face was comical when Charlie hadn't gone down but he'd been too angry to laugh. Teachers had broken up the fight before he could do any real damage to Dillon and they'd both been sent home for fighting. Now, he lay on his bed tossing the tennis ball at the wall and ceiling waiting for Julie to get home.

The monstrosity she called "Cafe Armstrong" rumbled into the driveway just after sunset. Julie and Josh came laughing into the living room as Charlie walked out to get something to eat.

"Oh Charlie! What happened to your face?" Like a mother hen, Julie lifted his chin for a better look at the bruise.

He batted her hands away. "It's nothing, I'm fine."

"It doesn't look fine to me," Josh said with concern, embarrassing Charlie. He didn't need Josh's pity.

"Did you ice it?" Julie opened the freezer door to scoop some out of the bin.

"I said I'm fine, damn it!" Charlie didn't care if he was yelling.

"Calm down, kid. Tell us what happened." Josh tried to put his arm around his shoulders.

Charlie hated being called a kid. He hadn't felt like one since the funeral. Rage boiled as he flung Josh's arms away and screamed, "Leave me alone!"

"What in the world is wrong with you, Charlie?" Julie asked. "You're always yelling or fighting. The social worker is coming tonight and now you have a bruise on your face. Do you want her to take you away?"

He was sick of his sister, sick of this house, sick of this town. He was sick of people looking at him like he was an orphan. "I don't give a crap about her. You don't understand!" He shoved Julie and her pitying face away from him. Not realizing his own strength, Julie tripped over the coffee table and landed hard on her ass. It'd felt good to release his rage—for about three seconds—before Josh had him pinned to the carpet face down.

"That's enough, Charlie." Josh brooked no argument while he held him to the floor, arms behind his back.

He probably learned that move from Jarod, Charlie thought bitterly. He struggled but it was no use. He wasn't going anywhere for a while.

"Are you all right, Julie?"

"Yeah," she said with a shaky breath. "He's never hit me before."

Great, now they spoke as if he wasn't laying on the floor with a giant on his back. "I can hear you, you know."

"Shut up," Josh said, gripping him tighter. "Not one word until you're asked."

"Josh. Let him up, please." Julie had gotten to her feet and checked herself for injuries. There was blood on her sleeve near the elbow.

Charlie was thrust up and tossed onto the sofa. "Stay right there." Charlie had never seen Josh so angry. It transformed the usually happy guy into something a little sinister. Charlie nodded and stayed on the couch, watching the scene play out before him:

Josh checking on Julie, asking her if she was hurt anywhere else, and then typing out a text on his cell phone.

Julie nodding, listening and then looking at Charlie as if he'd grown two heads.

Maybe he had.

She was right, though. He'd never lashed out at her before. Deep down, he knew he was a jerk but sometimes he just couldn't control himself. If he were being honest, when the rage took over everything turned black in his mind and his body just reacted. Maybe he was crazy. Maybe they should lock him up or, at least, take him away from his sister before he hurt her again.

He was still mad at her for dating Billy.

He was still angry his parents were dead.

A hot tear fell down his cheek and he viciously wiped it away before anyone saw it.

The front door opened and in walked Jason—and Jarod in full uniform.

Shit, they're sending me to jail.

REMANDED INTO CUSTODY

Warily, Charlie waited to be handcuffed. He crossed his arms sullenly over his chest and listened to the conversation going on around him.

"Are you all right, Julie?" Jason asked.

"I'm fine," she spat. "What are you doing here, Jason?"

"Everyone calm down, please," Jarod said. "When is the social worker coming?"

"About an hour."

Jarod nodded. "All right. Charlie, get your ass in your room now. Julie, you and Josh straighten up out here. Have you eaten?"

"Not yet. I was going to fix dinner when I got home," she trailed off.

"After cooking all day," Jason muttered under his breath.

"We got this, Jarod. Do what you need to do." Josh was already righting a lamp which had gotten knocked off the end table. Charlie hadn't even noticed it falling.

Jason put his big mitt around the back of Charlie's neck and steered him down the hallway and into his room, followed closely by Jarod.

They shut the door behind them.

This is it. They're going to kill me and bury the body before the social worker gets here.

"Have at it," Jarod said to Jason.

Charlie backed up until the backs of his knees hit his bed. Jason kept pace, crowding him. "If you ever hurt your sister again I will beat your ass so hard you'll need a pillow to sit on for a month. Understand?"

"Yep." He swallowed his spit and nodded.

"You were sent home from school today. What did Dillon do to cause the fight?"

"How'd you know about that?"

Jason smirked. "I told you I'd be keeping an eye on you, kid."

"Don't call me that!"

"Then don't act like one."

"Here's what's going to happen," Jarod interrupted. "After your meeting with the social worker, you're going to pack a bag and we're going away for the week. Since it's Spring Break, you won't be missing any school."

"I'm not—"

Again Jason interrupted. "We're going camping where you, me, Jarod, and Josh are going to straighten out your attitude, Charlie. You're the man of the house now and you need to start acting like it."

"I'm just a kid, remember?" he asked sullenly.

"Do you think age matters, or behavior?" Jarod asked.

That got Charlie's attention.

Jason nodded. "What do you think makes you a man? Maturity? Responsibility?"

"Family?" Jarod asked quietly.

"My family's dead." Charlie felt the tell-tell moisture filling his eyes but he ignored it.

"You still have your sister, Charlie. She is precious and should be the most important thing to you. But I guess you're still too immature to see it," Jason said with disgust.

Now that hurt. He wasn't immature, he was pissed... at her.

"It's her fault—" he began before Jason put a fist to his shoulder and leaned down to look him in the eyes.

"Nothing is Julie's fault and you know it. Do you have any idea what that woman has given up to take care of you? And this is the thanks you give her. If anything, you should show her respect just for being your guardian," Jason lectured.

Then Jarod said, "Midway through next week, I'm going to introduce you to some kids who aren't fortunate enough to have family who cares. Instead of acting like a spoiled jerk, you need to learn some respect and some gratitude. Now get cleaned up. I want you to eat before the social worker arrives." Jarod left the room but Jason stayed behind.

"Julie isn't your enemy, Charlie. And neither are we," he said before following his brother out the doorway.

DISAPPOINTED

Because of Charlie's behavior at school and at home, the social worker had agreed, on Judge Cook's behalf, to remand Charlie into the care of Deputy Jarod King. Julie tried to cover her tears but Charlie saw them anyway. The anger inside tried to convince him she was upset for her own selfish reasons but deep in his heart he knew it wasn't true. His sister may have unfortunate taste in men but she had a heart of gold. She'd loved their parents as much as Charlie had and she'd given up school for him.

And he'd let her down.

Swallowing his own tears he asked, "What now?"

Josh put his arm around Charlie's neck in a mock strangle hold. "Now you come with us. I'll help you pack a bag."

They left Julie standing in the middle of the living room listening to whatever plans Jason and Jarod had in store for him.

"How long will I be gone?"

"That all depends on you. My family's prepared to have you for the whole break, longer if necessary." Josh was back to his normal, smiling self, putting Charlie at ease.

"Your family?"

"You'll see. Hurry up so we can get this over with. The longer we drag it out, the more Julie will be upset—and Jason hates it when Julie's upset." Josh murmured the last part to himself.

"Yeah, what's up with that anyway?"

Josh laughed. "Ah, kid. That's a story for another time. Let's go."

Julie stood in the living room not bothering to hide her tears. Jason tried to hand her another tissue but she knocked his hand away and glared at Charlie. He put his bag down to face her wrath. Her disappointment in him hurt more than he thought it could.

She gave him the mean look she used to give him when he was little, when he'd taken something he shouldn't have. "You do everything they tell you to. So help me Charlie, if I find out you've disrespected Mr. and Mrs. King in anyway..." Her voice cracked and broke off as she swallowed a sob.

"I know. I'm sorry, Sis," Charlie said with meaning. His parents in Heaven now looked down on him with disappointment and the reminder filled his eyes with unshed tears.

"Just come back home, will ya?" she said before she threw her arms around him and hugged him hard.

Whoa, she's stronger than she looks.

"We got this, Julie," Josh said before he hugged her too. Jarod gave her shoulders a squeeze before he took Charlie by the elbow and led him outside. He turned back to see Jason thumb a tear from her cheek before following them out the door.

FAMILY

The barn was quiet while Charlie mucked the stall. The beautiful palomino that had filled it with poop was currently chewing on some alfalfa. Charlie grunted. He'd be mucking that alfalfa tomorrow. He'd learned a big lesson this week.

Horses shit a lot.

He sighed before continuing on with his work. He'd been

away from home for nine days. Was Julie doing all right? Did she miss him? He hadn't been allowed contact with her or his friends.

The palomino snorted, drawing Charlie's attention. Josh leaned on the rail.

"Almost done?"

"Yeah. What time is it?"

"Just about lunch time. Jarod wanted me to tell you after you're done here you need to get a shower and meet us in the dining room. Your sister and the social worker are here."

Charlie's stomach dropped. Would he be allowed to go home?

The brothers hadn't taken him to the palatial King estate right away. Instead, they'd taken him up the hill to Jason's parcel where they kept a camp site. During the week Charlie learned Jason still lived at home, Jarod was moving back home because his wife left him and, since Josh was still in school he only came home on the weekends. The campsite was their getaway to relax.

Charlie hadn't been allowed the privilege. He'd been put to work gathering wood, cutting wood, clearing wood. By the time they'd left Sunday evening, the camp site had a revamped fire pit, new Adirondack-style chairs, parking blocks, and a horseshoe pit. Not much talking had been done because Charlie's anger prevented him from being civil. So the physical labor mounted.

The chores hadn't let up once they were on The Estate. If Timbisha Township had a castle, the Kings lived in it. Town gossip had it that the Kings were pretentious snobs but Charlie found the opposite to be true. Right away Mrs. King welcomed his filthy self into her home and demanded he call her by her first name. Camille was anything but pretentious.

In her smile, Charlie saw the mother he missed, but she hadn't been easy on him either. She'd put him to work washing dishes! And not the easy stuff either but the industrial pots and pans she used for events. Camille did a lot of volunteer work for her church and the entire Timbisha Township community. There were enough pots to last forever.

He'd spent the majority of his time with Jason, who worked a construction crew for the family business, King Construction, during the week. Charlie was now very familiar with a shovel.

By Tuesday, he'd begun listening to what the guys had to say. Everyone had problems. Life wasn't fair and what mattered was how you reacted to the crap hands you were dealt. They believed family came first. Bullies weren't tolerated, which was something Charlie agreed with wholeheartedly. They looked out for the little guy. Mr. King had instilled all of that in his sons and now they passed their philosophy to Charlie.

Thursday night Jarod took him to the juvenile detention center for a tour, which was Jarod's version of *Scared Straight*.

It worked.

Charlie may have been orphaned but he still had free will. It was his choice to live in anger for the tragedy that stole his parents, or to live in gratitude for the people who cared about him now. He was learning there were quite a few.

Though they talked and worked and talked some more, Charlie never brought up the girl Billy hurt and his name was never mentioned again, except for Jason's admission he'd personally escorted the creep out of Timbisha Township. Even though he believed Jason, Billy's threat still lingered. Charlie still had a lot to lose. He could see it now that he'd let go of his anger. Maybe someday he would tell Julie about the rape, but not until he was positive she'd be safe. Besides, he still had no proof.

Julie stood in the dining room, while the rest of the Kings spoke with the social worker.

"I swear you've gotten taller." Julie's eyes misted with unshed tears.

"Have I?" He looked down at himself. He didn't feel taller but he did feel clear-headed. He sucked in a deep breath. "I'm sorry I hurt you, Julie. I promise I won't ever do that again."

She smiled sadly. "I know. And I promise to pay better attention to you." She took a step forward and this time she wrapped him in a hug. "You're the only family I've got, Charlie. I love you so much. You know that right?"

Feeling uncomfortable, and wanting desperately to get out of the hug, he murmured, "Yeah, I love you too, Sis." He released her then to see her smile. "Can I come home now?"

"That's what we're here to find out," she whispered, as the rest of the group took their seats.

"Charlie, I've been instructed to evaluate your past week. Having read Deputy King's report, I feel you can return to your home with your sister. But you're not out the woods yet. Though your behavior at school has been questionable, your saving grace is that your grades haven't slipped. Your principal also reported your fighting had been in defense of a fellow classmate who'd been bullied. Though your reasons were admirable, your actions were not. So, no more fighting. Understand?" The sternness of her voice didn't match the twinkle in her eyes.

"Yes, ma'am."

"Good. Then you are free to go home with your sister tonight. I'll be seeing you next week."

Charlie sighed with relief while Jason used the universal

signal he'd be keeping his eyes on Charlie by pointing to his own green ones and then pointing at Charlie. The gesture made him laugh but he nodded in understanding.

After thanking everyone for their help and receiving lots of pats on the back and promises to come visit, Charlie finally made it to Julie's little SUV.

He had a long way to go but he no longer felt the rage that had plagued him for so long. His sister was smiling while she talked non-stop about how well Cafe Armstrong was doing and Charlie couldn't help but feel a little excited himself. His sister's love for him would keep his rage in check. He was going home and, for the first time in weeks, he felt his parents smiling down upon him.

Acknowledgments

A special note of gratitude to Lynda Bailey, my partner in crime and all things Indie. Thank you for your patience, criticism, advice and, most of all, friendship.

You're the *Naughty* to my *Nice* ;)

Also by Elise Manion

Trouble In Timbisha Township Series

Jason's Princess; King Brothers Book 1

Jarod's Heart; King Brothers Book 2

Josh's Challenge; King Brothers Book 3

Marguerite's Redemption; Book 4

Applewood Series

Unwanted: Finding Where You're Loved

www.ingramcontent.com/pod-product-compliance
Lightning Source LLC
Chambersburg PA
CBHW011141310726
48972CB00009B/2802